The Bakery on Main

Famous in a Small Town

Book 2

M.L. Pennock

Also by M.L. Pennock

To Have series

To Have — Brian and Stella's story
To Hold (To Have #2) — Stephanie and Max's story
To Cherish (To Have #3) — Tommy and Jacelyn's story
Letters from Emily (To Have #4)

Famous in a Small Town series

Foster to Family (Book 1) — Delilah and Fisher's story
The Bakery on Main (Book 2) — Maggie and Maverick's story

Coming soon ...

Love Notes and Line Drives (Famous in a Small Town, Book 3)

Dedication

to coffee and preschool
without you, this book wouldn't have been possible

Table of Contents

Chapter 1

Maggie

My full name is Margaret Regina Florence Southard. Please. For the love of all things, call me Maggie. Or Mags.

Do. Not. Call. Me. Margaret.

"Margaret, will you be home for dinner tonight?"

"No, Gram, I have a food truck thing. I thought I told you."

"You might have. I just don't pay attention and you keep trying to get me to use that electronic calendar. I don't care for it."

"If you look at it, though, you'd see my whole schedule for the entire month, Gram."

Technology is going to kill us all. Just ask my grandmother. I introduced her to the Alexa a couple years ago and the first time it spoke without being spoken to she popped it under the tire of my car so I squashed it as I backed out of the driveway. In her defense, I still don't know why it was talking in the first place, so it was justifiable technocide.

"I don't like it one bit, Margaret."

"I know, Gram. I'll print out a copy for the fridge. Just try to remember I won't be home for dinner tonight."

"I'll leave a plate in the refrigerator for you. Don't need you going hungry, starving yourself like all those fancy ass supermodels you wanted to be when you were a child," she says, her voice trailing off until I hear the unmistakable sound of her rotary phone clunking down in the receiver.

Oh, yes, my Gram has a cellphone, but the government, as you should know, is absolutely watching everything she does. She's insistent on using the phone she had back before I was even born. It's not a horrible idea to have a landline that's actually connected to the wall, and I praise her for keeping it if nothing else for the fact she can literally slam the phone when hanging up on someone if they get her riled up.

That's one of those little quirks I love about Gram and now I'm able to enjoy them every day. You see, until recently, I was still living at home with my parents. Out of necessity, I've moved into my mom's childhood bedroom in the house she grew up in so someone can be with Gram more.

The necessity is partially me needing to be able to not live at home and also because Gram could use a roommate to hang out with.

She's the only one allowed to call me Margaret, by the way. Our relationship is unique.

I set my phone down and go back to the cupcakes I'm working on. My best friend, Lilah, owns this sweet little bakery on Main Street in the town I grew up in. When she started getting a lot of traction with her side gig — being an awesome pastry chef — I jumped ship with her. We were both stuck in dead end jobs at the local grocery store, which is fine if you're 20 and just want to use your paycheck to party with the college kids every weekend.

We are not 20. Nor do we party. I mean, partying to us is literally sitting in her kitchen with some hot chocolate designing new cake ideas with her teenage daughter, Genevieve.

But, I digress.

"I think these are done," I say as Gen walks in from school.

"That looks so amazing, Aunt Maggie. Your chocolate designs are some of my favorites," she says.

I don't get a chance to respond before she sneaks into the back room to dispose of her backpack and find an apron. I smile to myself, thankful she appreciates the weird shit I come up with. It's not weird to her and Lilah, though. They're doodles brought to life and shoved into little cakes. It's the talent that set my new career on its path.

"Gram having trouble with your schedule again?" Lilah asks quietly from the other end of the counter.

"Gram … is just having trouble," I say.

Some days I feel like I'm mourning my grandmother and she hasn't gone anywhere.

"I worry about her a lot. She called me by my mom's name the other day and brushed it off like it was nothing," I continue.

Trusting people with my personal info is difficult. Not because anyone ever really did anything to make me wary of oversharing, I just don't. I will talk anyone's ear off about anything, but when it comes to Gram? Nah. You have to be part of the inner circle to know the real her and my relationship with her. Lilah is like a sister to me, so she knows everything.

"Have you mentioned it to your parents? You've been living with her for a bit now so you're seeing patterns, Maggie."

She isn't telling me anything I wasn't already thinking. My mom is supposed to be coming over to have coffee with us in the morning before I come into work. The conversation is going to have to happen then and I don't want to alarm my mother with any of the information. It's just, I don't know. Seeing Gram go from sound mind and body to slowly forgetting where things are in the kitchen she's used for fifty years? It's hard.

"We don't have to talk about it. I'm here when you need me," Lilah says, squeezing my shoulders on her way past.

I'm grateful for her giving me an out this time. She's been watching me struggle with Gram's mortality for months. Gram is the last grandparent I have and she's gotten me to adulthood, which is an accomplishment in and of itself.

For now, I'm going to concentrate on getting work done, getting in the food truck we impulsively invested in, and getting to the high school. All my Gram concerns will still be here when I'm done with slinging cupcakes tonight.

Chapter 2

Maverick

Tonight is supposed to be one of those easy adventures. There isn't anything easy about selling your soul to a bunch of high schoolers and their uppity parents. This is why I stay out of the village, but business is struggling and I need to keep myself occupied and fed.

"So, you sell flowers now?"

Her voice comes from behind me and it makes the hair on the back of my neck stand up. I finish setting out the two buckets of roses in my hands before turning to find none other than my ex-wife.

"Sure would have been nice if you'd ever even bought me flowers when we were together, and now you sell the damn things," Hannah says, popping her gum. It's a tic she picked up after she quit smoking. I could handle the gum, but when she started popping it incessantly, I would hide in the garage.

"Did my child support pay for those? Or did the new boyfriend pony up the money? Pretty sure you weren't a D-cup last time I saw you," I say, wiping my hands down the front of my soil covered jeans.

She doesn't say anything, just stands there and pops her gum again. There might have been a little bit of murder in her eyes, but she doesn't scare me. Never has.

"You have a good night. Enjoy the event."

I walk away from her, needing to busy myself with anything other than talking to someone I wasted too many years on. The only reason I even stayed in this town was because I needed to be in my daughter's life. Just because her mother and I weren't right for one another doesn't mean I have to be a deadbeat dad and forget about my kid. I'm sure that's what her mother would have loved me to do, though, and I thoroughly enjoy pissing her off when I have to be in her presence.

The only good thing to come from getting her pregnant and getting married is my little girl. Well, Sawyer's not really little anymore.

"Daddy!"

I hear her yell to me from across the parking lot, but can't see where she is.

"Dad!"

I hear her again and when I finally see her, I'm ready to grab a jacket and throw it around her.

"Hey, Pumpkin. Are you warm enough? It's getting chilly out here," I say, trying to cover up my sudden and extremely protective mood.

"Yes, I'm fine. I'm going to be out there jumping around in a few minutes and get all sweaty and gross," she says.

She's supposed to still be five and in pigtails. Why is she fifteen and in a cheerleader skirt? What is that shit on her eyes? Is that glitter on her cheeks?

I rub the palm of my hand up and down my bristly cheek and groan under my breath.

"Do you have a sweatshirt just in case?"

She squints at me. She purses her glossed lips. She crosses her arms.

"God, you're so damn stubborn, Sawyer."

"It's the uniform, I know. Promise, I have a hoodie and my pepper spray."

She kisses me on the cheek and runs off to catch up with a group of girls all dressed just like her, bows and ribbons bouncing in their hair, and I wonder if all of their dads are worried, too. There's a small cluster of mom people walking behind them, insulated coffee mugs in hand, but my girl's mom isn't one of them.

Hannah is only involved to a point, and that point begins and ends with bringing Sawyer to me whenever she doesn't feel like being a parent. Those days are becoming more frequent and, even though I pretty much hate my ex-wife with a passion that burns as hot as the fire of a thousand suns, it makes me hurt for my kid. I've never parented a teenager. Parenting a teenage girl whose mother is less and less involved is getting difficult. She wants makeup and fancy hair and, for a while there, the skirts kept getting shorter. I want her to still be the kid with dirt smudged on her cheek from helping me on a job and her hair in a messy ponytail. Give me bib overalls any day instead of these itty-bitty clothes they're making for women now.

I watch as they all walk toward the stadium. The homecoming game is the most important fall event in this town. Lots of people come back to Brockport for the weekend, pack the stands, and fill the restaurants. I know I worry about the clothes and the people she's hanging out with, but I'm happy she gets this opportunity. When I was her age, I was busy not doing any of this stuff. My teen years were spent working at the tree farm to help my parents make ends meet.

Sawyer disappears in the crowd and I turn to get my mind back on track.

The lot where all the vendors are parked has filled to the brim with food trucks and crafts. We still have half an hour to kickoff, giving people plenty of time to mill around. There's a barbecue truck a few spots down from me and I'm pretty sure he's going to get all my money. Even further down is a guy about my age selling handmade onion crates and other wood crafts, and he catches me looking his way. I wave like a good neighbor would and he waves back. This is the epitome of "small town."

"Hey, Rick, what you got that's good today?"

Will has been around for years, but he's quiet and sticks to the background. His brother is a local priest who is used to being the center of attention. Will, however, is one of those guys who is extremely generous with his time and talent but doesn't advertise how talented he is.

"Man, everything is good. There are some baby blue spruces in the back of the truck if you want to check them out. Does Murph need anything for decorating the chapel?"

Reaching my hand out, he clasps it tightly and pulls me in for a half hug.

"I'm not sure, but I can ask him. Christmas is going to come quick," he says.

"Halloween and Thanksgiving first. Let's not rush St. Nick. Give him some time to check his list a few more times, you know?" We share a laugh and I motion for him to follow me to the bed of my pick-up where I have the bigger plants. "Prices are marked way down for the day. I've got to move some of this stuff out. It's all sitting in the spot where the new greenhouse is going up."

We team carry a few large trees to the front of my space, chatting about how business is and what he can help with out at the farm. It's comfortable conversation, and keeps my emotions in check when I see Hannah walking toward me once again.

"You're on dad duty for the rest of the weekend. I've got things to do," she says once she's within earshot, but she still says it much louder than necessary as if to draw attention to herself. She always draws attention, but it's not usually the good kind.

"I'm always on dad duty. When are you planning to act like a mother?"

The eye rolling and gum popping. It's difficult to explain in words how much I've come to hate her.

Will turns away from our interaction. He's not embarrassed by it, even if he wants to be. He wanders back to the bed of the truck and I see him trying to hide a smile. He's known Hannah since we were about Sawyer's age, so he knows what it's been like with her.

When I met Hannah, she was in her "good girl" phase and acting like a human being with a conscience. Hard to believe she was only four years older than our daughter is now when we found ourselves pregnant and getting married. That's the part that scares me.

Hannah still looks slightly taken aback by my question, but it's a game to her. She clutches her invisible pearls and covers the open-mouthed expression she paints on as if she's fooling me.

"I," she starts, then smiles, "am always acting like a mother."

My mouth opens, and I know it's because subconsciously I want to read her the riot act, but I close it and go about arranging buckets of flowers.

"Go. Do your things, Hannah. Sawyer will be fine with me. She understands," I say, not the least bit sarcastic.

"Good. Thanks," she says and walks away, slipping her hand through the arm of some man I've never seen before.

"Sawyer is a good kid. She's not going to end up like her mom, Rick," Will says from behind me. He's leaning against the grill of my truck, his arms crossed, and he looks just as sad as I feel. He would have made a fantastic dad.

"How do you do that? Read my mind? It's a little scary sometimes."

He shrugs, but smiles and wanders away to check out the other vendors.

Chapter 3

Maggie

So, there I was, just sitting in the food truck, when out of nowhere some fake-tittied ho with what looked like a barely out of high school guy on her arm swiped a cupcake. I wouldn't be fuming if she had actually paid for the food, but she just … took it.

"Deep breath, Mags. It's not worth getting upset about. It wasn't the prettiest cupcake anyway. Just like the woman who stole it."

I've been parked in the school parking lot for almost an hour. It's almost time for kickoff, so the only ones out here now are vendors checking their products and making food. The food smells delicious, and my mouth instantly waters as the scent of barbeque hits my nose. I should have eaten something before leaving the bakery, but I didn't because I was rushing. By the time I got here I was later than I normally would be because of all the traffic, because I didn't take into account the volume of people coming home for the weekend.

It's homecoming. Of course it's going to be a ridiculous number of people. Even with being late, I've still had to restock more than two dozen cupcakes because everyone loves Delilah's creations. My creations. I need to remind myself that these are mine, too.

"It's so pretty, Maggie," Will says, picking up a cupcake in its cute little package. "Not sure if I'll be able to eat this right away. I might need to Instagram it. Isn't that what all you younger people are doing these days?"

He makes me laugh every time I see him. Unlike a lot of the people in this town, I've known Will my entire life.

The best part is, his Instagram account is better than mine.

"How are you, Will? I haven't seen you in the bakery recently. Everything okay?" I ask, purely out of concern but also digging for info. He's always working on a project of some sort and I love hearing about all of them.

He pulls his phone from the pocket of his Carhartt jacket and sets the cupcake on the counter at the window. I attempt to slide out of the way, but he holds his hand up.

"You need to be in this one. I know you made these and you should get the credit," he says.

I cross my arms and lean on the counter so he can get me in the frame. Distracted by some guy hauling a tree out of his truck, I don't notice he's already taken the photo.

"Perfect, just like you," he says.

Sliding his phone back into his pocket, I give a questioning look. I'm used to people typing up a caption and posting things right away. It's sort of in the name of the app, you know?

"It might be called 'insta' but I do what I want," he says. Opening the package and pulling the cake out, he inhales deeply the scent of lemony sugar. "Oh, this is my favorite flavor."

Smiling as he takes a little bite, I wish I knew why he was unattached. His brother is a priest, but Will is just single. I've never understood it. He's a nice guy, handsome, and down to earth. You can't go wrong with Will.

"I'll need two more to go. You pick the flavors, though. They aren't for me." He takes another bite. "I had to take a break from visiting you and Lilah. My pants were starting to fit a little snug. But, to answer your question, yes everything is okay. I've been trying to visit the Veterans Home a little more often. This time of year is hard on a lot of the guys who don't have much family."

See? Awesome guy.

Turning to my stock of cupcakes, I pick two to send with him. I've started working more of the holiday flavors into the line-up, so I make sure to pull one that has peppermint mocha buttercream and choose pumpkin spice for the other.

"If you need a box of sweets to take with you when you go visit your friends again, just let me or Lilah know." I hand him the extra cupcakes and he passes me a wad of bills. "This is too much, let me get you some change."

"No need. I saw what happened."

"Why don't they make people like you anymore, Will?"

"They do. Everyday. You just have to pay attention." He winks at me and nods, taking another bite of his cupcake as he turns and wanders back in the direction he came.

*****

I hang out in my spot, crouched down in the window and watching a small crowd of vendors milling around after half time. They wander from one site to the next visiting with one another. Everyone else wants to chat and make small talk. I kind of hate small talk. It makes me so uncomfortable. I mean, there they all are talking about crafts and homemade soaps, and here I am just sitting in my truck acting like a creepy voyeur. I like it better this way right now.

The food truck thing kind of came out of left field. Lilah's husband is a restauranteur and caterer, so he was well acquainted with the idea of having food in a truck and taking it places. After we opened the bakery on Main Street and noticed how much business we were able to get just from walk in customers, I bravely mentioned expanding. Namely, expanding into the food on wheels arena.

Lilah was skeptical, Fisher thought it was the best idea ever, and I cried a lot because it was my idea and, therefore, I was in charge. I'm really quite okay with Lilah running the show and me being background noise. But, alas, I sucked it up and here I am running the food truck cupcake queendom.

Did I mention we had only been open officially for a couple months when I dreamed this up? I'm not going to complain, though. Not anymore. I'm in my element between the shop and the truck. We do these craft events and then there are food truck takeovers in various parking lots that I've gotten us signed up for, but with the weather starting to turn, those events are coming to a close for the season.

The group of crafters making their way around the parking lot loop around and head toward me. I try to make myself look busy, but I'm really not. The interaction is short and sweet. They come, they ooh and ahh over the confections, a couple of them grab bags and take business cards along with their change from the sale, and that's it. The extent to the small talk was asking me what the flavors were.

"I'm trying to watch how much sugar I eat, so I probably wouldn't have checked out her truck if it weren't for Ricky. He had a couple sitting on the hood of his pick-up and they just looked too delicious to not try," one woman says while walking away. "He's looking pretty delicious himself, if you know what I mean."

There's a short chorus of, "I know, right?" but that's all I hear before they're out of earshot.

One question, though. Who the hell is Ricky and if he's so delicious looking how did I not notice him buy something from me?

I scan the parking lot, set on finding this truck adorned with my cupcakes, when my eyes land on Will. He sees me looking his way and lifts his arm to wave. I give a little wave back just as the guy he's talking to turns his head in my direction.

He lifts his hand as well. I'm caught in a moment, turned to stone and unable to move because, holy shit, he's not delicious like a dessert. He's fucking scrumptious and I want to have him as a whole meal. It takes a split second for me to regain my composure and smile, whether he can see it from how far away we are from one another or not and the fact I'm pigeonholed in the window of a food tuck, who knows. That doesn't matter. What matters is there are two cupcake bags sitting on the hood of his pick-up truck and they ended up there because Will bought them.

The moment is over as quickly as it started and we all lower our arms. He turns his head and goes back to his conversation with Will. Will crosses his arms over his chest and gets a big grin on his face. He nods and the other guy looks my way quickly once more.

Maybe I need to be a bit more sociable? It's not like I don't have time. Pretty much everyone who wandered out to get food and shop during halftime has gone back in for the game. I could potentially have a conversation with a decent human being of the opposite sex. He has to be decent if Will is spending time with him. Those are the rules.

I work up the nerve to leave my station. The money is all secure and the cupcakes I had on display are the only ones out so if someone else come along and steals another one I won't be hurting too much from it. Slipping my keys and phone into my pockets, I climb out of the truck and check myself. It would suck to walk over there looking like a complete mess.

I hear him cuss as he starts toward the stadium, his steps hurried as he rushes toward someone coming out of the entrance to meet him.

"What's up?" I ask.

I was already most of the way across the parking lot to his truck, and turning around would have looked odd. Plus, I'm nosy. Asking Will for information is always a good idea.

"Not sure, but it sounds like his daughter got hurt. Someone sent him a message from inside," he says, taking a peek at his phone. "He said they had her up in the air and she twisted wrong coming down, so it's anyone's guess how bad or what actually happened."

I bump into a small evergreen tree and when I try to step out of its way, I knock another one over.

"That's horrible and scary. I hope she's going to be alright," I say, but what I'm actually thinking is I can't believe he's old enough to have a teenager. "Is his wife already in there with her?"

Will looks at me. It's almost one of those sad looks people give when they pity you for asking how someone is doing after they've passed away but you didn't know they had died.

"They aren't together anymore, but Sawyer's mom isn't here tonight anyway," he says, glancing at his phone again. "And Sawyer getting hurt doesn't mean she's going to bother to come back to check on her, either. Looks like they're going to head to the hospital to get checked out. Can you help me put all these trees in his truck?"

And that's the story of how I ended up briefly working landscape in October.

We work quickly, loading buckets of flowers and various little trees, and I've just finished moving the last bucket into the bed and closing the tailgate when I see him carrying his daughter through the parking lot.

Carrying. His. Daughter. A practically grown human. He's just carrying her through the lot like he lifts heavy things all day every day. My eyes drift to the bed of his truck where I just helped load a lot of nature. I can see the irony in my thinking now.

"Will, get the door for me?" he says.

"Daddy, I'm fine. I can walk on it. It'll be fine," Sawyer says, huffing and annoyed.

Standing at the back of the truck I watch as Rick sets her down and tells her to put pressure on her left foot. She does, but barely, and crumples from the pain.

"That's what I thought. Let's get you to the hospital," he says. "Will, man, thank you for loading everything up. You didn't have to. I would have come back for it."

"It's nothing. Maggie and I had it under control," Will says.

It's the first time Rick notices me standing there, all decked out in my Bakery on Main apron and boots straight out of the L.L. Bean catalog.

"I, uh … you're welcome. Don't forget your cupcakes," I say pointing to the hood of the truck where the bags still sit and it's very much a when Baby meets Johnny for the first time moment. I'm damn glad I don't have a watermelon in my arms.

He squints at me, nods, shakes Will's hand, grabs the bags, and gets in the driver's seat of his truck. The engine roars to life. When they pull away from his parking spot, Sawyer waves to me and Will, then holds up one of the bags and mouths, "Thank you," as Rick turns to head toward the exit.

Chapter 4

Maverick

"I don't like you being held up in the air by one leg, Sawyer. It's not safe," I say as I pull into the hospital parking lot.

She smiles sadly, because she knows how I feel about it. This isn't the first time she's been hurt doing a stunt of some sort. I could find a way to excuse it if it hadn't happened before, but here we are at the hospital again and the season just started.

"Dad, I'll be fine. It's just a bad sprain. It feels a lot like the last one," she says, looking at her ankle which is already pretty swollen. "You weren't this protective when I was doing dance and tumbling. Not even when I broke my arm from landing wrong. At least this injury is less severe."

"You hope. Sawyer, you hope it's less severe," I say emphatically.

My tone says I'm angry. I see it all over her face, too. She thinks she's done something wrong by doing a thing she loves and I don't want her to feel that way at all.

I pull into a spot and put the truck in park facing the entrance marked "Emergency" in bright red letters. Leaning into and wrapping my arms around the steering wheel, I drop my forehead onto my hands. Parenting just keeps getting harder as she gets older. Wasn't it supposed to get easier? Someone lied to me about this part.

"I saw Mom talking to you before the game. What happened?"

I don't give her enough credit for how easily she picks up on what's actually wrong. It's not her getting hurt and she knows it.

"You're home with me this weekend. She's got something else to do," I say, turning my head to watch her expression.

She covers her disappointment quickly with a smile. It's a mask she's learned to wear often and I hate it.

"Well, good. Then we can work on the design for the new greenhouse. I want a little section for tiny plants. All of your plants are big," she says, pulling her braids over her shoulders so they curve around her ears. "Plus, we need to start thinking about Christmas. Tree season is upon us."

"You been talking to Will?"

She rolls her eyes, but the smile tells me everything.

"A little. We want to do big decorations at the farm, maybe add a horse drawn sleigh once the ground freezes and a cocoa shop," she says.

Her face lights up like it used to when she was little and my anger about her mother and her injury dissipates.

I look at her foot where she's propped it up on the console between us and see the bruising that's already started.

"Alright, Pumpkin, let's get you in there and checked over."

I pull the keys from the ignition and shove them in the pocket of my jeans as I climb out of the truck. Sawyer already has her door open when I get to the other side and is attempting to get out by herself.

"They're going to give me crutches again," she says, hopping on one foot while holding the side of the truck.

"Probably. Unless they see something more on X-rays and they boot you," I say, and silently send up a prayer that isn't the case.

We're close enough to the entrance she could probably handle hobbling her way through to the waiting area, but I notice she keeps trying to put pressure on that foot.

"I'm not a baby, you know," she says as I lift her in a cradle hold.

"I know you aren't a baby, but you are my baby and you're hurt, so deal with it," I say, picking up speed to get us into the hospital and out of the chill that's taking over the early October air.

The nice thing about this place is no one really knows me. We live outside of town so I don't have to deal with the villagers. I've always been a bit of a loner anyway and it doesn't bother me. My kid is a social butterfly, though, and is saying hello to every nurse we pass and they're calling her by name.

"How do they all know you?"

"Well ... I'm not a hermit like you. I go to school with most of their kids, or they volunteer at the school." The tone tells me these are things I should have known. The message she's sending me is that I'm the clueless father. "Don't feel bad about it. Mom doesn't know anyone either. She's involved less than you."

Ouch. That stings more than I think I'm willing to admit, but it's definitely something I'm going to start working on. I don't want to be absent, not during these years when things get even crazier between school and boys and hormones. I stop my thoughts. I don't want to jump down that rabbit hole.

"Well, you just earned yourself more involvement from me. I don't like not knowing what's going on with my kid," I say close to her ear.

"I know. That's why I make sure you know all the important details," she says softly. "Mom doesn't care and I don't tell her anything unless it's necessary. Why do you think all the emergency contact forms only have you listed on them?"

I drop my head to hers. She's a tough kid.

A nurse calls Sawyer into an exam room. She's looking at us with an expression I can't quite place, but I'm sure it's because she knows the home situation and isn't letting on.

"I love you, Pumpkin. Let's get checked out so we can get home," I say, carrying her into the room.

*****

Sawyer has earned herself a six-week hiatus from cheer, a wrapped and booted ankle, and a decent dose of pain reliever. That break from cheer gets her through the football season and maybe, if I'm lucky, I can talk her out of being on the squad for basketball season. If I can't, maybe the doctor will be able to.

I get her home and settled on the couch with a mug of hot chocolate, hand her the remote to the TV and her cell phone, kiss her on the forehead, and head back out to the truck to unload.

The few hours I was at the school weren't as profitable as I had hoped, but they were better than nothing. I had a few people from our rival school take business cards. Good for me because it's a pretty wealthy district out of Rochester. They seemed like the kind of families who can afford to get quoted for a project that costs thousands of dollars.

I open the back door to the cab and begin pulling smaller potted plants from the seat and floor when I notice a brown paper bag with a cellophane front. I grab it thinking Sawyer left something behind, but an empty bag falls on the floor when I move it. Cupcakes from Will. In all the chaos of getting her to the hospital I forgot he brought food over for us. They would have been left on the hood if that woman hadn't reminded me they were there.

I feel my eyebrows pull together as I try to place where I could know her from, but come up empty. Who was she? Will seemed to know her, but he knows everyone. The way she was dressed tells me she was definitely a food vendor, but I'm clueless. We've established this. There's only one way to find out.

The phone rings three times before he answers with a, "Yeeellow." I shake my head, but proceed.

"Who was the lady helping you get the plants in the truck?"

"Oh, her? That was Maggie," he says, as if I am supposed to know who that is. He waits a beat before saying, "The cupcakes."

"The cupcakes."

"Have you tried them yet? She and Delilah make the best," he says.

I can hear him practically drooling over the thought of them and it gets a short chuckle out of me.

"Not yet, but Sawyer ate one on our way to the hospital. She's got a pretty nasty sprain, but should be okay with some rest. They booted her anyway for when she's out and about because she's such a repeat offender and we know she'll listen to the doctor. It's only for a week, but hopefully that's all it needs," I say. "I guess I should try this other cupcake so she doesn't steal it on me."

"And then go buy yourself a dozen because one just isn't enough," he says. "Tell Sawyer to get better quickly. I'm going to want her to help with the greenhouse as soon as she's mobile."

She's going to love that. Sawyer has been excited about getting the new greenhouse up since I first mentioned it. This business is as much her life as it is mine and we're hopeful it'll be ready before the first heavy snowfall. Now that she's injured, we'll just have to play it by ear.

I grunt a response and we hang up so I can continue putting plants back where they belong, but keep glancing at the bag I placed on the tailgate. Will knows everyone here and I'm a transplant. Sort of. I grew up closer to the Finger Lakes, so I always went to Rochester or Syracuse for anything I couldn't get locally.

When I met Hannah, I was working with my parent's business still. They owned a Christmas tree farm and always did a great job, but I wanted more than just one season to work. Not that working only happened in the fall and winter. There was plenty of planting and tending to the trees during the rest of the year, but the only time we were busy was the end of November and December.

But Hannah … I had just turned 20, and we were overrun with families trying to get their trees right after Thanksgiving. My dad sent me out to help anyone who needed a hand and I happened across her family. Before I knew it, we were exchanging numbers and had made plans to go see a movie the next night. She was almost 19. Things moved quickly with us and before I knew it, we were staring at a positive pregnancy test and the expectation that we were going to get married to raise this baby "the right way," as her father so eloquently put it.

In hindsight, I don't think he really knew much about his daughter. That's a mistake I'm not willing to repeat.

At first, I tried to make it work. Her family lived on the other side of Rochester near a college town on the edge of Monroe County, so that's where I went. We started our little family in a two-bedroom single-wide trailer on a 3-acre lot and I commuted every day back to my parent's house to work the farm. Eventually they asked if I wanted to plant some trees on the property I'd bought. There was plenty of room, so I said sure. I was 22 when I made the shift from working for the family business to damn near taking it over. The original farm is still operating with the help of my sister and brother, but where I planted those first trees just outside of Brockport has blossomed into so much more than just a Christmas tree farm. We've slowly turned it into a proper landscaping outfit with trees, flowers, mulch, and pretty much anything else you can imagine. Sawyer likes to get on the computer and see what the trends are, then she gets to designing something new. More than once I've had someone come in with one idea and leave choosing something my kid originally drew up on a napkin.

I tell you what, though. It's worth it. I wouldn't change a thing. It's happened the way it was supposed to and changed as it needed to so we could evolve. Over the years, I've divorced the wife, expanded the acreage and changed the business name just enough to make it mine. I also took that single-wide and turned it into the business office after Sawyer and I built what is now our home. Since she was a little girl, she has dreamed of living in a log cabin and I was able to make it happen for her. It's big enough for us and maybe a couple others if life ever gives us someone else to fill the extra rooms.

The cupcake catches my eye again as I walk past with a clipboard tucked in my armpit and a mug of cold coffee in my hand. I snatch the bag from the tailgate, open it, and inhale deeply. Chocolate and oranges … and mint. That's an interesting combination. I open the door to the office and kick it shut once inside. Dropping the clipboard on the table, I reach into the bag and pull the cutest little cake from inside. Peeling the wrapper down the sides, I take a large bite and am surprised by how spongey it is after sitting out all day. A bit of frosting gets caught in the stubble along my upper lip and I wipe it away with my hand. I don't remember the last time I had something from a bakery — a real bakery. I get doughnuts and muffins from the grocery store once in a while, but this is no grocery store cupcake.

Grabbing the bag, I look at the back and then turn it over searching for the name of this place.

"The Bakery on Main," I read aloud. "Not a very unique name, but I'm sure no one forgets it."

I take another bite, savoring the taste of mint and orange mixed with the richness of dark chocolate. I tack the bag up on my corkboard, then stand staring at some of Sawyer's designs. It's more than her landscape designs that decorate the board. There's a note telling me she'll be late to work because she has homework. Then there's the drawing she did when she was eight of Santa and a few elves with a tree in the sleigh. Having Sawyer as a kid has been the biggest gift I ever could have received.

"You're studying the wall again," she says from the door.

I heard it open but didn't acknowledge it. If I had, it might have come out sounding more like I was scolding for being off the couch and I don't want to make her think she shouldn't be out here.

"I am," I respond without turning. "You're really good at this. Have you thought about doing it after high school?"

"Dad, I'm fifteen. I haven't thought about much past this cheer season," she says, but I know my kid better than that. I turn and tilt my head as I look at her. She rolls her eyes and says, "Okay, so I've thought about it a little. I don't know how someone goes to college for landscape design though. We need to look into it."

She shrugs and adjusts her crutches, brushing a piece of hair behind her ear.

"You ate your cupcake?" she asks, pointing to the board where I've pinned the bag.

"It was the best cupcake I've ever eaten. I think that's where I'm getting your birthday cake from next year," I say. "What flavor did you have?"

We swap reviews of the treats Will sent home with us and I flip through the pages attached to my clipboard. They're all orders I've looked at a hundred times, most I can't do much about until spring. I grab a folder so I can put them in the file cabinet to review in a couple months. Some people like to plan way far ahead. I'm thankful for that. It's job security, and when your job often depends on the weather security is necessary.

"The woman from the cupcake truck was really pretty," Sawyer says, fiddling with a pen on the desk.

Closing the cabinet, I look at my daughter. This kid ran off most of the women I thought about dating from the time I started dating again until last month.

"I hadn't noticed," I say. It's not a lie. When she was standing at the truck with Will, I was kind of in a hurry to get out of there and get Sawyer to the hospital.

"You should take notice next time you meet her," she says.

"You don't like when I date," I say matter-of-factly, moving back to the table where I shuffle more papers and don't look at my daughter's face.

"Not true. I just haven't liked any of the women you've picked. There's a difference. Stop picking people who give off bad vibes like Mom and I'll stop making them not want to date a guy with a teenager," she says, quirking an eyebrow.

I can't help but laugh.

"Fair enough. I do tend to date people who remind me way too much of your mom, but it's not on purpose."

Sawyer turns and starts back out the door, but looks over her shoulder to say, "Time to break that cycle, Daddy. She's not worth it."

Chapter 5

Maggie

"He has a kid, Lilah. Not just a kid … she's practically grown," I say into the phone as I unpack what's left from the day.

"So? A lot of people have children young and are our age with teenagers," she says. "I think what's thrown you off is you want to get to know landscaper man but don't know how because you're afraid to let anyone know the real you."

I stand up straight, smack my head on the roof of the food truck, and call her a liar. She laughs at me. Always laughing at me.

"Okay, say I do want to get to know him. I don't think it's for lack of wanting anyone to really know me. I think, in this situation, it's more because I have a first name to go off of and that's it. I don't even know the name of his business." I rub the spot I hit on the top of my head and think about the complexity of dating in my thirties. Well, my almost thirties. "No, actually, I don't want to find out more about him. I'm perfectly fine waiting for him to randomly show up at the bakery after pining for me and my cupcakes."

"You're delusional. I love you. Goodnight, Maggie," she says, but I hear the teasing tone.

"See you in the morning, boss lady. Love you, too," I respond and end the call.

Working quickly, I finish moving food back into the bakery through the rear entrance. There isn't much left and once everything is inside, I place half-price stickers on each of the bags. We never sell yesterday's goods for full price. If it's still there after two days, it all goes to Father Murphy for his soup kitchen initiative. We don't usually have a lot that's been left for two days in a row, but what does go to Murph is definitely appreciated.

There isn't a whole lot to get done before fully shutting down for the night since Lilah and her daughter took care of most of it, but I waste no time in turning on the audio system and blaring a little Taylor Swift while I wipe down a counter and premeasure dry ingredients for tomorrow's specialty flavor cupcake. I would tell you what flavor that is, but it's a secret and I'm good at keeping secrets.

Humming along with the music, I let my mind wander and it wanders right into manly man, landscaper territory. He really does not look old enough to have a teenager and I'm not sure why I have such a difficult time wrapping my head around that. Growing up here, I know plenty of people who started families when they were in their late teens. Maybe it's hard to comprehend because I haven't seen myself as being ready for kids and I'm as old as I am. Not that there's ever even been a guy I want to raise a family with, but that's beside the point.

I'm mid-thought when my phone starts ringing. It's Gram's ringtone, and I immediately get a sinking feeling in my gut. She doesn't usually call me after 7 p.m. because she's busy watching reruns of M*A*S*H and Golden Girls, and lord help you if you interrupt her TV time.

"Gram, what's wrong?" I say as soon as I answer.

"Why would anything be wrong, Rebecca? I can't give a call to my favorite daughter for no reason?"

Rebecca. Daughter. I had started to smile, calmness washing over me, until she said those words. I feel my face fall as I pivot and try to put the smile back in my voice, hiding the concern. It's getting more difficult.

"You can call me any time, Gram. How are you tonight?"

I don't correct her, because the last time I did it stressed her out and I don't want to do that to Gram, especially not over the phone when she's home alone. I begin quickly putting my ingredients away, making sure lids are on tight and lights are off, as my grandmother tells me about her day shopping in the city.

The only issue is, Gram doesn't drive anymore, she hasn't been to Rochester or Buffalo to shop in over a year, and she's called me during her programs. Nothing feels okay right now.

I keep her on the phone, chit-chatting away like it's a normal conversation, as I slowly pull out of my parking space behind the bakery and drive the ten minutes it takes to get back to her house. When I turn into the driveway, my headlights sweep across the living room windows.

"Oh, it would seem someone is at the house. I'll let you go, dear. We'll talk again soon," she says.

"That sounds like a wonderful idea," I say. "Goodnight."

"Goodnight, sweetheart."

I turn off the car and watch as her silhouette appears in the window. Gram pushes the sheer curtains to the side, peering out into the dim evening light as I sit quietly in my car in the dark. What if this isn't a fluke? She waves at me, prompting me to grab my bags and pull myself from safety. I was safe from reality until she called. It wasn't a thing that I needed to think about for just a few hours. Things were fine when I talked to her earlier today.

Letting myself in through the breezeway that attaches the garage to the house, I want to be six again. I want to not acknowledge what's been slowly creeping into our lives for months. Reaching for the doorknob, I breathe in deeply. The door opens and my nose is filled with the smell of homemade pasta sauce and garlic bread.

"Margaret! Finally, you're home. I made dinner," she says, wandering into the kitchen, an apron tied around her waist.

The pasta bowl is filled with enough spaghetti for a family of ten. She's used her biggest stock pot and it's closer to full with sauce than not.

"Gram, who all were you cooking for tonight?" I ask, smiling at her.

"Well, just us."

"You seem to have gotten a bit carried away," I say, smiling while trying to conceal the concern.

My grandmother's face scrunches as she looks mournfully at the stove. "I didn't think I made that much. Did you add more puree when you came in?"

I shake my head, but grab a plate from the cupboard and kiss her on the cheek as I walk past to the silverware.

"Thank you for making pasta, Gram. It's my favorite."

She smiles as I scoop noodles onto my dish and spoon sauce from the pot, taking a few meatballs with it. She sticks a slice of garlic bread on the side of the plate as I make my way over to the kitchen table where I spent my childhood coloring pictures.

"Did you eat, Gram?" I ask, twirling a forkful of pasta until it's practically the size of the meatballs.

Waiting for her to respond makes me uneasy and I say her name again.

"What, dear?" She slides into the seat across from me, a look on her face I can't place.

"Did you eat?"

"Of course, I ate, Margaret. You said you weren't going to be home for supper, and I wasn't going to wait."

Chewing and swallowing the bite in my mouth, I wait to respond so she doesn't scold me for talking with my mouth full.

"Good. I was worried you waited for me anyway," I say. "Have you talked to Mom this evening?"

She crosses her arms and props her elbows on the table, a confused look drawing a shadow on the wrinkling skin of her face.

"No. I haven't talked to her in a couple of days. Was I supposed to call her for something?" she says curiously.

"Uh … no. No, Gram, I don't think you were. I just wasn't sure if you had gotten lonely and needed someone to chat with while I was at work," I say.

Wiping the sauce off my plate with a slice of bread, I stand to take care of my dishes and begin putting dinner away. I don't know where I'm going to find enough dishes to store this much sauce, but I'll figure it out. Even if I have to get her into bed and then run to the store for containers, I'm not going to waste homemade sauce from Gram.

I begin searching the cupboard for enough dishes, and when I turn to ask her where she hides the biggest Tupperware bowls, she's disappeared from the kitchen.

My search doesn't last long as I find her in the bedroom down the hall, already slipped into a cotton nightgown and brushing her hair. From the door, I watch as she turns the bed down and nestles into her side of the mattress. For as long as I can remember she's left room for my grandfather who's been gone since I was a child. It's sweet, but lonely, too.

"I'll get the light, Gram," I say, walking into the room and around the foot of the bed. I lean down and gently kiss her on the forehead. "Get some rest. I love you."

"I love you, too, Margaret. Let's have sausage gravy and biscuits for breakfast. I want to talk to you about the flower beds," she says.

I chuckle, but agree to the food and conversation she wants.

"That sounds like a great plan for a Sunday."

*****

Wrapped up in a heavy blanket, I carry a mug of coffee and my cell phone out to the screened-in porch. There's an oversized armchair that Gram bought in the 70s and, ever since I was a kid, I come out here and curl up when I need to disappear. I've put the winter window covers on, but they only cut down slightly on the chill once cold weather really sets in and I end up huddled under a comforter while trying to breathe in some sort of calm. Tonight, I don't think calm is the word I would use.

"Mom? We need to talk about Gram," I say when she answers, her voice already concerned because it's kind of late for me to call.

She launches into her list of concerns, making sure Gram didn't fall or have a stroke, because I would absolutely call her and say we need to talk without giving that information first, I think sarcastically. I roll my eyes as I respond to her, but since she can't see me do it, I can't get in trouble for it.

"I think we're dealing with some dementia," I say. "Or at the very least, confusion."

"What makes you think that?" she asks.

I'm worried she's in denial, but begin explaining some of the smaller things — Gram slipping and calling me the wrong name, talking about my grandpa coming home soon from work, asking what time the Tonight Show with Johnny Carson comes on.

"She's just getting old, Maggie. Sometimes things get a little mixed up," she says.

I knew she would say that. There's a difference between mixing things up on occasion and what I'm talking about though. Plus, I've kept it between me and Lilah for more than a few months now as the occurrences become more frequent.

"I was planning to talk to you about all of this tomorrow when you come over for brunch, but that plan obviously changed," I say. "She called me tonight and had a full conversation believing I was you, saying she'd been shopping in the city."

"Oh," I hear her quietly say as if she didn't mean for me to hear.

"Gram also knew I wouldn't be home for dinner. I walked in and she had made like five pounds of pasta and her large stockpot was full of homemade sauce. She doesn't remember making that much and thought I had added to the pot," I say. "She hasn't made homemade sauce in a few years because we haven't had a huge family dinner with all of us together. There's enough leftovers I'm going to have to have Will take some down to Murph for his guys. It'll feed them for the rest of the week."

We're both quiet. I want to wait for her to say something, but the fact she hasn't is not making this easier. I breathe in and out deeply to release the rock in my chest.

"It might be time to consider having an extra hand or two to come in throughout the day while I'm at work. Just to check on her, nothing more. Someone to come over and have a cup of tea or make a batch of cookies with," I say to break the silence.

She's still so quiet. I pull my blanket tighter around my shoulders, unsure if I'm cold because it's October or because I know we're beginning to travel down a road that won't necessarily be easy.

"I think that would be a good idea. I'll start coming by every day again on my way home and maybe some of the ladies she used to play Scrabble with can fill in the gaps," she says.

"Thank you. It'll help put us both at ease knowing she's safe, Mom. It's been getting worse and I just … This was a difficult phone call to make."

We sit in silence again until I hear the unmistakable sound of her sniffling.

"I'm sorry, Maggie."

Taking a sip of my now lukewarm coffee, I wonder how to respond. Like, how do you say it's okay when you're 27 and would like to have a social life but instead you hang out at home with your 85-year-old Gram playing board games on the weekend?

That's the thing with us though. It really is okay.

"Mom, I chose to move in with her. I'm not here just to help her, I'm here because I love her and we're both fucking lonely," I say without thinking about my language. I mean, it's my mom. She knows I cuss like a truck driver, but it's different when I start letting it fly in conversation with her. "Look, I couldn't care less about the massive pile of pasta or the sauce, because it's going to get eaten one way or another. What I do care about is making sure she's safe when having a confused moment while using the stove. Neither of us can be home with her all the time."

"When did you grow up?"

A smile breaks the tension I feel forming where my eyebrows are drawn together.

"I'm not sure, but I like the person I've grown up to be."

"Me, too, sweet girl. Me, too."

Chapter 6

Maverick

It's been a week since she messed up her ankle. Sawyer is doing better and isn't required to wear the boot anymore, but she's still taking it easy so things can heal completely. In the meantime, I'm trying to get as much done around the house and prep for Christmas tree season while making sure she's not overdoing things at home. I'm positive she's not taking it easy when she's at school, but I can't control that unless I go there and walk her to every class. That would be embarrassing.

Maybe I should do that. Embarrassing for her, but hilarious for me.

I shake my head. No, that wouldn't be nice. I'm better than that. Plus, she's already been back for a week and it would be awfully strange if I just showed up and asked if I could shadow my kid.

Besides, there is just too much to get done at the farm. We had an unexpected first snow last night, so I've been clearing driveways and paths out to the grove. I'm not completely sure why I'm bothering since it's probably all going to melt tomorrow.

Climbing out of the truck I hear an ATV nearby and feel my mouth droop a bit as Sawyer pulls up beside me at the gate to the back lot where we're planning to build one of the greenhouses.

"You're supposed to be resting that foot."

I try to ignore her eyeroll by putting on my work gloves, but she knows I saw it, just like she wanted me to.

"It's a sprain, not a break. It's still wrapped and I've got my boot on for extra protection," she says, lifting her leg as high as she can to prove she is in fact wearing the boot.

It doesn't make me happier. She's supposed to be keeping calm for a few more weeks. This is the opposite.

"Anyway," she says, crossing her arms as best she can in an old Carhartt jacket of mine I keep on hand. "I wondered if you wanted to go into town for lunch. You've been working since dawn and it looks like you're almost done. Maybe we can pop into that bakery and grab dessert for later."

I nod, pull my cap down tight, and wait. She knows I always come back to the house around lunch. There was no reason for her to come out to find me. Discussing food could have waited another thirty minutes.

"We could spend the rest of the day watching movies," she continues.

Again, something we could have discussed at the house. I peek at her from under the brim of my cap and see hesitancy on her face just before she speaks again.

"Mom's not coming to get me tonight like she was supposed to," she says.

There it is. This is where the rebellion is coming from, regardless how small the act.

I grunt a response. I'm not shocked. Hannah has put off coming to get Sawyer all week. Called twice to check on her after I let her know about our trip to the emergency room, but hasn't bothered to come see her.

"Thoughts?"

"Pumpkin, I don't think you want to know what my thoughts are when it comes to your mother."

"I meant lunch, cupcakes, and movies, but okay. How about thoughts about me moving in full time and she can see me when she wants to instead of breaking promises all the fucking time? That's kind of what she's been doing anyway," she says. "She doesn't give a shit about me."

"Language. Her actions leave a lot to be desired. You moving in full time is fine with me, but we've got to talk to her about it first."

Her cheeks flush, no doubt embarrassed about her nonchalant use of cuss words. She presses her lips together and gives me half a smile. She was worried about asking me? What am I going to tell her? No? That would never happen. Not when it's something like this.

"I hate the idea of talking to her about it. Can you do it?"

Pulling open the gate so I can drive through and have some thoughts to myself about the upcoming projects, the air feels thick with my daughter's emotions.

"I wasn't going to ask you to do it. This is something I need to talk to her about. If she's not going to step up and be available like she's supposed to be for you, then she's going to deal with me," I say. My tone is harsher than I intended, but this shit gets to me as much if not more than it does to Sawyer. "We'll get it figured out, Sawyer. I promise."

31

*****

Lunch at Canal Side. Hot cocoa from the Jumping Bean. Half a dozen cupcakes from the Bakery on Main.

After a morning full of emotions about Hannah's lack of give a damn for our kid, we kept busy visiting the shops along Main Street. It has been oddly enjoyable. I don't think the food has everything to do with that. Spending time with Sawyer away from the tree farm is rare because there's so much to do there that I forget I'm allowed to have fun.

"What movie were you thinking of starting with?"

"Avengers!" she yells back from her bedroom. When I look up from the cabinet that houses our massive collection of DVDs, she's limping her way back toward the living room, but has changed into sweatpants and an old hoodie from when I attempted college. Wrapping her hair up into a bun, she adds, "We could just start with the first one in the MCU and see how far we get this weekend."

"Nerd," I say, shaking my head.

"No one said I had to be an airhead to be a cheerleader, Daddy."

That stops me cold. She's incredibly intelligent and I hope no one is treating her like she's less than because she puts on a skirt and yells the loudest for her team.

"I didn't see her at the bakery when we stopped there. I'm kind of sad about that," she continues, switching topics as if I'm not inside my head trying to decide if I need to fight some kid who called my daughter an airhead.

"Wait. What? Who?"

She gives me an "oh good lord you can't be this dense" look and points to the box of cupcakes.

"Her."

I mouth an "Oh," but don't have anything else to say.

"Maybe I'll go in after school one day and do some recon work," she says, laughing.

"Yeah, you go right ahead. I'm not introducing myself to some woman I don't know until you give your stamp of approval. If it doesn't work for you, it doesn't work for me," I say.

Pulling a stack of cases from the cupboard, I make my way over to the television.

"You know I will, Dad. I'll get the info and her number for you," she says, flopping onto the couch in a fit of giggles.

"Yeah, you do that. Just make sure you find out all the details, if that's your plan. All her favorite things, her best friend's mother's first boyfriend's name, how she likes her eggs ... all of it," I say, the words lightly laced with sarcasm.

I find myself laughing along with her, but wonder if she really will do what she says. It feels weird to have my teen daughter scouting dates for me. I'm not even really interested in dating.

Am I?

"Popcorn?" I ask as the movie menu comes onto the screen and I shake away the idea of sharing my days with someone other than Sawyer.

In charge of the remote, she starts clicking around but I catch a brief nod and make my way to the kitchen. She hasn't spoken to her mother yet. I know she doesn't want to and I honestly can't blame her. My opinion of her mom really is none of her business, but she knows it's been rough for a lot of years. I try to keep it civil with Hannah, especially when Sawyer is close by, but she likes to argue and twist things to get her way. For the majority of our marriage, I found myself just agreeing with her about things that would have caused a fight otherwise.

Grabbing my phone from the counter after tossing a second bag of popcorn in to nuke, I open my messages and find the conversation with her. My kid deserves so much better than what Hannah is providing right now and I need to start the conversation. Firing off a text and not thinking twice before sending it causes a sinking feeling in my gut I'd rather ignore.

All it said was, "We need to discuss Sawyer's living situation."

It's nothing bad.

But when the phone rings a minute later as I'm pulling a steaming bag of popcorn from the microwave, it feels like I jumped into a river of lava. My entire body is on fire when the call connects and I hear her voice.

"Why the hell do we need to talk about her living situation," she says. "There's nothing wrong with the situation."

It's the way she says "situation" that upsets me. I envision her using air quotes to go along with the way she changes her tone from annoyed to mocking.

"I want her to live with me full-time," I say. No sense tiptoeing around the reason I contacted her in the first place.

I will try to play nice, though.

"What's wrong with the way it is now?"

Dumping popcorn into two large bowls, I try to figure out how to be polite while also despising the fact I have to answer this question at all.

"The way it is now is Sawyer's with me ninety percent of the time anyway and she'd like to have her belongings with her, but they're at your house," I say. "She wants to bring her stuff home."

Holding the phone in the crook of my neck, I take snacks to the living room where Sawyer is still waiting to press play. She looks up at me and sees the phone. I quietly tell her I'm talking to her mother. Without a word, she clicks the button to start the movie. She knows this could take a while.

"Are you saying my house isn't home to her?"

"No. I think she feels like it's become less of her home because she's rarely there," I say. "Look, Hannah, I don't want to fight with you about this. I just want our daughter to be happy. You don't seem to have the time to spend with her right now and she's going to be helping get the greenhouses designed and built. I'll need her here anyway."

She laughs, but not a funny "I understand" laugh. Nope.

"Oh, I see. Maverick Rogers wants to have his kid around more for the free labor."

I scrub my free hand across my eyes and pinch the bridge of my nose. She's insane.

"Not even close to the truth, and you know it," I say, hearing the frustration build in my own voice.

It's quiet between us and I hear the distinct sound of billiard balls hitting against one another. I listen more closely and can make out other background noise reminiscent of my very brief bar hopping days. This was a bad idea. I should have waited to talk to her until daylight. It's a Saturday night, so of course she's out drinking.

"You know what, never mind. We'll talk about it when you're sober," I say.

"Blah blah blah. Whatever, Rick. You know what, she can live with you. If that's what she wants, so be it. You never were able to tell her no, so why should this be any different."

She must think I always give in to Sawyer. I don't. There are rules at my house. There's routine. She has boundaries and we respect the hell out of each other. That's why my relationship with my daughter is fucking awesome.

"We'll be by tomorrow for her stuff. I'll make sure she leaves some clothes and toiletries for when she spends the night."

"You know she won't want to. She's always chosen you," she says. She quietly adds, "I wish I wasn't such a shit parent."

And I wish I could say I tell her she's not, but I don't. Because I think she is. One of the advantages to our divorce was we were nice to one another through it and never had a formal custody agreement or child support arrangement. We just worked things out since we live close to each other. Sawyer's primary residence was Hannah's house because I felt she needed her mom in those early years. But now? Now she's going to be home to stay.

"We'll be over tomorrow. Goodbye, Hannah."

I press the red button to hang up, feeling okay with the way the conversation went, and walk back into the living room. As I situate myself on the couch, I hear her phone make a noise and look at her out of the corner of my eye. It's too much of a coincidence that I hang up with her mother and she gets a text message.

She sighs deeply as she reads it then presses a button to make the screen go dark.

"Everything alright?" I ask, knowing it's possible she won't want to talk to me about it.

Without answering me, she pauses the movie and turns so we're face-to-face. It takes less than a second for my brain to register the tears welling up in her eyes.

"Thank you for dealing with this. She's pissed at me, but I don't care. She's barely there when I'm with her anyway so I don't know why she's upset. Is she afraid you're going to take away her child support?"

I hadn't even thought about that. Over the years the amount I give her has been fluid. Sawyer and I will go shopping for school clothes and I pay for all of them. When I drop her off some weekends, we hit the grocery store and stock up on things she likes to have for dinners or snacks at school. Hannah has never complained that what I do give her on top of that isn't enough and if she's going to start now, I'm not sure how we're going to remedy the issue without getting lawyers involved. If Sawyer is living with me full time, paying her any child support feels wrong and if there isn't a written agreement she shouldn't expect any at all.

"No idea, but that's not something you need to be concerned about. Right this second, you need to worry about what's going to happen to Captain America and Iron Man and leave the grown up shit to me."

I hate being a grown up.

"He is America's ass, after all. We must be concerned about that. It's way more important than Mom and her nonsense," she remarks.

I smile at my kid and wonder how I got so lucky the first time around. I know she's going to try to figure out how to solve whatever her mom is piling onto her, but she's going to have me to help her navigate through it.

"He really is. I wonder if women think about my butt like they think about Chris Evans'?"

She cracks a smile and starts laughing, wheezing out an, "Ew."

"Right. I need to start working out more," I say, smiling at her even bigger. "This stuff with your mom is going to be resolved. If she's mad about it, that's on her. You are old enough to make this decision and as long as we're all in agreement, we're good. I'll talk to her more tomorrow when we go pick up some of your stuff, but I don't want you freaking out thinking about what Mom thinks or how she's going to act. I'll handle it."

I hold my fist out and she bumps it. Good. Great. Conversation over. The rest of our movie marathon is boring and mundane, which is perfect for a Saturday night at home.

Chapter 7

Maggie

Gram wants the bushes in the front yard ripped out, a tree in the back cut down and the stump ground out, and a small garden for vegetables put in.

Right now.

She doesn't want to hear that it's almost November and the time to do all of this would be in the spring.

"Margaret, I don't think it's unreasonable to at least call some places and see what can be done now."

"Who should I call? There are a ton of tree services and a handful of landscapers close by. Do you have one in mind?" I wish I could talk her out of this, but she makes a good point. If some of the work can be started now, then we can make a reasonable plan for springtime.

She gets up from the table, walks to the stove and picks up the kettle, turning slowly to fill it at the sink to her right. I watch her movements and hope she stays accident proof for longer than I anticipate.

Returning the kettle to the stove, she turns on the burner. Two mugs are pulled from the cupboard and a box of teas on the counter is opened. She chooses for both of us, and I don't mind one bit. I'm just watching quietly to make a memory.

"When you stare at me, I can feel it on my skin," she says, her back still turned to me. "You've seen me do this a thousand times. It's no different this time."

"I know, but that doesn't mean I don't want to remember it forever," I say.

There's no time to not be completely honest with her. Some weeks I feel like I'm losing a piece of her every day; other weeks the days go by without incident.

"You say it like I'm going to die tomorrow," she shakes her head as the kettle begins to heat. Listening to the water boil, I wish she didn't think about her death even if the idea doesn't scare her. "Even if I did kick it tomorrow, it's okay. I have had a pretty good life. My memory isn't quite what it was, but I'm doing okay for an old lady."

I smile and reach for the mug of steaming tea as she walks the short distance to the table.

"Yeah, you are. So, let's talk about who to call for these projects …"

*****

Sitting down at the counter in the back of the bakery, I look through the short list of landscape companies Gram and I decided to try calling first.

Delilah usually works on specialty orders on Mondays, so we open midmorning instead of a normal time to catch the early crowd. My Mondays are spent baking cookies. Nothing too exciting or difficult, so I'll be making phone calls while waiting for timers to ring.

Staring at the list again, I start with the first name. I leave a message. Pull two trays of cookies out to cool, put two more in. Set the timer. Call the next number and talk to a receptionist who sounds like she doesn't love her job. I leave my name and number, but hope they don't call me back.

"What are you working on today?" Delilah asks as she walks through the kitchen to stick her bags in the office.

"Chocolate chip, oatmeal raisin, snickerdoodle, and white chocolate macadamia. You?"

"Cupcakes for a sweet sixteen, wedding cake sampler for a couple coming in later in the week, anniversary cake that includes lots of fondant," she says, sipping from a thermal mug.

It sounds like we both have a busy morning.

"I need to find a landscaper for Gram. We made this list and I just don't even know who is good and who to avoid."

I hand Delilah the notepad I wrote on while explaining in more detail what the project entails. She grabs my pen and starts making notes. She crosses one out completely.

"That one, just no. They like to give quotes, take a down payment, start a job, and never come back. I don't even know how they're still allowed to be in business. This one, though, I would trust. His family has been in the tree business for years and he expanded out here about 15 years ago."

I look at her, and I know I'm doing something with my face. She hasn't lived here long enough to know all the details about all the people. I mean, I grew up here and have no idea what or where this farm is other than not in the village or on a main road I normally travel. I've kind of lived a sheltered life since high school, though, so maybe that shouldn't be a surprise to me.

"Fisher and I get our Christmas tree from his farm. He's got some greenhouses planned, but no clue what he's going to offer," she continues. Taking another sip from her cup, she hands the list back to me, smiling a little too much. "Just call him. Even if he can't get to it before the end of the year, he can give you an idea when the work could be done."

I nod and set the notebook on a shelf just as my timer rings and I have to get back to work.

"I'll call between flavors," I say, really to myself more than Delilah. "I just need to get these cookies done first."

Delilah offers me a smile and turns on our Monday morning playlist, then begins working on her projects. The music soothes a piece of me and I begin sorting the cooled cookies to put out in the display case.

"His name is Maverick, by the way," she says, passing behind me to grab something from the counter I'm working at. "A lot of people call him Rick, though."

That gets my attention and she damn well knew it would. I stare at her. She stares back, a sly grin playing at the corners of her mouth.

"My landscaper man? That Rick?"

"Your landscaper man," she says, laughing. "You should tell him you call him that when you ask him about pulling out your bushes and planting your garden. I bet he'd jump at the chance to work for you."

My eyes roll so hard I think I see the inside of my skull, but I start laughing, too.

"I don't think I'll be able to call him at all now. This is embarrassing."

"You will call him and you will ask him to come give you a quote. This isn't for you. It's for Gram. Take one for the team, Mags."

Is she fucking with me? I feel like she's fucking with me and using my grandmother as bait.

"I should just have Gram call. It's her project, after all. I really don't need to be taking up my work time to make personal calls. It's unprofessional," I say, but even I don't believe anything I just said.

She grabs her cell phone and the notepad with all the information on it.

"Delilah, no. Don't pull a Maggie," I say as she walks past me typing numbers into the phone.

Once upon a time Lilah and Fisher were enemies until I called him and forced her to apologize for her wrongdoing. It's a whole story.

"I'm not, but the fact you're afraid I might is fun for me," she says as I follow her from the kitchen through to the front of the bakery. "I wouldn't actually call him, but you need to do this for Gram. Think about how happy it would make her."

She turns to me to say something else, but the bell hung over the front door rings and we both look at the man who sheepishly enters. He looks like he doesn't belong in a cute little bakery in the middle of town. He belongs on a farm, tending trees and working the land.

Lilah grabs my arm and I look at her, my mouth slightly open in surprise.

"I guess the Universe is intervening. I'm going to go check on your cookies," she says and quietly leaves me standing behind the counter looking like a fool.

Naturally I do the first thing that comes to mind. I say something stupid.

"We're not open yet," I blurt out.

He steps closer to the counter, eyeing the few things in the display. They're leftovers from yesterday and marked down, but I know for a fact they're still delicious.

"Oh. My apologies. The door was unlocked, so I assumed you were. What time do you actually open? I can come back."

He smells so good. There are only a few feet and a counter between us, but I want to jump over it and stick my nose against his neck. Taking a deep breath, I close my eyes for just a moment and when I open them again, he's smiling at me. It's crooked and adorable, and there's a hint of a dimple in his left cheek hidden by the dark stubble.

"Are you okay?" he asks, but I'm still full of stupid. "Maggie, isn't it? You were at the high school a couple weeks ago."

Oh God, he knows my name. I just nod. That's all I'm capable of.

"My friend, Will, gave me a couple of the cupcakes you were selling. I've been meaning to come in ever since. Well, I did come in, but I don't think you were here that day," he says. Tapping his fingers on the counter, he glances at the display again, "So … what time does your bakery open? I'd like to come back and try something else."

41

I do that fish thing with my mouth — it opens and closes like I'm drinking water, and don't pretend you don't know what I'm talking about — while I try to get my brain working.

"Um, we technically open at 11, but if there's something you see that you like, I'm sure we can work out a deal," I say.

I feel my face immediately heat. Why did I say that? I sound so dumb. Why is this man making me sound like a lovestruck pre-teen? I close my eyes and hope when I open them, I've actually died because that would be better than this debacle.

I open them. He's standing there, but now he's wearing a smile that reaches his eyes and his shoulders are visibly relaxed beneath his Carhartt jacket. Unfortunately, I continue to debate if death would still be better than trying to crawl back from this.

"I think I'd like to make a deal," he says, his voice gruff and filled with an emotion I cannot read.

Moving down the counter to get a closer look at what's available, he begins selecting one thing after another until he's filled a large bakery box with a dozen cupcakes and pastries.

"How is your daughter's ankle?" I ask, finally retrieving my head from my rectum.

Delilah wanders out as I'm ringing up the items Maverick has chosen, and carefully places half a dozen fresh cookies in the box.

"Hi, Rick. Getting ready for Christmas yet?" she asks.

"Trying to, but Sawyer messed up her ankle during cheer so my number one helper is having some trouble keeping up," he responds. Turning his attention back to me, he continues, "It was just a bad sprain, but I want her to take it easy. Doctor said to stay off it a bit and no cheer for a while, so at least I have one less thing to worry about."

"Well, I'm glad she's healing. I know how much she loves working the farm with you," Delilah says. She gives me the "have you asked him yet" look and I respond with a look that clearly tells her I'm chicken. "We know you're about to get super busy, but Maggie was saying this morning she needs a landscaper. Maybe you could grab a cup of coffee and talk about her project?"

How did she get so good at this talking to people thing? She wasn't good at this when we first met. Oh, right, I taught her everything she knows. Really. I haven't always been this ridiculous.

They're both looking at me.

"Yes. Please." That's it. I don't tell him what the project is. Just confirm and be polite.

My ears are on fire and I need to leave. So, I do. I push the box of goodies across the counter and walk back to the kitchen.

"Is she okay? Did I say something?" I hear.

"She's fine. It's just been a long time …" and her voice trails off until I can't make out what's being said.

Opening the freezer door, I shove my whole head in as far as I can. This should help speed up my death from mortification. Freeze my brain. It doesn't work, anyway.

"Don't most people stick their heads in the oven?" she asks from behind me.

"That's only if it's a gas oven and we don't have one of those. This would work better if you slam the door on my neck, okay? Just put me out of my misery."

Her hand starts cautiously rubbing my shoulder. Then she pulls me back out of the freezer to get a good look at me.

"He's going to meet you at the Bean in a half hour. Get yourself together, fix your eyeliner, shotgun a Red Bull, and do the thing."

"Do the thing. Right, yes, I can go to the coffeehouse and talk to Mr. Landscaper Man with the gorgeous eyes and amazing stubble about Gram's landscaping. I can do this," I say in an attempt to pump myself up. "Oh my god, what if I make an even bigger fool of myself there? There will be witnesses."

I cover my face as she begins laughing at me.

"Stop it. You're a big girl. He's a businessman and you want to give him business. It'll be fine."

It'll be fine.

Delilah returns to her projects, ignoring my potential for messing things up.

I just repeat that it'll be fine over and over while I finish baking what I need to get done in the short timeframe I have. I'm back in the groove when a timer goes off.

"That's not my timer. What timer is that?" I ask, nervously.

"Hey, Mags? Calm the fuck down," Delilah says, her head down as she concentrates on a design for the anniversary cake she's planning. "That was the timer I set for you so you can't use the excuse you lost track of time."

Oh. That's what I was afraid of.

"Go on," she says, waving her hand toward the door. "Coffee. Handsome man. Vegetable gardens and trees. I can't wait to hear about it when you get back."

"Damn, you're bossy. Are you in competition with Gram?"

"Where do you think I learned it? Now, go, or I'm dragging you down the block by your earlobe."

I untie my apron and hang it by the sink, smiling.

"You're the best friend I've ever had, Lilah."

"I love you, too. See you in a bit."

Chapter 8

Maverick

Sawyer's right. She is pretty.

I wish I had the opportunity to meet her for real when we were at the vendor event, though. I feel like it would have been neutral territory and maybe the conversation wouldn't have been so quick. All things happen when they're meant to, though, right? You don't close the door when opportunity knocks, which is why when Delilah told me what was going on, I jumped at the chance to meet with Maggie.

My daughter's opinion of her has nothing to do with it.

Sitting in the local coffee shop, I wait for her to show up. I'm not entirely sure she's going to after the way she acted at the bakery. It seemed the conversation was moving in a good direction until Delilah came out from the kitchen. Not that I didn't enjoy talking to her and catching up a bit, but I went to the bakery for a reason.

To buy cupcakes.

And meet a woman.

She's also a woman who appears to be much younger than I'm used to checking out. I try really hard to date in my age bracket and Maggie appears well below that. She's probably not outside my acceptable range, but straddling the line.

Picking up my cup of black coffee, I blow gently across the top of the mug to cool my next sip before setting it against my lip, and I hear the door open.

Now, I'm not going to say I have any feelings in particular, but there's definitely something happening when I watch her walk through the entrance and stop to read a sandwich sign. Maggie's smile lights up the space surrounding her when she hears someone call out her name. I'm watching her every move as she waves to a man behind the counter and slowly pulls her arm back to her side.

Then she's looking around the room for me as her smile fades.

And her eyes lock on mine and the grip around my coffee mug tightens.

Her smile reappears as she pushes a lock of dark blonde hair behind her ear.

Before I can think too much about it, I leave my drink behind and slide out of my chair to say hello. She takes my outstretched hand and shakes it gently, and her soft fingers fit damn near perfectly against my rough palm.

"We didn't have a chance for proper introductions. I'm Maverick Rogers. I own Sugar Shack Landscaping just outside of town," I say.

"I know," she says. "It's nice to meet you, Maverick. I'm Maggie Southard, and please don't ever call me Margaret."

"Why shouldn't I call you Margaret?" I ask as I release her hand and motion to the seat across from me.

"Because there's only one person on the planet who I allow to call me that, and she's the reason we're sitting here," she says. "I'm not sure how much Lilah told you."

Lilah told me enough to know this job is important. Tearing out some bushes, cutting down a tree, tilling and planting a garden for an elderly lady. It isn't too much, but what she said about Maggie's grandmother's recent struggles made the work jump to the top of my priority list. We can work on finishing up the greenhouse in the evenings.

"She gave me an idea." I pick up my mug for another sip and ask her a question I already know the answer to. "Did you have a chance to order a drink? What would you like?"

Maggie shakes her head.

"I'm okay. I'll grab something in a bit," she says. Fidgeting with the sleeve of her sweater, she begins again, "So, basically, my grandmother told me over the weekend she wants to overhaul half the property and I don't know where or how to begin. Gram's mental status has started to deteriorate, but I want to be sure she's still allowed to control what's going on as long as she can. It's important to me that she make the decisions she can while she's able to."

Oh. Delilah did not tell me all of that. I feel my smile fall a little, but I put it back in place and nod my agreement. She's intense and I see a fiery side I'd like to explore more. The fact she's doing this for her grandmother and making sure Gram is the one calling the shots? That's the sign of a good woman as far as I'm concerned.

"I haven't eaten yet. Have you?"

I ask the question as I lift my hand to get the attention of someone who looks like he works here. After tilting his chin at me, he meanders over to the table.

He smiles at Maggie and ignores me. Interesting. Not in a good way, though. I don't like it.

"Hey, Mags," he says, drawing out her name. "How've you been?"

She doesn't seem to enjoy the attention and I'm grateful for it. I want to give her my undivided attention, and it hits hard how quickly my emotions jumped when he spoke to her. The server looks like a college sophomore trying way too hard to be liked by beautiful patrons and it makes me extremely uneasy.

"I'm fine."

Maggie's body language went from wide open as if she was saying, "Let me tell you everything you need to know about me," to closed in seconds. She clearly doesn't want to talk to him, so I clear my throat to remind him I'm sitting right here.

"What can I get ya?" he asks, but hardly glances in my direction before he looks at Maggie again and gives her a smile that leaves a really bad taste in my mouth.

"Eyes over here, kid," I say. Watching as he slowly turns back to me, I realize I've used my dad voice. It's the tone that only comes out when Sawyer is getting a little too smart with me. "I'd like a refill and two of the chocolate chip scones. Could you also bring my friend a caramel macchiato? Thanks."

He knows he's been dismissed and walks back toward the counter. Despite wanting to pat myself on the back, I'm not sure I should. I don't know Maggie and now I've potentially overstepped.

"I'm sorry," I begin, but stop because I'm not sure what I'm apologizing for exactly. "He didn't give me the best feeling and you seemed uncomfortable. I didn't mean to speak for you."

Her lips part slightly as if she's about to say something. Anything. *Say anything, Maggie.* I'm feeling a little out of place as it is and she's still not saying anything.

"I don't come into town all that often, at least not to sit in coffeeshops and bakeries, so when I see a kid being rude and disrespectful it's a huge red flag," I say, rambling. "Manners were a really important part of my upbringing, mostly because the whole family essentially worked in customer service. No one wants to buy their Christmas tree from a bratty teenager, you know?"

She makes me nervous. I wrap my hands around my near empty mug again and don't miss her watching my every movement. Her eyes follow my fingers as they lace together, as I rub my right thumb across the left.

"Thank you," she says, meekly. "He's kind of a creep. I try not to stop in here when I know he's working because he gives off such a strange vibe. I can handle strange, but his strange is stalker vibe, not tie me up and make me blush strange."

She seems to realize a moment too late what she says and she covers her flushed face, peeking out at me from between her fingers.

"I haven't heard that one before," I say, trying to ignore the blood rushing from my brain to my boxers.

"I think I'm going to die right here. I thought I had made it weird enough at work, but nope. Now we can add the Jumping Bean to the growing list of places where I've been extremely awkward today."

The creep comes wandering back over, a coffee pot in one hand and plate of scones in the other, so I make a point of saying, "I think it's cute. There's nothing wrong with being awkward when you're in good company."

He fills my mug while practically dropping the plate on the table. Maybe I'm laying it on a little too thick, but she doesn't seem to mind. Plus, it's not a lie. She's really cute.

"Your macchiato will be right out," he says, quietly.

I must have hit a nerve when I called him "kid," but seriously. I cannot understand how someone can be so full of themselves to not pick up on social cues. There could be more at play, and I try to be conscious of that, but her reaction to his behavior hit me in a way I wouldn't have expected it to. I feel like I need to be protective of this woman I barely know and it all boils down to my experiences with my own daughter. I would never want a guy to make Sawyer feel the way Maggie seems to around him. It's as simple as that. He's the kind of guy that makes women choose the bear.

Once he's further from the table, Maggie smiles at me.

"Why did you order that for me, anyway? You just met me a minute ago. You don't know what I like and don't like," she says, playfully.

Tapping the tabletop with my middle finger, I see I have to admit how closely I was watching her when she walked in.

"You stopped to read the specials listed on that chalkboard over there when you walked in, so I took a shot in the dark. Was it a good choice?"

I don't bother mentioning that I saw her reach her arm out like she was showing someone what she wanted to order and point to the drink written on the board, or that I had studied it before sitting down and therefore had a good idea what she was reading. It's intriguing to see what they're doing to make a simple beverage so complicated these days, but anything beyond a cup of black coffee or a little cream and sugar are outside my comfort zone. However, she works in a bakery so I'm comfortable making the assumption she's sometimes into elaborate drinks.

"The best. I don't usually spend the extra money on the special drinks, but this one is a favorite," she says. "Tommy usually adds extra caramel sauce if he's working, which is exactly what the drink needs and sets it apart from other places as far as I'm concerned."

I slide the plate to the middle of the table and watch her lift a scone, break it in half, and take a bite. Handing her a napkin, it takes just a split second for me to go from being a gentleman to wanting to kiss the crumbs off the corner of her mouth. I turn my head away to keep myself from staring. My brain needs to get back on track.

"So, tell me about this project your grandmother is planning," I say.

Sliding my coffee mug to the middle of the table, I reach for my pen and notepad as she begins telling me about the job she needs done. We sketch out a rough draft of where things are on the property. I remind her it's already October. This project, depending on how detailed she wants to get, could take a few weeks.

"That's okay. I'm prepared to have this be a huge undertaking as long as it's something you'd be able to do. Even if you can't start until spring, I understand and so will Gram. If it's something we can put on a calendar for her to look forward to, that's worth all the money it's going to cost."

Does she think I'm going to charge a million dollars for this? I'm all about keeping food on my table, but I also know I undercharge compared to other companies nearby.

"I'd like to come out and see the area before we talk prices," I say, sidestepping that part of the conversation. "If the weather holds out a bit longer, we could get started now and then discuss coming back to get your garden ready in early April."

The concerned look she wore as she spoke about her grandmother's health never really went away but now it begins to fade. In its place, she puts on a smile I'm quickly becoming accustomed to.

"It's a deal," she says.
I hope to see her smile more tomorrow.

Chapter 9

Maggie

"How'd it go?" she asks when I've barely stepped through the door.

Taking my time, I pull my sweater off and hang it on my hook by the back entrance.

"Good. I think. He's going to come out to Gram's tomorrow to look at the scope of the project. Then we'll talk prices and timeframe, but it seems if we move quickly Gram will be shrubbery free by the end of the month."

I shrug like it's no big deal that Maverick is going to come have a cup of coffee with my grandmother in the morning. However, in my head I'm thinking through what outfit I might wear, how I'll have my hair, and if I'm going to put makeup on and how much makeup. This is not like me. I don't usually care much about what people think of me. I'm generally loud and ridiculous, my filter is often dismantled, and I find it hard to tell a person something just because it's what they want to hear. I have an honesty glitch.

Today, though, I was mild mannered and almost shy once I sat down across from him. I watched the way he held his pencil and wondered why he didn't use a pen. I listened as he confidently told the jerk at the coffeehouse to do his job and marveled at the way his tone of voice went from friendly to making me want to beg *please, please, please do something naughty to me*. I instantly agreed to having him come to my house tomorrow without trying to get the upper hand. I just … submitted to his request to arrive by 9 a.m.

Walking back to the bakery was a feat of strength because my legs were wobbly after he held the door open for me and then touched the small of my back on our way out of the coffee shop. Holy. Shit. I was unaware I could have that kind of physical reaction from a man doing something so benign. It's never happened. Ever. That's not to say I haven't been attracted to men, but this was so different from any of those times. I'm not even sure how to describe it.

To save face I kindly refused a ride from him back up the street so I could get my wits about me before being inundated with questions by Delilah. It was needed. That time to decompress was definitely needed.

"That sounds exciting," she exclaims. "Gram is going to be so happy to have this done to the yard."

"I still can't understand why she wants it done. It's silly to me after all these years to pull them out now. I think my grandpa planted them when my mom was a baby," I say, wrapping my apron strings around my waist to tie them at my belly button. "There's nothing wrong with them and they get trimmed every year so they don't get all unmanageable."

I don't particularly love them, and the tree Gram wants taken down is half dead, so I'm not opposed to the work she wants done by any means. We had a conversation about the yard a few months ago before cool weather was even on the horizon and I mentioned my non-attachment to the things she decided she wants taken care of. I'm sure that might have played a role in her decision, but that was never my intention.

"Well, at least it's one less thing you'll have to worry about if and when her health declines," Delilah says.

I hadn't thought about that. I would rather not think about it.

"Moving on," I say, and Lilah gives me a look. It's the one that reminds me she's a safe place to feel my emotions. I have no desire to feel them right now, so I justify. "I need to get back to baking. I didn't realize I was gone as long as I was and now, I'm behind."

She continues working on the tasting cakes in front of her on a table behind the main counter, nodding her head.

"You're really not, but okay."

I feel like I'm behind, though, and that's the thing stuck in my head. So, I duck into the kitchen and submerge myself in all the scents in the room. The chocolate, the vanilla, the sweetness of sugar floating through the air, and let it all fill me with happiness, because working at Delilah's bakery is my happy place. She's given me creative license and right now that's what I need.

I start with a simple cookie base — it's the same one we use for chocolate chip — and then I throw in butterscotch chips, unsweetened coconut flakes, and slivered almonds. I put in enough of everything it becomes questionable if there's enough dough to hold it all together, but I know my guess-and-by-gosh measurements well. There's actually plenty of dough. The first two trays go in the oven and I watch as the glob slowly and precariously melts into flat deliciousness. These would go wonderfully with that caramel macchiato … and I think I know the perfect person to taste test them.

*****

I'm used to staying late to help close up shop, but tonight I promised Mom I would be home for dinner with her and Gram. She's taken Mondays as her day to spend hanging out at the house since it's one of her days off work, but it's her first day and me being at work all day didn't drive the worry away. I'm grateful she's there, though. I don't mean to sound like I'm worried she can't handle the situation. It also isn't that I think my mother wouldn't have come and spent more time with her mother if I had just said Gram was lonely during the day, but her knowing just how concerned I am was imperative.

Pulling into the driveway, I see my mom standing at the window over the kitchen sink doing something. She's not really paying attention to what's going on outside and it gives me a few breaths to watch her. I imagine Gram in that same position for years and years waiting for Mom or my uncles to get home. The stance of a parent waiting, but not really waiting. She's just always conveniently been there when the car pulls in the yard.

What if I'm the next one to stand there waiting for my own daughter to come home, but not really be waiting?

That's crazy thinking. I'm not even remotely ready to have kids. Like, it's not a thing I'm in a hurry to do. I have Delilah and Fisher's kids to love on and I adore being Aunt Maggie. I'm okay with that.

Mom looks up from the sink and sees me sitting there, staring off into space, and waves at me with a smile. A tired smile. I gather up my things and push the car door open.

"Hey. How was your day?" she asks as I set my bag on the kitchen table.

Do I jump right into sexy landscaper man coming to see us tomorrow or …

"It was good. I created a new cookie," I say, pulling a takeaway box from my bag. I always bring a dozen home of anything new I make.

She takes a cookie from the opened box and tastes it. Her eyes widen.

"Oh, sweetie, this is one of the best cookies I've had in a long time," she says, taking another bite. "Take one in for Gram."

I love my mom, but I adore her for raising me to eat sweets even if it's right before dinner.

"Gram, I have something for you to try," I say, walking into the living room. She's sitting in her rocking chair, slowly knitting one, purling two, and repeat. I should have her teach me before … "Here."

She reaches for the cookie, places it between her lips, and continues to work silently. I watch as she occasionally reaches up to bite, chew, and hold it between her lips again. When she finishes, she doesn't look up at me, and then I wonder if they aren't as good as I thought.

"I'd like another, please," she says. I catch a glimpse of her hiding a smile as she tucks her chin in an attempt to keep me from seeing.

I hand her a second cookie, and place a third on the table beside her.

"Just in case you can't decide if you like them after the first two."

She tips her head to the side and we smile at each other. It's the kind of smile that makes me feel warm, as if she hugged my whole being.

Back in the kitchen, I take the short stack of plates and forks from the counter and set them out before moving my bag and taking it to my bedroom. There's a box labeled "pictures" sitting on my bed that I know I didn't put there. But, it's in my room. I open it and am greeted by my grandfather's enormous grin, a fedora sitting high atop his head, as his arm holds tight to a tiny baby in a christening gown. Beneath it is a picture of Gram sitting at the edge of a pool in a two-piece bathing suit, a can of beer beside her, and a cigarette hanging from her mouth. I had no idea Gram used to smoke, but I smile at the picture of her full of life and enjoying it, too. Beneath that one is one of her and Grandpa beside one another at the pool, looking at each other as if no one is paying them any attention. I can feel the love radiate from the black and white image.

"Ah yes, the summer I was conceived," Mom says behind me.

"That's more information than I needed, I think," I say, but we laugh together because, like me, Mom's filter often is broken.

"Regardless, that's the summer she quit smoking, from what I'm told. Things were different back then and the science against smoking during pregnancy wasn't there, but she was so sick with me she kicked the habit because it made her more nauseous," she says, tugging the photo free from my grasp. "They always looked at each other like that. Right up until the moment he took his last breath."

That hurts. I feel how much that hurts her, but not because she and Dad don't have a similar love. I think she fears a time when they reach their end, when a last breath is taken and memories are only alive in photographs. Hopefully we have a lot more years before she really needs to let thoughts like that steal her smile.

I pull her in for a hug, wishing life didn't take away from us the things that make us so fucking happy.

"I want to find joy like that."

"You will. He'll surprise you and show up out of nowhere to sweep you off your feet," she says. I look at her and a small, slightly cynical, laugh escapes my lips. "Maybe? Maybe. Let's go eat."

She pulls me down the hall to the living room to gather Gram before we make it to the kitchen. Gram insists on saying grace even though I've already shoved a forkful of mashed potatoes in my mouth. I swallow just about the same time as I'm supposed to say, "Amen," and grab my cup of water to wash the food down.

"What's going on with my plants?" she asks, her tone rather demanding for something as innocuous as redesigning her yard.

I look at Mom, who knows nothing about the landscaper search unless Gram told her after I left this morning.

"Oh, what plants are you thinking about?" Mom asks, and it's clear she doesn't know a thing.

"No. We're going to get rid of a bunch and then make a garden. We'll talk about what goes in it later."

Mom looks from Gram to me and back. Gram scoops peas onto her plate like it's any other day. Might as well get into the details now while we're all here.

"Since you brought it up, I have a guy coming tomorrow morning to see what you want done and to give us ideas of how long it'll take and the cost," I say, and immediately take another bite of meatloaf.

My mother's gaze settles on me again.

"Who did you call? Someone reputable? Are they insured?" She fires the questions at me one after another without giving me a chance to respond.

Setting my fork down, I pick up the napkin beside my plate and wipe my mouth. Part of me is feeling a little bit like a teenager who's not trusted with her own decisions … but then I also realize Mom isn't used to me making decisions like this. She's still accustomed to me having trouble remembering where I put my car keys. There's been a lot of maturing since moving in with Gram.

"Actually," I begin, pausing slightly to get my bearings as the image of Maverick flashes through my mind, "actually, it's a local tree farmer."

Mom looks at me, confused, probably because I said tree farmer and not landscaper, but I'll get to all the bits and pieces if she stops making me feel like I'm twelve.

"So, he owns Sugar Shack Landscaping. It's outside of town and I had no idea it existed," I say.

Her face is still doing that thing where I'm not sure if she's listening intently or judging silently and it makes me squirm now just like it did when I was a kid. Who am I kidding? She still looks at me like I'm a toddler. I might act goofy and ridiculous a lot, but that's because I don't want to be so serious I forget how to be happy. People who are serious all the time make me feel sad. Where do you find your happiness if you never smile?

She lifts an eyebrow. I was lost in my thoughts and she knows it.

"Plus, Delilah and Fisher get their Christmas tree from him and she recommended the service, so we met this morning to talk briefly about what you want done."

"He must be pretty handsome," Gram says, pointing her fork in my direction.

"Why would you think that?"

"Your face is red."

Feeling my left cheek with my free hand, the heat radiates off my skin.

"He's a little handsome, I guess."

Mom and Gram share a look, but it's one of those secret mother-daughter kind of looks, and then they both look at me.

"A little?" Mom asks. "No, baby, Maverick is definitely more than a little handsome."

"You know him?"

"Of him, mostly. He's had his picture in the paper a few times over the years and I've gone out to look at trees on occasion. Remember the magnolia tree we planted when you graduated high school? That came from his farm," she says, lifting her drink to her lips. Before taking a sip, she adds, "Uncle Will recommended him to me back then."

Will. Of course. I could have just asked him about trees and shit. But, no. I had to go and make a list and then get weird when Maverick walked in this morning like he'd been reading my mind.

"Right, so this has been fun. Yes, he's a lot handsome. He'll also be here at like nine tomorrow morning and I'm trying to decide how to do the hair and the makeup," I say. I said too much. I always say too much. "Because I want to make a good impression on him so he'll take our business."

It's like a chorus of "mm hmms" from the two of them. Thank goodness I'm done with my food. I stand and begin clearing my plate and silverware. The box with the rest of the cookies I brought home is sitting beside the stove and I grab it before going back to the table.

This is slightly embarrassing. The last thing I want is Gram knowing this random tree man can get me hot and bothered without even doing a damn thing to me. I'm getting way ahead of myself, and take a bite out of the cookie in my hand.

There is nothing wrong with thinking a grown man is attractive. I, too, am a grown person and that makes it not only okay but also legal in all 50 states.

"Do you want to talk about something else?" Mom asks.

I stop chewing.

"No. It's okay. Do you want to know what Gram was planning to have done?" Maybe that will get us back on track since this whole conversation derailed way too easily.

She nods and Gram begins excitedly talking about tearing out bushes she says she never really liked and taking down the half-dead tree to let more sunlight into the house. The property is large, some might say huge, but we live in farm country and "huge" is really a relative term. The few things she's going to have done will impact the yard greatly.

"This way, when Margaret owns the house after I die, she doesn't have to worry about all this nonsense. I want her to be able to live here and enjoy it without things falling apart around her," she announces.

"Mom, don't talk like that. You've still got plenty of years left," my mom says.

She tries to keep her voice upbeat, but the reality is, aging happens. So does death. She picks at the cookie in her hand, staring at her fingers as they turn it into crumbs on her plate.

"Oh, Rebecca, you know as well as I do that nothing is guaranteed. I might as well talk about it like it's going to happen because it's going to happen," Gram says.

We have good conversations a lot, but this is the hardest and most lucid one we've had in a really long time.

"Are you worried?"

Gram reaches for my mother's hand and I feel slightly voyeuristic as they have a silent moment together. Maybe I should excuse myself?

"Worried about what? Dying? Nope. When it's my time, it's my time. But, that's why I want to get things in order now so you and Margaret don't have to worry about it when that time arrives. I'm not going to leave you to make big decisions while trying to celebrate the life we had together," she says. "I expect a celebration, too. None of that boo-hooing bullshit where everyone stands around being sad and stupid. I want cakes and tea and liquor flowing. Make it magical."

She cracks a smile to break the emotional tension that's built while she was speaking. The reality is still there, though, and that's the part Mom and I will need to tackle later.

"So, the plan is to get the yard in the best condition as we can now so we can do a garden because I know Miss Maggie loves to get her hands dirty just like her mind and it sounds like she found the perfect person to help create that space for her," she says.

"I don't have a dirty mind," I say, stuck on that part of her speech.

Gram laughs at me and says, "Liar. You're filthy."

I feel my face flush again. I am a little filthy. I'd like to get filthy with Maverick.

"Okay, fine. I'm not innocent. Now, what kind of plants do you want to put out front once that's all cleared?"

Chapter 10

Maverick

"But it's a school day! I want to go with you. You have no clue how to design a garden," Sawyer yells from her bedroom.

When she got home from school, I was out working on the frame for one of the new greenhouses. By the time I got to the main house, she was deep into homework with ear buds in and ignoring everything around her.

"Excuse me, young lady, I've been designing gardens and planting trees since before you were born," I yell back.

It might be a slight bend of the truth, but that's not the point. Stirring the pasta so it doesn't stick to the bottom of the pan, I consider letting her be tardy tomorrow and having her go with me to see Maggie and her grandmother. No, I shouldn't do that. I can, however, admit to both of us what we're both thinking.

"I'm just not ..." I raise my voice to yell to her down the hallway again, but reduce my volume when I realize she's standing right beside me. "Sorry. Didn't see you there. I'm just not as good at it as you are."

"Thanks for the compliment. So, you're going to map out the yard and then bring me all the info so I can do what I do?"

I laugh and move to the sink to pour water off the noodles. Catching her eye, I don't see her laughing with me.

"Oh. You're serious."

"Uh, yeah, I'm serious, Dad. I want to help with this job. From what you've said about your meeting with her this morning, this job is super important. Not just for you because we're in a lull, but also because it's for her."

"I just met her, Sawyer. You make it sound like we're fated to be together and this garden is going to make or break the deal," I say.

"Who's to say it won't?"

That stops me. I don't think I want to have this conversation right now. I don't believe in fate.

"What are you having on your fettuccine?"

"Butter and parm. The store-bought red sauce tastes weird lately. We need to make homemade again," she says, holding her plate out for me.

"Okay, then, Betty Crocker, I guess we'll make a real grocery list this week."

"Can we get ice cream and marshmallows, too?"

"Sure. What are you thinking?"

She carries the container of grated parmesan and her plate to the table. I used to shake the cheese on for her and she'd tell me when to stop. I wonder if she remembers that? It's scary how grown up she is all of a sudden. But I guess it isn't really sudden. It's been coming for a few years. She was eleven when she began taking care of herself for the most part when at her mom's house. That was before I found out how much she was taking care of herself.

"S'mores ice cream sundaes."

"Sounds delicious," I say, setting my plate at the seat across from her.

Stirring the sauce into the pasta with my fork, I pick up a piece of garlic bread to hold the noodles in place while I twist them up onto the tines. My mind drifts a little. I like when she still acts like a kid. I love when she gets excited about things. Even things like ice cream sundaes. However, it's really nice when I see her finding her groove in something we both love.

"The answer is yes," I say without context.

"Great! I'll add all that stuff to the list, plus we need graham crackers and chocolate, too. These are going to be amazing," she says.

My mouth is full of food, so I shake my head. I didn't mean yes to ice cream.

Swallowing, I wipe my mouth and take a drink of the water in front of me.

"I didn't mean that. No, I did mean yes to that, but I mean yes to the other thing. I'll bring the drawings to you and a list of possible trees or plants they want. Do your magic. I'll let Maggie know you'll be helping," I say, quickly twirling more pasta and taking a bite.

This is the first time she has asked me if she can design for someone. Usually, she just does it. I'm humbled by the fact she asked, even if it is partially because she sees this job ending with me getting a girlfriend. That's the amusing part ... well, that and me stopping in for food when Maggie was going to call me for a quote. That was amusing and just plain weird.

"I can't wait to see what we have to work with," Sawyer says, grinning from ear to ear.

*****

Sleep was not my friend last night. I tossed and turned so much that I finally just got up for the day around 4 a.m.

I caught myself thinking about her while I was standing at the counter waiting for the coffee to brew. Her wavy, dirty blonde hair. The way her eyes brightened when she asked me about ordering her coffee for her. Those extremely kissable and crumb coated lips. The way she cares about her family apparent in every sentence.

"You need to brew faster."

Talking to the coffee. That's what it's come to.

The pot isn't even full yet and I pull it from the burner to fill the biggest mug I have in the house. The trailer is calling my name. I need to go over my notes from yesterday and finish putting together a list of potential native plants and trees we can use. It's going to be a short list to hopefully help her grandmother when choosing. If she wants her grandma to be making the decisions, I'm going to attempt to make it as easy as possible and not overwhelm her.

I step up into what used to be our living room when Hannah and I tried to make this place a home. It never felt like home with her. When she lived here, I was more at home checking the evergreens and maple trees. I spent as much time with Sawyer as I could when I wasn't working. But, in those early years of lifting a new business off the ground, I was working a lot. I was up before the sun, just like today, and writing up business plans and marketing. I was out in the field planting what I could until I knew the baby would be awake and Hannah would want a break. It wasn't long after Sawyer was born that she started coming to work with me. I even went out and got one of those baby carriers that you strap to your body, and she did literally everything with me.

I haven't moved since walking in the door. Memories hitting me out of nowhere usually leave me feeling like I've been punched in the gut, but not this time. My baby still does everything with me, she's just a lot more grown now.

My phone buzzes in the back pocket of my jeans, but it's 4:30 in the morning. It's a little early for someone to text me.

"Ask her about a butterfly garden." I read out loud the message from my daughter, who should still be sleeping.

Why aren't you sleeping?

Her response is almost immediate.

"Sleep is for the weak. Remember, butterflies."

I've never been asked to do one of those, but now I have a little direction for this morning. Sipping my coffee, I press the power button on the desktop computer sitting on a desk I hardly use. I generally use information I've requested from the Department of Environmental Conservation and books about landscaping for my projects. This is going to require some savvier searching. At least, it feels like it does.

Butterflies.

I text Sawyer back before digging into my search. *I'll remember. Go back to sleep.*

I don't get another message from her, so I'm going to assume she's still in bed as I begin clicking on blog posts and Pinterest pins about gardens designed for pollinators. It's wild the amount of stuff I still don't know even after all these years. I guess that's the beauty of learning — it never stops.

Setting an alarm on my phone, I allow myself to work until six in the morning before heading back to the house to wake Sawyer up for school. The rabbit hole of information sucked me in and if I didn't have something to pull me out, I would have been gone forever.

"Hey, Pumpkin, you awake?" I knock gently on her bedroom door.

"I'm up," she says and a second later pulls the door open. She immediately turns and walks back to her desk where her computer is open to a page filled with plant varieties. "I found this thing called a butterfly bush, but there are too many sources saying it's invasive and I don't want to do something like that if possible."

That cancels all thought that she went back to sleep after her last message.

"I found the same thing, but there are some non-invasive ones we could get," I argue.

Watching her face scrunch up, I guess that idea won't fly.

"Okay, what else did you find?"

I pivot, mostly because I know she's got a whole list of other, better plants to put in a garden Maggie might not even want.

"Thought you would never ask," she says with a huge smile. "Hosta, hibiscus, zinnia, coneflower, petunias, columbine, bleeding heart, bee balm. That's just some I found, but I feel like it's a good start."

A good start? Why did I just spend more than an hour researching when she did all the work? I let a small laugh slip through and put my hand up for a high five.

"That is most definitely a good start. I'll stick to trees. You can do flowers. Get ready for school. Breakfast will be ready in ten."

She smacks my hand and returns my smile as I leave the room.

There are still more than two hours before I'm supposed to go to Maggie's grandma's house. I can kill the first hour with Sawyer as she gets ready for school and waits for the bus, but then what? I'm caught up in the trailer, but could work on the greenhouse as long as I have everything else ready to go in the event I lose track of time.

I'm staring off into space as Sawyer walks up next to me and pushes me away from the stove.

"You're burning the pancakes."

I look down as she pulls the spatula from my hand and goes to work flipping her breakfast.

"What's on your mind? Thinking about … her?" she questions, a lilt to her voice. She glances at me before turning her attention back to the stove. "Are you worried this job will be too much for you?"

"Nah. The job will be fine. I was trying to figure out what I can get done around here between you leaving for school and me leaving to go to her house. If I get in too deep working on the greenhouse, I'm worried I'll forget and be late getting there. If I'm late, that will make her later getting to work. If I don't do anything, I'm afraid I'll show up too early and look desperate for work," I admit. Then, sheepishly, I add, "I'm not sure if I should wear a ball cap or not."

"Weird. You've never worried about any of this stuff before," she says, pouring more batter in the pan. Handing me a plate with a short stack, she purses her lips and says, "I wonder if it's because you know you're going to get sweaty palms and be awkward once you're in her space instead of somewhere neutral like the coffeeshop?"

Chewing my food and swallowing before I choke is crucial in this moment.

"Sweaty palms and awkward? You forget that back in the day, I was a total ladies man. I don't get awkward."

"Maybe before Mom did a number on you and all those other loser women you've tried to date turned out so, so wrong for you. But that was then and they weren't Maggie, who you obviously find attractive now that you've actually seen her and talked to her."

"You've met her all of once for ten seconds while in excruciating pain. I'm not nervous about this job," I say, stubbornly.

It's a weak attempt to end the conversation.

"Who says I've only met her once?"

I stop chewing and look up from my plate. Her back is to me, so I can't tell what her face is doing.

"You've seen her since the vendor event?"

Sawyer turns around, a plate of pancakes in one hand and the spatula in the other, and stares at me. I hate when she does this because I can never figure out what's happening inside her head.

"I have not, but ..." she pauses, collecting her thoughts. Then she sighs so dramatically I'm not sure what it's supposed to mean, so I wait. "What if you go and do the estimate for her this morning and I just happen to stop by the bakery instead of coming home on the bus and then, whoops, you have to come pick me up because I don't have a way home? And then while you're there to pick me up you ask her out to dinner."

"You're crazy and need to stop reading romance novels," I say.

Pushing my chair away from the table, I stand to refill my coffee cup and give her a kiss on the forehead as she sets the spatula down and fills her mouth with a bite that is way too big.

"I love you, Pumpkin. How about wait until I've had a little more time to get to know her before you start planning the first date?" I lift her chin to look her in the eyes. "I appreciate that you like this woman and think she'd be a great match for us, but I'm not stressing about finding someone right now. I have you and we have a lot going on."

Sawyer gives me sad eyes, but I'm not falling for it. She doesn't need to go getting involved in her dad's lacking love life.

"I love you, too. I just don't want you to grow old and die alone," she says and keeps a straight face for half a second longer than I'm comfortable with.

"Ha. Ha. Go pack your backpack. The bus will be here before you know it."

I pull the empty plate from her hand. She gives me a big smile before attempting to skip off to the other room to finish putting her school stuff together. This kid ... I could almost put money on it that at some point this week she's going to be calling me for a ride from the bakery regardless of anything I just said.

A few minutes later, the bus pulls up in front of the house and she hustles out the front door.

Turning her head, she yells over her shoulder, "Wear the hat, but backwards!"

Chapter 11

Maggie

It's almost nine in the morning and I've already had more caffeine than I usually allow myself to have all day. I probably shouldn't have chased my coffee with a Mt. Dew. This should be interesting.

My leg won't stop bouncing as I sit on the porch waiting for him to come over, but my heart doesn't start racing until I see his truck roll up in front of the house. I've decided I'll wait until he's out of the vehicle before I stand up, mostly because I worry that I'm going to wobble.

He takes his time getting out of the cab of the pick-up. When he does, there's a clipboard under one arm and he's carrying a bottle of water. In the other hand he carries a baseball cap and effortlessly puts it on his head before spinning it around so the visor covers his neck. My thighs press together instinctively, as if I've never seen anything even remotely as sexy as that move.

Maverick hasn't noticed me yet, so I take my time watching him, soaking up the way his legs move in his jeans as he looks at the clipboard and slowly walks along the edge of the property to the driveway. He checks the address on his papers and glances at the porch where Gram and I hung her house numbers when I was in high school. They need to be repainted, and I should do that before too long, but the thought is interrupted when I look back in his direction and lock eyes with him.

It's his smile that undoes me a little more. Instead of feeling my heart race, my stomach drops, but not in the "I'm so anxious I could throw up" kind of way. I don't know how to describe it other than I feel like my legs can't lift me and so I just sit, waiting for him to reach the door.

He knows I see him. He sees me. We are literally looking at each other, but he still lifts his hand, curls it into a fist, and gently knocks on the doorframe.

"I can't believe you just did that when you see me sitting right here," I say, but my smile is big and stupid and I kind of love that he's a man with manners. Too many either don't use them or don't have them and I have no time for any of those people.

The door creaks open slowly and he steps into my domain.

"It's not my home. I'm not going to enter unless invited," he remarks.

I want to invite him to do more than enter the porch. But …

"Are you a vampire? Should I be concerned?"

He laughs and it's wonderful the way the sound washes over me.

"May I sit?" he asks, and the butterflies are back.

"Of course. Would you like a cup of coffee?"

"I'm okay for now, unless you're having a cup."

I'm already hearing colors, but if a cup of coffee means sitting with him a little longer, I see no reason to not have another one. I excuse myself to grab two mugs from the kitchen and, when I return, he's staring intently at the side yard.

"This was a nice hardwood at one point, I'm sure. What happened to it?"

Maverick asks the question but I'm stuck on his use of the word "hardwood" and look at him blankly as he turns his attention back to me.

"Maggie?"

I snap out of it. Handing him his cup, I pull my brain out of the gutter it crawled into.

"The ice storm we had several years ago. The trunk split up high, a bunch broke off and came down. Thankfully, it all fell away from the house and the damage was minimal. But it just slowly started dying after that and now we're at a point where it needs to be removed. It's not really part of what Gram wanted done during this project, though," I say, as if he asked me to explain why I hadn't mentioned it before.

He nods slowly as I take a seat and curl my legs up underneath me, cupping my mug in order to keep the liquid from splashing over the edge.

"I can take care of it for you if you want. I really don't like the way it's hanging over the house, especially if it's rotting away. If we get another early storm with that wet, heavy snow, it could fall and cause more damage than it's worth." He glances back at the tree, concern marring his features. "I'm worried about it coming down on your roof and taking out the chimney."

Now he's overexplaining, when it truly isn't necessary. I agree with him and nod as I pull my cup from my mouth and swallow. He watches my throat and then turns away, his ears turning the darkest shade of pink.

Trying to not laugh — because it's really quite comical — I look back at the tree.

"I won't argue with you. It needs to come down sooner rather than later, but if you don't have time to do it as part of this project, we can plan to do it next year," I say.

"I'll take care of it," he says, matter-of-factly.

I love the way he does that. I react to it more than all the things combined my last boyfriend attempted to do. Maybe it's because I haven't had any attention in a very long time, but I think it has more to do with the person who is giving the attention.

We sit a little longer in comfortable silence drinking our coffee. We reach to set our empty mugs down at the same time. Then, he clears his throat and I'm all eyes on him again.

"Yes?"

"Would you like to show me the backyard?"

I begin moving before answering him but, as I stand up, trip over my own feet. He's so smooth I don't even realize he's out of his chair before his arms are around my waist and my hands are on his shoulders.

"I am so sorry," I say, willing my heart to not pound out of my chest. It's not doing that because he caught me. It's because I was pretty sure I was falling to my death. This isn't the first time I've tripped over myself with the potential to get hurt. Last time I ended up with stitches on the underside of my chin. That was a fun one.

"I'm not." Again, with the succinct tone.

I feel my body against him for the first time as I look up. Every hard muscle in his chest presses against every soft curve of mine.

I. Can't. Breathe.

His lips part slightly and he pulls the bottom into his mouth, biting it gently. He smells like pancake batter and maple syrup. I want to taste his mouth on mine and, as if he's reading my thoughts, he inches closer to my lips.

"Does this mean the tree's getting cut down for free?"

Maverick and I both freeze, his nose nestled gently against mine as we stare at each other.

My life is one comedy after another and Gram has a "haha I caught you" grin on her face as Maverick and I turn to meet her gaze.

She lifts a mug to her mouth, and takes a long, thoughtful sip before saying, "I'll take that as a yes, young man. Now, let's go talk about the back yard."

Before either of us can react, Gram turns and wanders away from the door. Maverick's fingers gently squeeze my waist. My fingers graze the back of his neck, up into the short hair peeking out from under his hat. I don't want to let go, but …

"I should go talk to your grandmother about this project," he says, his tone a gruff whisper, his lips still a heartbeat away from mine.

"Yeah. You should."

It takes another few seconds for me to pull my arms from his neck, and even longer for him to slide his hands from my waist. We both make ourselves busy — me picking up empty coffee cups and him grabbing his clipboard and bottled water.

We stand, awkwardly looking anywhere but at each other for a moment before finally I say, "I'm going to take care of these dishes. If you want to walk around, I'll meet you out back."

For a split second I question whether I should have led him through the house to the back door. That probably wouldn't be a good idea. Not because I don't want him in the house … but because for the first time in years I want to show a boy my bedroom.

"Perfect. I'll go get started," he says. He smiles warmly and looks at me in a way a guy who wants to complete a job at my house wouldn't if he was just interested in getting paid.

He pulls the door to the house open for me and, as I slip past him to take the dishes in, his free hand softly brushes my hip when I step up into the front entryway from the porch.

Chapter 12

Maverick

I've never acted so unprofessionally in my entire adult life.

The best part, though, is now we've gotten it out of the way and we obviously are both attracted to the other without having to have any sort of weird conversation about it. I hope. Plus, her grandmother is hilarious.

The worst part? Needing to keep this from my kid. Not because she's a teenager and my romantic life is really none of her business. It's because she's going to ask how it went the second she gets home from school and if I give any indication there was a chance of a move being made, she's going to start planning a wedding or something. Honestly, she doesn't need my life drama influencing her, especially since she's in high school and that's enough drama on its own.

My ears are still on fire as I make my way around the house and to the back yard where Maggie's grandmother is waiting for me.

"Good morning," I say, reaching out my hand to shake hers and attempting to break the ice, though she certainly took care of that on the front porch. "I'm Rick."

"I know," she says with a smile that reaches her eyes. "I'm Gram. Everyone calls me that so you might as well, too."

I chuckle, grateful she seems to be leaving the scene from a few minutes ago right where she found it.

"Well, Gram, what are we thinking of doing with this yard? Maggie mentioned a garden, but not necessarily what kind," I say. "There's a lot of potential back here. I didn't realize how much land you had."

She sips her coffee and a contemplative look creases her brow.

"My late husband wanted a houseful of children and plenty of space for them to explore. When we bought this land, it was nothin' but trees. All fifty acres. We did what we wanted with it back then, and left the rest wild … kind of like my granddaughter," she says, making a point to sip her coffee again and look over the rim of the mug at me. A smirk lifts the edge of her mouth as she pulls the mug away and she continues, "I like vegetables, but I also love flowers. And Margaret really loves flowers, too. You got anything you can do with that?"

I smile broadly, getting a really good feeling about this job, and say, "I think I can work with that."

*****

Gram and Maggie decided that taking down the tree damaged in the storm was a priority. That will be the first step along with cutting a couple other small trees that offer more shade than they'd like directly behind the house. Then we'll set our sights on putting in some flower beds and go from there as they decide what best suits their needs.

Sawyer is going to be ecstatic. A vegetable garden in the spring is a definite go, but for now since we're into autumn we're also doing a fall flower bed in the front yard. Maggie wants pops of color, so we're starting with mums and dianthus out front this year. Then she can add more as she wishes. Gram gave her approval of a butterfly garden, which will go out back along with an arbor and small seating area for her to sit and relax.

"So, I just want to run one more thing by you both," I say as we're walking back toward the front of the house.

Maggie's got her arms crossed. Her hands are tucked in the armpits of her flannel shirt and that's when I realize how cold she might be. I'm used to working in the cold, so it never occurred to me she might not have a heavy enough jacket on to be outside as long as we have been. I thought it was supposed to stay warm this week, but so far today the weather guy is being proven wrong. She gives me a small smile when she notices me looking, and my ears start burning again because I know it looks like I'm staring at her chest.

Clearing my throat, I drop my eyes to my notes and try to not let her see how much she affects me.

"What did you want to run by us?" she asks, humor in her voice.

I look up, making eye contact first with Gram and then with Maggie.

"Sawyer is kind of my garden design guru. I know she's only a kid, but if you're willing to give her a chance, I'd like her to put together a few concepts for you to look at before we start on the flower beds," I say. "It will give you some more time to choose which plants you'd like and she can give you ideas of what would work well together while I focus on getting the trees down and stumps ground out. Is that something you both would be interested in?"

They exchange a glance. There's obviously a conversation happening that doesn't require words and then Maggie turns back to me, a smile that reaches her eyes making her even more beautiful.

"We'd love that. But, why the signifier? Who cares that she's a kid?"

I open my mouth, but realize I don't know how to respond. Letting out a small laugh, I say, "I don't actually know. I'm just not used to offering her abilities, I guess. Her entire life she's helped with the tree farm and doodled when people ask about landscaping. Part of me wants her to stay a kid and not worry about work, you know? I've got to tell you, though, she's probably sitting in study hall today drawing up plans even without knowing you'd like her help on the project."

"We can't wait to see what she comes up with," Gram says. As she turns and begins walking back toward the house, she adds, "I'm going back inside. It's colder than a witch's tit out here and I need to get warm."

Maggie covers her face with her right hand in an attempt to hide her laughter.

"Sorry about that," she says, motioning toward her grandmother. "If you can't love her honesty, you can't love her."

"I completely understand that sentiment. The kid is like that, too, so I live it every day."

With my clipboard up under my arm, I shove my hands in the pockets of my Carhartt jacket. It's less to keep them warm and more about keeping them from reaching out to brush the hair out of her eyes.

"Sawyer really does love designing this kind of stuff. Half the time she's coming up with ideas for gardens no one has asked us to do. There's a bookshelf in her bedroom dedicated to landscape design and plants."

I'm not sure why I feel like I have to reassure Maggie that this is a hundred percent my kid's choice to help, but I need her to know.

"Sawyer seems like a very smart young lady. I wish I'd had a chance to meet her before she was rushed off to the hospital," she says.

It's not the normal response I get when talking about my daughter. Usually, a comment about meeting her is in passing, like she's a second thought and unimportant. When Maggie says it, though, everything about it is genuine.

"I have a feeling you'll get properly introduced to her soon." I laugh, but her quizzical look prompts me to explain. "She made a mild threat this morning to walk to the bakery today instead of riding the bus home so I'd have to come pick her up and see you again."

Maggie begins laughing along with me, but stops short when she says, "Your child is my favorite teenager. Well, aside from Fisher and Lilah's kids, that is. Sawyer sounds like she'd fit right in with those two."

I watch her as she looks at her watch and a concerned look crosses her features.

"I really hate to cut this short, but I should get ready for work. Let me know when you need the down payment for what we're doing here, okay? I'm excited to have Gram's visions come to life," she says. "And, um, if Sawyer shows up at the bakery this afternoon and you're busy, I can always bring her home if you need me to. I have a thing tonight with the food truck anyway, so ..."

She's cute when she's nervous. Really cute. I don't stop myself this time when a lock of her hair falls across her face. I just reach out and gently tuck it back behind her ear. Her head naturally tilts into my palm, her eyes closing softly, right before she realizes what she's doing and lifts her head.

I pull my hand away, but don't miss the empty feeling squeezing my chest.

"Right. Yes. If she comes to visit, just have her shoot me a message. If I can't get back to town right away and you don't mind dropping her off, that would be ..." I trail off as I get caught up in her gaze again. "That would be wonderful."

"Thank you, Maverick," she says softly. "I'm excited about this project with you and Sawyer."

And then she turns away, walking toward the house like she didn't just obliterate all of my willpower with one sentence.

Chapter 13

Maggie

Don't turn around. Don't turn around. Do not stop and turn to see if he's still watching you walk away.

I just keep that on repeat in my head until I get into the breezeway and then force myself into the kitchen where I can look out the window like a nosy neighbor because I don't want him to think I think he should still be watching me.

"Whatcha looking at?" Gram says from behind me, close enough to make me jump.

She's caught me leaning over the sink trying to be inconspicuous by also washing my mug from earlier. Obviously, she knows me better than to think I'm just washing dishes.

"No one. I mean, nothing. I'm not looking at anything," I say, pulling a towel from the drawer beside me to dry my hands off.

Gram sighs as she steps up beside me and peeks out the window.

"He is a handsome young man. He reminds me of your granddad. Works with his hands and smart. Rick seems like a smart guy," she says. Then she sighs again and I wonder if she's still thinking about Maverick or if she's consumed with thoughts of Grandpa. "You two would make a cute couple. I'm very sorry for interrupting this morning."

Our eyes follow as Maverick starts his truck and ever so slowly begins to pull away from the house. He turns his head and I know he's caught us watching from the window, so we lift our hands in unison to return a wave he offers.

"Did you interrupt, though? I mean, I think it would have been way more awkward to have him doing this job if he'd actually kissed me."

"But you wanted him to kiss you. There's nothing weird about it if you wanted him to and he did it," she says. "People kiss other people all the time."

I laugh and turn to lean against the counter.

"Gram, we aren't just talking about any person. This is Maverick freaking Rogers who, apparently, half the town's women are infatuated with," I say, rolling my eyes just a little. "I guess we'll just have to see what happens. Who knows? Maybe Sawyer will come into the shop like she told her dad she was going to and she'll decide she doesn't like me. That will certainly put an end to anything that could happen."

She narrows her eyes at me.

"You would let a teenager come between you and the possibility of a good time with a cute boy?"

Oh my gosh, is this actually happening right now? Gram is challenging me. I love her spunky attitude and never want her to lose it. Ever.

"It's not that I would let her come between me and Maverick if there was really something there between us. If Sawyer doesn't like me, though, I refuse to come between her and her dad," I say, crossing my arms. I bite the inside of my lip. My thinking face. "She is his entire world and that was evident the first and only time I've seen him with her. I don't want to be the thing to break that bond just like I would never want someone to do that with me and my dad."

Gram reaches her hands out and cups my cheeks.

"You are such a beautiful and wise woman. I hope his talented, young protégé sees how amazing you are just like I do."

I place my hand over hers and offer a small smile. I hope she's right. Even though we know so little about one another right now, I really want to spend more time with Maverick.

"I need to get ready for work," I say softly. "If I'm not there, how will we ever know if she approves of me or not?"

A smile lights up her face as she drops her hands and turns to go into the living room.

"That's my favorite girl."

The smile I wear falters slightly. That's what she calls my mom.

"And don't forget my ladies are coming over to play poker later. I don't want your mother worrying much, so I'll give her a call after you leave for the bakery."

"Right. I almost forgot your friends are coming by to spend the day with you," I say loudly from where I stand in the middle of the kitchen. I need to know if she meant to call me that though. I'm second guessing everything and it's going to make me nervous if I don't ask. "Hey Gram? Did you mean to call me your 'favorite girl'?"

I lean against the doorway to the living room and watch her closely.

"Of course, I did, Margaret. Just don't tell your mom you're my favorite now. She'll get jealous."

*****

It's almost three in the afternoon and no sign of any high schoolers in the bakery. I'm not sure if I'm scared she'll show up or afraid she won't.

"What is the matter? You've been standing at the front window for ten minutes now," Lilah scolds from behind the counter. "Who are you waiting for. Rather impatiently, I might add."

I haven't told her everything from this morning and I'm not sure if I want to. I mean, I do want to, but I don't want to make it a bigger thing than it really is. That would be weird if it turned out to be nothing. But … I don't want it to be nothing.

I go for the safe answer.

"Just wondering when it's going to snow. The clouds are dark and it's definitely starting to smell like winter," I say turning to look at her and hoping she won't call me on my bullshit.

"Smell like winter. Okay," she says, pursing her lips and rolling her eyes before I turn back to the window. "You're not good at lying, just so you know. Like, really, really not good at it."

I let out a small gasp when I see her. She's wearing jeans with rips in them, but not the kind that look like they came from a manufacturer. These look like jeans she's worn to work with her dad on the tree farm. The knees are ragged and torn compared to the rest of her put together look. Her backpack is slung over one shoulder and her tan flannel shirt complements her brown hair.

"Who is it?" Lilah asks curiously as I walk over to hold the door open as Maverick's daughter hobbles up to the shop.

I toss a look at Lilah, but the message isn't clear to her — and why would it be when I stupidly haven't told her about this part of the morning's conversation? She tips her head to the side, silently questioning me seconds before her eyes go wide with recognition of the young girl who just came into view.

"Good afternoon, Sawyer. How are you today?" I say with a smile, probably louder than necessary but I want Lilah to hear me, too.

She stops in the doorway.

"My dad told you I might stop by didn't he?" she asks, letting out a small laugh and stepping further into the bakery as she waves to Lilah.

"He may have mentioned it when he came to do the estimate this morning," I say. "But it's okay because this gives us a chance to chat about what you're thinking for the gardens at Gram's house."

I let the door swing closed as I move through the front of the bakery.

"Pull up a seat and show me what you've got," I say to Sawyer as I slide a chair over to a table in the corner.

When Lilah and I first set up shop, we knew we wanted a cozy atmosphere but didn't want to even come close to competing with the Jumping Bean. We don't offer coffee or sandwiches because that's not our thing. But we have set up a couple small tables for tastings or people who want to sit with their treats before venturing on their way. Occasionally, regulars will come in with their coffee from the Bean, sit to visit with us while we work, and catch a snack in the process.

Sawyer shifts her weight and says, "Huh?"

"What?"

"You really want me to help Dad with your project?"

"He didn't tell you?" I ask, slightly embarrassed. "You've been at school all day. Of course, he hasn't told you yet. I'm so sorry, I should have waited to say anything."

She pulls the chair out across from me and holds her hand up as she sits, dropping her bag on the floor. She unzips her backpack and pulls a spiral bound notebook from its interior, flipping it open to a page filled with color.

"I've been up since like four this morning working on different designs," she begins. "Everything is changeable, we can swap out plants I've chosen for something more your style, and the extra landscaping concepts are just that. Concepts. You don't have to do any of this. I just wanted to give you an idea of what could be done with the space."

Holy. Shit. This fifteen-year-old has her life together more than I ever did at that age or still do at almost thirty.

I must be giving her that deer-in-the-headlights look because she stops talking and immediately starts to backpedal.

"Stop. No. I love all of this. Tell me what plants you were thinking," I say before she can talk herself out of the ideas she's come up with.

Her shoulders visibly relax and it makes me curious who in their right mind would have given her so much doubt. Sawyer's creativity is boundless and endless and I want to wrap her up in a hug just because she's taken all this time to put something together for me and Gram before she even knew Maverick was going to let her work on the job.

"You're fucking amazing," I say before she begins her presentation. And as soon as the cuss word leaves my mouth, I slap a hand across my lips and apologize.

It doesn't even seem to phase her. Sawyer's smile grows to megawatt levels.

"Thank you. I really love making things like this," she says. "Even if the design isn't used, it still makes me happy to draw the ideas and think that maybe someday someone will want it. I have an entire album of sketches waiting for homes with gardens to create."

For the next half hour, she points to different areas on her page, flips to other pages, and talks non-stop about what plants are native to the area that would also help the local pollinators. How is she only in high school? She speaks like a college-educated adult when she's in her element and I am loving every second of it.

She takes a deep breath as she finishes going through the last page of designs.

"And that's as far as I've gotten," she says.

"That's as far as you've gotten?" Lilah says as she stands over my shoulder. "How has your father not got you employed full-time doing this?"

"Well, I assume it's because I'm a kid and he wants me to focus on finishing school, but we did talk about the possibility of me going to college to master the craft. Sort of." Sawyer bites her lip and I don't miss the resemblance she has to Maverick. Her eyes connect with mine. A bit unsure of herself, she asks, "Do you like it?"

"I love it. Gram's going to be so excited when I tell her you showed me your concepts. For whatever reason this is a really important project for her," I say. "I feel like it's really important to you, too."

I don't question her because I can tell by the way she's talked about plants and placement since the minute she opened her mouth that this is a big thing for her. So big I nearly forgot she's only fifteen.

"What have you got going on the rest of the afternoon?" I ask as I stand from my chair and head toward the counter. Lilah's already retreated to the kitchen and it's nearing four in the afternoon, so Genevieve and Jaxon will be here shortly. Then Delilah will take them home, have family dinner, and then come back to close up for the night. "Want to hang for a bit and then I'll take you home before the event I have to set up at?"

She's poring over her notebook, a pack of colored pencils sitting on the page she's working on, but looks up when I offer to take her home.

"Um, I don't know. I should probably call my dad and see if he can come get me," Sawyer says, but seems nervous.

"What if I told you I already told him I would bring you home and he was cool with it? You're welcome to have him come get you if that's what you'd prefer, though. I just figured if you were to stop in then I would try to help him out since I'm going in that direction tonight anyway."

Waiting patiently is not my strong suit, so I put my hands to work while I listen for her to respond. She chews on the end of her pencil, picks her phone up to check the time, sets it back down again, and nods.

"Yeah, that would be awesome then. I'll just text him and let him know the plan," she says, beaming.

I smile back at her and start working on putting together the food I have to load into the truck. Since everything is made at the bakery and then transported, I don't have to worry so much about having ingredients with me. Making sure I have all the cookies and cupcakes I've listed on our social media and the white board for the parking lot, though, is a completely different ballgame.

Sawyer continues to work in her notebook and we share the quiet as if we've been in each other's space a thousand times. This is contentment? I think so. I'm content.

Around five I start loading the truck. When I come back in to grab the next bin of cupcakes, Sawyer asks if she can help me and I gladly accept the offer.

"You know, when you drop me off, you should see if Dad wants some dessert. He really loved the pastries we picked up a couple weekends ago," she says.

That stops me in my tracks as I'm climbing up into the food truck. The only time I've seen him in the bakery was the day we ended up having coffee and talking about Gram's project, and Sawyer most definitely was not with him during that visit.

"It was the weekend after I hurt my ankle," she says, handing me a bin of cookies.

I mouth an "oh" and turn to secure the cookies so they don't fly all over the truck when I drive.

"My mom's kind of horrible and I was just having a really rough day, so we did this whole thing where we came into town and got lunch and cupcakes and then went to the bookshop and ..." she trails off when she notices me staring. "Sorry. Sometimes I start rambling because it's too quiet."

Oh, my goodness, this kid would fit in perfectly with me, Lilah, and Gen. I notice a bit of sadness in her eyes as I step down out of the truck. Without thinking too much about it, I reach out and place my hands on her biceps so she's an arm's length away from me.

"Listen, rambling is one hundred percent acceptable here. You can ramble on and on here, because you're in a safe space. Being a teenager comes with its own special kind of bullshit, and having issues with your mom is definitely something that's going to happen," I say, looking directly into her eyes. "But, I had the pleasure of seeing your mother in action at the football game and let's just say I'm not going to talk bad about her, but I was not impressed."

I know I probably crossed a line somewhere because I have no right to say anything about her mom, but she left an impression on me. Not a good one, either.

"She breaks all her promises," Sawyer says, and I see the emotion begin to well up in her eyes. "Daddy doesn't."

I've known this child for a few hours. I feel like I've known her forever and I know some of that could just be because she's in need of a female role model. I stop short of telling her I also don't break promises, but don't want to overstep more than I already have. Instead, I pull her to me and give her the best hug I can offer. She doesn't hesitate to wrap her arms around me and bury her head in my shoulder.

A few minutes pass when she finally eases her grip on the back of my shirt, so I loosen my arms as well.

"You okay?" I look directly into her eyes again when I ask, knowing she's not going to lie to me when she answers if she's looking at me.

"I'm better."

"That's all I can ask for. Why don't we finish loading the truck and then we'll head for home? I have less than an hour before I need to be at the winery."

Sawyer nods and I follow her through the back door into the bakery kitchen. Lilah's returned from dinner with the kids and has the stereo turned up as she starts prepping ingredients for tomorrow. I smile at the sight of my partner dancing around the kitchen because she's such a grown up, but such a kid at heart still, and I'm so fortunate to have all these women in my life who are completely amazing.

"Does she always do that?" Sawyer asks quietly as we walk out with the last load of food.

"Always," I say, shooting a smile in her direction.

"I want to be like that when I grow up."

"Me, too, kid. Me, too."

*****

I pull up the driveway to a gorgeous log cabin and get a little lost in the what ifs. What if I came on too strong this morning? What if I came on too strong this evening? What if Sawyer tells Maverick about our interaction and he panics because he has no idea who I am and I've completely walked all over his boundaries? What if I've misread all of the chemistry that seems to be between us? What if …

It's daunting and I don't want to be in my head. I want to stay in my heart about everything with this kid and her dad. In the span of two days, I've gone from what-the-fuck-ever about men and my future as far as a love life or parenting is concerned to wanting to step in and give all my fucks to this little family I just met. It's … a lot. On top of everything else, it's almost too much.

It's so much more when he steps out the front door. I smile like a fool, but his daughter's face lights up when she sees him coming down the steps of the small deck on the front of their home.

"Don't forget the treats," I say as she opens her door.

We made up a box of desserts for the two of them to share tonight. I let her think we were going to toss them out if they weren't sold, but I'm covering the cost. Neither of them needs to know. After all, if they weren't sold tonight or before lunchtime tomorrow, they'd go to Murph.

I'm still focusing on Sawyer and making sure she has her backpack when I hear a tapping at my window.

My brain didn't register him walking around the truck while I was focused on Sawyer, so I jump a bit at the sound and laugh in spite of myself. This guy is going to think I'm a complete headcase.

"Sorry, I didn't see you," I say, rolling down the window with a smile on my face. "Sawyer has some dessert for you to share."

His scruffy face catches me off guard. This morning he wasn't nearly as stubbly and I catch myself wondering what it would feel like to run my hand up his cheek.

"Hi," he says, his voice gruff and scratchy and it pulls at something deep inside me. "Thanks for bringing her home. I don't think either of us were surprised by this, were we?"

I shake my head, but am caught in his eyes. He's looking for words and I don't think he has any idea which ones to use, so I try to figure out what words are and use them instead because if I don't say something I might crawl out the window of my truck and attack his beautiful mouth.

"I really wasn't. I would have been sad if she hadn't showed up," I say. Quietly, I add, "She's a really amazing kid, Maverick. She showed me and Lilah her notebook, the sketches and plans she's come up with, and I'm just completely blown away by her talent. I mean, I can whip up hella good cupcakes and cookies, but what she was putting together? My brain would not comprehend some of it."

Maverick shoves his hands into the pockets of his jeans and a bashful look crosses his face, but is quickly replaced by pride.

"She's always been like that. Some days I wish she'd just be an ornery teenager, but I kind of lucked out with a kid who wants to hang with her old man and still play in the dirt," he says.

While we've talked, Sawyer has gone into the house, deposited her school supplies, and returned with one of the cookies from the box we put together.

"Try this," she says, shoving the cookie in her dad's face. He willingly opens his mouth and takes a bite. "Peppermint mocha chocolate chip. Amazing."

He looks at her, then looks at me.

"There's something going on and I don't know what it is, but I think I like it," he says. "Did you get your homework done?"

"Not yet, but I just have to review notes for a math test. Everything else I was able to get finished during the day," she says around bites of cookie. She holds her hand out to Maverick, the last bite resting in her palm, and asks, "Want the rest?"

He shakes his head and she pops the remaining cookie in her mouth before heading back to the house.

"So, you're not going to be surprised if this becomes a thing, are you?" he asks, watching her go into the house. "Because I can see her coming to the bakery more often now that she's done it once."

"Would that be a bad thing? If you would rather she not do that, you're welcome to tell her not to, but I really don't have a problem with it. I mean, you're her dad, so of course you'll tell her if she can or can't, but Delilah's daughter is there with us a lot and we love having the extra company when it's a slow day or we need taste testers," I ramble. "I'll understand if you don't want her to since we have a business arrangement and that might be crossing a line or something."

He abandoned the hands in pocket look and is now leaning on the open window and I can't help but look at his forearms. The rolled-up sleeves of his flannel shirt leave them on display and I suddenly realize what was wrong with every guy I ever dated. They weren't like Maverick Rogers.

He's so close to me I can smell pine and dirt.

Absentmindedly, I close my eyes and take a deep breath.

"Maggie?" he attempts to get my attention, but if I open my eyes I'm afraid I'm just going to make it weird. My brain has left the building. "I know you have things to do tonight, but would you like to have dinner one night this week when you aren't busy?"

Okay, that gets my attention and I open my left eye to look at him, afraid if I open them both it will break the spell.

"Of course, I'd understand if you say no since it might be crossing a line. Or something."

His smile reveals deep lines that reach up to a set of dimples that weren't as noticeable this morning. They seem more prominent with the extra facial hair he's sporting and I feel a little swoony about it all.

"I would very much like that. To have dinner with you. One night this week would be perfect. Any night, really, because tonight is the only event I have and then the rest of the week is probably dinner with Gram and watching Wheel of Fortune," I say.

85

"Perfect. Maybe Thursday?"

I sigh. Oh my god, I audibly sigh. I'm such a fool. And he smiles at me anyway.

"Thursday would be lovely."

Did I just bat my eyelashes at him? Why is being an adult so fucking hard? I feel like I'm being asked out by my longtime crush back in high school and I'm totally going to screw it up by being myself.

"I'll text you the details," he says, stepping back from the truck, indicating the end of our time together. "But maybe I'll see you tomorrow."

Putting the truck in reverse, I begin slowly backing down the driveway. He's making me have feelings that I'm not sure what to do with, but I know I'm going to figure it out. Before I roll my window up against the chill in the evening air, I smile at him again.

"Maybe you will."

Chapter 14

Maverick

Last night I had to take a cold shower before going to bed. After all the interactions I had with Maggie, I couldn't get her out of my head. Can't get her out of my head. Even my dreams were about her and I am not used to remembering those, but these were unforgettable.

Exhausted, I pull a hoodie over my head, put my phone in the pocket, and shuffle out of the bedroom, making my way to the kitchen where the coffee maker greets me like a long-lost best friend. On mornings like this, I'm grateful for the me from the night before when I set up the machine and remembered to set the timer.

Pulling a mug from the cupboard and filling it almost to overflowing, I look out over the front yard. The sun is starting to lighten the horizon and I have a clear view of it since there's nothing but empty corn field across the way. When we found this property, it was almost too good to be true. Being successful in this business and having the chance to build and expand here with my little girl, it's like a dream.

I push my feet into a pair of worn boots and make my way to the door so I can enjoy the morning on the deck before checking on Sawyer. There's still plenty of time before she needs to be up for school and I'm going to take advantage of it today.

She was so excited last night telling me about her afternoon with Maggie and Delilah, and getting to briefly meet Delilah's daughter, but I think it was more than just being able to talk about her ideas for this project we're starting today. Her eyes changed when she talked about these women. They were supportive of her, they took her in and let her just be while they did what they needed to do at the bakery, and the reality of Sawyer needing that in her life hit me square in the chest. If she makes it a regular habit to go spend time in town after school, as long as I know where she is and who she's with, I want her to take advantage of it. Especially if it means she's going to be visiting the same spots we did when we had our day out.

Taking a long sip of my coffee, I try not to think about what that means to me. I know the fact she would be with Maggie has something to do with it. If I jump the gun on something with Maggie, though, I don't want it to interfere with what my daughter could be building with her, too.

I lean my head on the cushioned back of the chair I'm sitting in and slip my phone from my sweatshirt. I'll check the weather and catch up on the news before the day really starts. It's my routine.

My routine just got derailed.

Maggie Southard: When you said maybe you'd see me today, did you have an idea what time you maybe will see me?

I smile. She knows I'll be over to start on the trees this morning. I thought I told Gram what time, but maybe I didn't. My brain was a little distracted during the entire conversation.

Me: You're up early. Probably around 8. I'll head over after Sawyer leaves for school and I finish packing the trailer. How was your event last night?

While I wait for her response, I scroll through my calendar and start blocking off the time for Gram's project. I was going to do it yesterday, but then Will and I got busy getting part of the new greenhouse up. Sawyer wasn't too upset she wasn't home to help, and I made it acceptable when I told her she and Will are in charge of the second one now that her ankle is better. I'll supervise.

My phone alerts to a new message and I see the beginning of it pop onto the screen before I open to read the entire thing.

Maggie Southard: Event was good. I had trouble sleeping and gave head

She what? That can't be the entire message. Finding myself instantly upset but also aroused at the thought of her doing that, I open the message. Breathing out a sigh of relief when I read the whole text, I will my heart rate to slow down.

Maggie Southard: Event was good. I had trouble sleeping and gave headache so was up half the night with an icepack on my neck. Pain meds haven't touched it, so I'm assuming the weather is about to shift and it's time to get more lemons for my tea.

I laugh at the absurdity of autocorrect and where the text preview cut off. I assume she meant she had a headache, but for my amusement I point out her mishap.

Me: Autocorrect is not your friend, Maggie. For the headache, though, take a warm shower and massage where you have sinus pressure. The steam should help a little until you can get something better.

Maggie Southard: Autocorrect?

How do I say this without making it awkward? Are we at a point in knowing each other where this won't be taken as me coming on stronger than I actually am? Here goes nothing, I guess.

Me: Gave instead of have. When your text first came through, I read it as you had trouble sleeping and gave head. The message preview decided to give me a heart attack. I did not need that this morning.

She responds with a shocked face emoji and, "::palm-face::" which gives me a good laugh.

Maggie Southard: That's ... embarrassing. I'm so sorry. It's too early for me to catch that shit. For the record, I haven't done that in a very long time. Kind of happens when you're eternally single.

She went there and I'm going to follow.

Me: If we're going on the record, it has been a very long time since I've had that done. So, I guess that makes us even. Somehow. It's been a long time for a lot of things. Even enjoying talking to a woman is new for me.

I contemplate how much is too much. Bravery got the best of me last night when I asked her to dinner, but maybe this was more than she bargained for first thing in the morning. It's the truth, though. I don't make a habit of seeking women out. And dating? There's no time. The few dates I've had over the years since Hannah and I divorced ended in me home alone. Second dates have been rare. There was one girlfriend, but that lasted all of a few months once I saw how she was with Sawyer.

I've moved back to the kitchen to refill my mug and start the morning dad routine when my phone dings with a new message.

*Maggie Southard: Just so you know, the woman you're talking to hasn't stopped smiling since you asked her to dinner. There's plenty of time to make up for all those things neither of us seems to have done in a long time. I'm off to shower. Some cute guy told me it'll help my headache. *heart emoji**

What is she doing to me? I can't even respond to that. She knows I can't. It'll get really dirty really fast. Plus, I kind of like letting her have the last word.

"What are you smiling about?" Sawyer asks as she walks into the kitchen, pushing hair out of her face.

The surprise of her coming in the room causes a reflex and my phone goes clattering to the floor where she reaches down and picks it up. The messages are still open. Please don't let my teenager read it, I silently beg.

"Oh, I see," she says. Laughing at me, she adds, "Don't worry. I won't scroll through. Your face tells a whole story about how embarrassing it is to be caught texting a girl, by your kid no less."

Taking the phone from her outstretched hand, I stick my tongue out at her. She sticks hers out at me and thumbs her nose at me.

"Don't be sassy," I say, but it's all in play.

"Daddy, I like her. It's okay."

Sticking the phone into my hoodie, I nod at Sawyer. It takes a lot for her to say she likes most grownups other than me, Will, and Murph. The fact she has openly attempted to meet Maggie on her own terms is nothing short of amazing.

"I like her, too, Pumpkin. But let's take it slow, okay?" I say and try to gauge her reaction. "It's been a long time since we've had any sort of serious relationship with a woman. Plus, you're the most important girl in my life, so if something changes you need to tell me so we can work through it together."

She pops a bagel in the toaster and pulls a gallon of milk from the fridge. With her back to me, I see her tense up. Her shoulders aren't relaxed anymore and I wonder what I said to garner a reaction like that. This raising a teenager thing is really hard. I don't know how my mother dealt with three of us at one time.

Rehashing what I said, I lean against the counter and drink my coffee in silence.

Sawyer puts peanut butter on her bagel, fills a mug with milk and puts it in the microwave to warm up, and then she stands and stares at me.

"What?"

"What?" she parrots. "Nothing. It's nothing."

"Hmm. No. My lie detector says otherwise. Out with it."

She isn't going to win this one. I'm starting to worry because this isn't normal "I don't want to talk about it" behavior from her. That I'm used to, especially when it comes to boys or friends or friends that are boys who want to be more than friends.

"She's already a better mom than Mom," she blurts out, then immediately takes a bite of bagel, grabs her mug from the microwave, and makes a beeline for the table.

My coffee mug is halfway to my mouth and my brain has ceased to function. This calls for a heavy morning conversation, so I make my way over to the table and sit across from her.

"Sawyer, look at me, okay?" and I wait until I can see her eyes. "The way your mom has behaved lately—"

"Most of my life, you mean."

"Doesn't mean she doesn't care about you. I'm glad you like Maggie, but right now she's a person I'd like to get to know better who I'm also contracted to do work for."

"I told her about the day we went to town and I just … Dad, she not only listened to me, but she didn't talk shit about Mom, which is huge because Hannah is easy to talk nasty about. We had a moment, and that moment included her hugging me and it was the kind of hug you give me where I can feel all of the unsaid things," she says as fast as she can, as if I might stop her and not let her finish if she spoke slower. "Even if nothing comes of you and her, there's a reason she's in my life and I plan to keep her."

Well, then. I wasn't wrong thinking something happened when they spent yesterday afternoon together. I was just way off about who and what they had discussed.

"We're doing dinner Thursday," I say. "Should I make it just me and Maggie, or do you want to join us?"

When I asked her to dinner, I figured it would be a date for just the two of us, but if Sawyer wants to come with us, I'm not going to tell her no. Something tells me Maggie wouldn't tell her no either, and maybe I'm wrong for not talking to Maggie about it first, but I can let her know when I see her this morning.

The look on Sawyer's face is unreadable at first and quickly shifts to her thinking face, before she takes another bite of bagel.

"You need time with just her, too," she says, after swallowing her food. "Maybe you can plan date number two for a weekend day and we can all do something together?"

"Settled then. I'm not planning on us being out too late tomorrow night. Will you be okay home alone?"

She rolls her eyes at me. Then looks at me like I have an extra ear growing from my forehead. I don't know what's so weird about the question. It's a normal question, isn't it?

"Yeah, Daddy, I'll be fine on my own for a few hours. It's not like you're leaving me for an entire weekend to fend for myself," she says.

It clicks as I watch her finish her milk. It might be a normal question for me, but it's not normal for her to be asked her thoughts or opinions on something as innocuous as being alone for an evening while I go out.

"Understood." I stand from my position at the table so I can go get dressed and ready for my day. Placing my mug on the counter, I refill it and leave it to begin cooling, then walk over and kiss my daughter on the crown of her head. "I love you, Sawyer. You're safe here."

Without waiting for a response, I take my chances with having the last word and leave the room.

*****

Somehow, I missed her this morning, but it's fine. I pulled up to Gram's shortly after eight and I needed to focus on getting these trees down. It's cool enough and the forecast is saying we could see snow in the next couple of weeks. The last thing I want to see happen is the mostly dead oak take on a heavy load and not be able to withstand the weight. It would come right down on the house and then Gram would be in a bigger predicament than just having a little landscaping done.

I'm up in the tree cutting limbs to make it easier to take down the trunk when I see Will pull up. He climbs out of his truck with two coffees and a pastry bag. I keep cutting away while he pulls his coveralls and Carhartt on over a thermal shirt. I'm covered in sweat already and dropped my jacket down through the tree limbs not long after starting. He must have noticed it laying in the yard because he wanders over under where I'm hooked to the tree and grabs it along with a handful of branches.

"Thank you!" I yell down. He lifts the hand with my coat in it so I know he heard me.

We work in the quiet of nature for another hour before I begin making my way down the tree trunk. Will meets me at the base of the trunk with one of the cups of coffee and a muffin.

93

"You got a head start this morning. I thought you told me to be here by nine-thirty," he says, taking a pull from his to-go cup.

"I did. And you're still early. If I told you I was planning to be here earlier, you would have beat me to the job," I say.

"If you're not early you might as well be late, Rick. You know that's how I live," Will says, chuckling. "I would have been here even earlier if I hadn't stopped at the Bean. I ran into Maggie."

At the mention of her name, I swallow wrong and start coughing as coffee goes down my windpipe.

"You good?" I nod. "She said you asked her to dinner. I just have to say, I'm impressed."

Raising my eyebrow at him, I question what he means.

"I figured it would take you longer to ask her out. I know you tend to play it safe because of Sawyer," he says, lifting his cup up again.

I take a bite of my muffin and contemplate. I do play it safe. There isn't a person alive who knows me well who doesn't know that. Will and I have known each other long enough I can share pretty much everything with him, though.

"Well, actually, it would have taken me longer to find the nerve if it wasn't for Sawyer. She went and spent the afternoon with Maggie at the bakery, so when she brought Sawyer home, I just went with my gut."

The entire time I've talked I have tried not to make eye contact with Will. He's one of those friends who keeps to himself, but he can read people like a fucking book and I'm not sure I want to know what he sees right now.

"You're smitten," he says.

"Smitten." I bark out a laugh, then I release a sigh and continue, "Yeah, you're probably right. I just hope it doesn't come back to bite me in the ass, you know."

As quickly as he mentioned Maggie, he changes the subject back to the job at hand. We make quick work of getting the rest of the white oak down before taking another short break for lunch and creating a plan for the rest of the trees that need to be removed.

Spending the afternoon climbing trees doesn't sound that exciting, but for a guy who spent his entire childhood wandering through pine trees with my dad and helping the neighbor when they were tapping maples for syrup, this is next level. I love the adrenaline rush of scaling to the highest spot.

It's the best seat in the house being 50 feet up in the air looking out over the neighborhood or a grove of trees. Plus, up here it's quiet and I can think.

Making my way down the last tree so we can finish it off, cutting the trunk down so it's short enough to grind out, I see Gram peeking through a window in the back of the house. I smile and wave, and in return she waves and then places her hand on her chest above her heart. I'm close enough to the house to see her take a deep breath, but it catches me off guard when I see her wipe at her eyes as though there are tears falling.

Looking up at the tree I'm about to completely remove, it hits me how much history is here for her. This tree has been here as long as she has been. I imagine Maggie's grandfather sitting beneath it in the summer, Maggie's mom playing in the shade it provided when she was a little girl, Maggie cleaning up the leaves it dropped every fall when she was a teenager. I'm lost in thought, busy saying my thanks to Mother Nature for providing for this family, when Will wanders into view.

"Where are you taking her tomorrow?" he asks out of the blue as we each grab handfuls of branches.

We drag more limbs from the back of the house so I can cut them up smaller and take them back to my property. Unless Gram has a use for the wood, it'll go in the pile for summer bonfires.

"Haven't really thought about it," I respond.

We've gotten a lot done in a short amount of time, and once we clear out the rest of the branches I've taken down behind the house we'll just have stumps to grind.

"You might want to get on that."

"Yeah. I'm just not sure what she might be in the mood for. I don't even know if she likes low-key or fancy."

There's a lot I don't know about her, but I want to. All in due time, I suppose.

Dropping an armful of small branches into the bed of the truck, I grab the side of the box and turn to look at Will.

"Where do you think I should take her?"

I squint against the sun so I can see him and pull the brim of my ball cap down over my eyes to shield them as I wait for him to answer.

"She's not super fancy, but she's always seemed to enjoy having a reason to dress up," he says. "But, she's also just as content to be in sweatpants and a hoodie with a bowl of popcorn. I guess it depends on what your end game is."

"What do mean?"

He cocks his head and gives me a look that says I should know exactly what he's talking about.

"No," I say. "That's not even on my mind at this point. I mean, yes, I would like to very much at some point. Not on a first date, though. I'm more of a gentleman than that, Will."

He raises his hands in surrender.

"Then take her to that upscale burger joint in the next town over and see what happens. If she's not loving the place, she'll tell you, and this way you can talk about what you both like," he says. Walking away, I hear him say to himself, "You'd think the guy never took a girl anywhere. Didn't think he was this out of practice."

I smirk, and wonder if he'll ever figure out that I ask him things like this because his opinion means a lot to me. I look at him like I would an older brother.

Chapter 15

Maggie

It's date day with the hot landscaper man. I wish I wasn't nervous, but I absolutely am. Maybe I wouldn't be if I had seen him between him asking me and today.

Long story short, I skipped out and left for the bakery way earlier than I usually do on a Wednesday, not because I didn't want to see him yesterday but because after that text exchange first thing in the morning, I was afraid if I saw him, I might not leave the house at all. If I did, I might have dragged him back inside cavewoman style and had my way with him.

So, the smartest thing to do was throw on my clothes, pack up my makeup, and head to work a couple hours ahead of schedule. It's not the worst decision I've ever made. Delilah and I were able to get ahead on some things and start planning for the holiday season.

But now, it's the day of the date, and he's supposed to pick me up at Gram's after he goes home to shower and get ready. Then we're going to get burgers and beers. He didn't say if the place we're going to is a fancy place or has a dress code, so I'm going for cute but casual. Jeans, a flowy top with a strappy tank top underneath, boots, and I've double Dutch braided my hair.

My brain is spinning through scenarios faster than I can comprehend them. What if we decide we just don't click? I don't think that's going to be the case, but there's always a possibility that the initial attraction won't be there once you get to know a person. I'm not the type to just be like, "Thanks, this was fun, but see ya," and it would take a lot of unattractive things about a person to make me up and walk away instead of forging something of a friendship with them. There would have to be absolutely no redeeming qualities for me to not even allow the potential for anything to play out. For instance, maybe it's not a romantic thing for us but a friend thing, and what a disservice that would be for me to not find out.

This is what my head is like right now. It's as if I'm trying to talk myself out of liking him. As if I might get hurt if I put myself out there. I don't put myself out there with guys, ever.

Last time I tried to go on a date with a nice guy, it was my friend Alex. He's an adjunct music professor at the college here in town. He's great. Totally down to earth, a sweetheart, one of those guys who opens the door for you and pulls out your chair at dinner, but we didn't click in that way. I was really hoping that would change because when we started seeing each other Delilah and Fisher were in the midst of planning their wedding and adopting Gen and Jax. Part of me worried I was missing out on life without having a partner.

That truly isn't the case though. Alex turned out to be a fabulous guy to be friends with and hopefully he finds his one sometime in the near future. Hopefully I find mine, too. He just didn't have magical forearms, you know?

"Okay, Gram, how does this look?" I stand in the kitchen doorway, hands on my hips.

She motions for me to turn around so she can see my back.

"Your hair looks cute. Might want to make sure he's not one of those men who like to pull your braids, though" she says, attempting to hide a snicker.

"Gram! That's so dirty. And nothing like that is happening tonight. Jesus, it's a first date," I say, turning back around after schooling my smile. "The shirt? Does it look good or is it too much?"

"It's perfect. You're beautiful, Margaret. If he doesn't fall in love with you, well then, he's just the stupidest man on earth," she says, walking closer to pull me into a hug.

I breathe her in and whisper a "thank you."

*****

"Just us?" I question when he leads me out to his truck.

He laughs and scratches at the back of his neck before reaching for the passenger door handle.

"You know, it's funny. I thought about seeing if you'd mind Sawyer coming with us, but she told me not to," he says. "She assured me she would be fine at home for a few hours while we spent time together alone."

Placing my hand over my heart, I'm not sure if I'm sad Sawyer isn't joining us or really happy she's mature enough to understand her dad and I should take a little bit to get to know one another better.

"She's really sweet, Maverick," I say, climbing up into the seat.

He closes the door and walks around to the driver's side, a smile on his freshly shaven face. Pulling his phone from his jacket pocket, he checks something before getting in the truck.

The drive to the restaurant and then while we wait for drinks to arrive is filled with easy conversation — where we went to school, what years we graduated, how it's possible we never ran into one another before the homecoming game, why I chose baking and why he chose trees. Despite the age difference, he makes me feel at home.

"I wasn't sure if this was going to be okay," he says after our plates of food arrive.

"If what was going to be okay?" I question. Everything so far has been perfection. The scenery, the guy, the food, and the little bit of alcohol has made it all seem dream-like.

"Burgers and beer. It just seems like a cop-out for a nice first date," he says. "Honestly, I asked Will for his advice because I wanted to make sure we were going somewhere you'd like."

"Are you … nervous? Maverick Rogers, I really didn't expect you to be the kind of man to be nervous about taking a woman out. For real, though, this is the best first date. Will gave you good advice," I say.

His smile warms my heart the way it reaches his eyes, the way his ears turn a deeper shade of pink. The more I look at him the more I wonder how I've spent so long without knowing him.

"How is Gram doing?"

I laugh because, really, she's been amazing the last few days. She talked a blue streak last night at dinner when I asked about the trees. She got a little misty-eyed when telling me about taking down the ones in the back of the house. When she and Grandpa first started clearing more of the land to build the house, she insisted those stay. Grandpa wanted to take them down to give more room for a backyard, but she didn't want to lose the shade they provided.

"I saw her when I was getting ready to take the trunk down. Is she okay with the decision to cut them down?" he asks, worry marring his face.

"I think she is. She knows we're going to put something there to replace what's been taken, but the initial shock was a lot."

She may have had some regret at first, but after I talked to her about the plans Sawyer showed me and Lilah, there was a very obvious calm that came over her. Like she knew it was the right decision. Plus, I don't think Grandpa would be upset about taking them down if it means a safer environment for me and Gram.

"I was telling her about all the plans your daughter has come up with for the back yard and the bed out front and Gram seemed to be very excited at the possibility of updating the property. I don't know if it's for my benefit or not, but I'm glad she's got this to look forward to," I say.

There's a lull in conversation, but it's so comfortable I don't even notice. As we finish dinner and the waitress comes to take our plates, he questions me about dessert. Typically, I'm not a dessert when I eat out person because I eat so many sweet treats at work. But …

"How about one dessert to share?" he asks. "And two to take with us? One for Gram and one for Sawyer."

That is something I can get behind.

I'm quickly learning that chasing any guy my age was the wrong decision on my part for a lot of years. I should have known an older man would be the one to capture my heart.

Maverick reaches across the table and gently covers my hand with his. The electric charge I feel from his touch is stronger than the last time he placed his hand on mine, it draws me in and my eyes meet his. There's desire there, but something more. He has so much more to offer than a fun evening out. His gaze is a security blanket I didn't realize I needed, and now I understand what Sawyer meant when she said he doesn't break promises.

"You're different than other guys I've tried first dates with," I say without thinking about it. The words just tumble out.

"How so?" he asks, his calloused thumb softly brushing against my knuckles.

He glances at my mouth and I catch myself licking my bottom lip. Maybe that first date rule will get broken after all. Perhaps something will happen.

"Well, you aren't overbearing. You haven't really talked about yourself, at least not in a way that makes me want to go to the bathroom and not come back to dinner. I've gotten to know you enough already to know you're kind and you care about the company you keep," I say, stopping to think a moment. "However, I think there's a bad boy side to you that's mysterious and that has me intrigued."

He picks my hand up and pulls it closer to him as he leans toward the center of the table. Kissing my hand, he looks directly in my eyes and it feels like he's seeing the deepest parts of me.

"I wouldn't call it a bad boy side, but it's definitely not choir boy, either," he says. "I can certainly be rough around the edges and hard to live with at times."

"Everyone can be difficult. What matters is making sure you're difficult for the right reasons."

As we stare at each other, dessert arrives. He lets go of my hand and I miss him immediately. Maverick must feel the loss as well, because he reaches his left hand across the tabletop for my left hand and we stay that way while eating our shared dessert. It's awkward, but neither of us moves to change position.

I would rather starve than let go, and that is not a feeling I'm accustomed to.

*****

As he drives us back to Gram's, I wonder if she's going to still be awake. She's been going to bed early, and Mom was going to stop by while I was out so I shouldn't have anything to worry about. Unfortunately, that doesn't keep the intrusive thoughts at bay.

Maverick pulls in the driveway behind my car and kills the engine. Mom's car is parked beside mine. This won't be weird at all.

"I'd like very much for you to come in, if you'd like," I say in the darkness of his truck. It's so quiet.

"I would very much like that," he says.

I feel like a teenager all over again. Our entire evening was magical and not one time did it feel awkward. But now that we're sitting in the driveway it feels like if we do anything we're bound to get caught. Inviting him in while Mom is here and Gram is potentially still awake could be a recipe for disaster.

The outside light is on, as if the house is waiting for our arrival. Trying not to think about what's going to greet us inside, we open our doors at the same time and make our way to the breezeway that connects the garage to the house.

Gram and Mom are standing in silhouette at the door to the back yard when we enter. The sight catches me off guard. I'm not used to being a voyeur where the women in my life are concerned, but as Maverick and I walk into the room I'm struck by the scene. There aren't many chances I've had to spend with just the two of them recently, but I also rarely get to watch them interact without being part of the interaction.

Maverick touches the small of my back and I motion toward the door that leads to the kitchen. He must have noticed what stopped me from moving further into the room as he doesn't say a word. I want to give them this time together, so we quietly make our way into the house hoping not to disturb them.

Once inside, I close the door and set the take away container with Gram's dessert on the counter. When I turn, Maverick is standing beside the table with his hands in his pockets watching me.

"You okay?" he asks.

I think about the question for a moment, biting my lip and wondering what is the best way to answer it. Truthfully. That's the only way to answer something like that.

"Honestly, not really. She's been great since you came to look at the trees and talk about her project, but I'm scared those non-lucid moments are still going to become more frequent," I say, crossing my arms over my chest. "She's confused me for my mom more than a few times recently, you know? And seeing them standing out there together ..."

My voice fades away as I hear Gram's and Mom's voices coming closer to the door.

"It's a moment you need to make a memory, Maggie," he says as the doorknob begins to turn.

We lock into a silent conversation as my mom walks into the room and is startled by us being there. Apologies are exchanged, but there's also a look of gratitude that flashes in Mom's eyes.

"Did you have a nice dinner?" Gram asks. She notices the food container on the counter and makes a beeline for it before either of us can answer. "Leftovers?"

"Dessert for you," Maverick says before I can respond. "Maggie said it was one of your favorites."

She pops the top on the container and holds her hand out to me for a fork.

"You're a good boy, Rick. I do love a good cheesecake." Gram motions to Mom and makes her way to the living room. Popping a bite into her mouth, she says to Mom, "Come on. We'll let them have a few minutes alone to say goodnight. I'll even share this with you."

Maverick and I laugh at the silliness of it all, but really it wouldn't be my Gram if it was any other way.

He's still standing on the opposite side of the room and I wish he wouldn't. I wish he would come closer.

"I had a really nice time tonight," he says, his voice low and growly.

I know I heard him, and he knows I heard him, but I play stupid and place my index finger up by my ear. "What was that? You're so far away I could hardly make out what you said," I say, playfully.

It makes his feet move in my direction. Painstakingly slow. Then all at once the energy in my space changes and he's a breath away. He reaches out and his hands grip the counter on either side of my waist, and he leans in close to my ear and whispers.

"I had a nice time tonight," he says.

The barely there stubble on his jawline brushes against my cheek and sends a shiver down my spine. I place my hands on his hips and plant my feet to keep myself from wobbling too much.

"I would like to have another evening with you sometime soon," he whispers, his lips inching closer to mine. "Maybe I could cook. We could make it a family thing. Me, you, Sawyer, and Gram?"

"Gram would love that," I whisper back. "Now, are you going to give me a proper kiss or do I need to take it from you?"

Abandoning his good boy persona for a moment, Maverick's mouth crashes against mine. He moves his hands to cup my face and I grasp the beltloops on his jeans. He pulls my bottom lip with his teeth and then gently nips it before letting go. My fingers find his chest and I want to forget we aren't alone in the house as I push my hands inside the warmth of his jacket. He presses his hips against me and I could melt into a puddle right here.

A small moan escapes my mouth and he quickly steals the sound from me, then reaches behind me and tugs on my braids. I drop my head back giving him full access to my neck and he takes the hint, laying soft kisses along the tender skin beneath my ear.

"I should probably go home soon," he whispers, giving my hair one more gentle tug before letting go. I tip my head up and find his lips again, knowing I want to savor this experience for as long as I can until I can have it again.

I shift my weight from one foot to another, subtly brushing against the front of his jeans knowing full well what I'm doing.

"I agree, you should. I promised Gram nothing naughty was going to happen on the first date," I say, gently nibbling his chin.

"What are the rules for the second date?" he asks.

"No idea. I'm making this up as I go. It's been a very long time since there was a second date worthy of having rules for," I say. "But I can't wait for a second date with you."

He presses his lips to my forehead and I breathe him in as I grip his shirt in my hands, wishing suddenly things were easier. We're both tied down in ways we can't control.

One thing is for sure — anything worth having with him is worth the work we'll put into it.

Chapter 16

Maverick

The last time I was with a woman and left with a hard-on was never. This is a first for me. I adjust myself as I climb up into the cab of the truck and take a few deep breaths because this woman ... she's doing things to me that no one else ever has.

Driving home, I take my time and relish the feelings from my night with Maggie. When I roll up into the driveway, I'm not surprised to see the front light on. I figured Sawyer would turn it on after I left.

What I don't expect is to see her sitting on the deck wrapped up in a blanket with a mug of hot chocolate waiting for me. It's not too late, but for a school night I would have expected her to be inside winding down for the night.

"Hey, Pumpkin, what are you doing up still?"

"I thought about going to bed early, but then I wanted to make sure you got home safely. I thought about leaving you a note to wake me when you got here so I knew you were home, but that seemed like a lot of extra work," she says.

Her downcast glance at her mug tells me something more is going on, but I don't want to push her too hard for information.

"Mind if I join you?" She shakes her head. "I'm going to change out of these clothes real quick and I'll be back."

The house is picked up, not that there's much clutter anyway but sometimes the mail is scattered on the counter and the blankets aren't folded on the back of the couch. The dishes are done. Again, not that there are too many since it's just the two of us. There's a pot on the stove with enough hot chocolate in it for another mug, maybe a little more. I fill my biggest coffee mug with what's left and place the dish in the sink with a bit of water before shedding my jacket and going up to my bedroom.

My clothes smell like her. Whatever cologne she uses, is infused into my shirt. I toss it on the bed instead of putting it directly in the hamper and pull a hoodie over my white undershirt. I sit and unlace my dress boots, which are really just work boots that I haven't worn for work so they're still in perfect condition and not a muddy mess. The jeans come off, the grey sweatpants go on, and I make my way back to the kitchen to grab my cocoa.

"Okay, spill," I say to her as I step back out onto the deck. "You didn't text me at all, but you're still up at almost ten at night and you're sitting out here like a worried parent."

Sawyer shrugs and pulls her blanket around her shoulders tighter.

"It was the first night since I moved in that we didn't spend the evening together. I think it bothered me more than I thought it would," she says. "How was your date?"

That hit me right in the heart. Damn. She's right, though. A couple nights before I told Hannah Sawyer was moving in with me permanently was the last time we spent an evening apart.

Handing her the takeout container and a fork I brought out of the house with me, I say, "Peace offering?"

"Cheesecake?" she asks without opening it.

"Turns out you and Gram are both lovers of the cake of cheese. Maggie and I made sure to get you both a piece."

"Have I mentioned I really like her, Daddy?"

"Well, then you're going to really like the good news I have to share. There's going to be a second date," I say, lifting my mug to my lips. She smiles despite her mouth being full of food. "Even better news is we're going to have dinner here with you and she's going to bring Gram so we can make it a family thing."

Family events are pretty rare for me and Sawyer since my parents and siblings are a couple hours away in the Finger Lakes. We just don't see them frequently. I talk to them regularly, but it's not like they live just up the street and we can get together on a whim, you know? It makes it difficult. It's more difficult since Hannah's parents live out of state now and don't have the level of give a damn I thought they would where their granddaughter is concerned. If Sawyer gets Christmas and birthday cards, that a small miracle.

But I see her eyes light up when I mention us hosting dinner with Maggie and Gram and it makes the lack on other people's parts a little easier to digest for the moment.

"When are we doing this and what are we making? You should grill something," she says. "And I can make apple crisp."

Sitting back and crossing my right ankle over my left knee, I take a swig of my now chilled cocoa. Picking at a fuzz on my sweatshirt, I take my time before telling her I think that sounds like a fantastic idea. I love to grill and she's figured out the perfect ratio of brown sugar, flour, and butter for the crumbly topping on her apple crisp. It's a win for all of us.

"We're going to need more than steak and dessert, but we've definitely got a decent start."

Sawyer lets a yawn slip and I encourage her to call it a night.

"Hey, Sawyer?" She turns to look at me, expectantly, her hand on the door. "Thank you for waiting up for me. I'm not used to being gone in the evening, or not spending the evening with you either."

She pulls the blanket up around her shoulders again and steps over to my chair, giving me the best hug she can in her mummified state and kissing the top of my head.

"I love you, Dad."

"Love you, too, Pumpkin."

*****

I stay up way later than I should. Initially it was so I could plan out the next step for Gram's project, which is going to be the fall inspired flower bed in the front yard. Then I found myself having trouble falling asleep and instead revisiting the biggest parts of my night with Maggie — the way her eyes sparkled, the way her lips tasted, how she left me covered in her scent.

When I woke up in the night for the third time, I might have shoved my button-down shirt under my pillow so I could feel her close to me.

Perhaps things are getting way more serious way faster than I anticipated, but I'm not going to question it unless she does. The second date feels like it's forever away. Even though we haven't made our plans yet, I want it to be soon. As soon as possible, actually. I wonder if she'll think I'm being too forward if I ask her to do dinner here on Saturday?

I'll take my chances.

Sending her a text this early might get me in trouble with her considering she told me how much she loves her sleep, but I'm willing to take my chances with that, too. I'm pleasantly surprised when I get a message back within minutes, but hardly have a chance to read it before her name lights my phone up in the dark of my bedroom.

"For a woman who insists on loving sleep, I really didn't expect to hear back from you at —" I sit up to look at my alarm clock, "Five-fifteen in the morning."

"I couldn't sleep. There were too many things on my mind," she says.

Her voice is lovely to listen to in person, but on the phone when she's being quiet because the house is silent? It hits deep in my gut in a way that makes me want to bury myself deep inside her.

"What sort of things?" I prod. "Because I was having the same issue last night."

She chuckles, it's low and throaty, and when I close my eyes, I see the beautiful curve of her throat as her head dropped back to give me access to her neck.

"Oh, you know, cookies, cupcakes, Thanksgiving decorations," she says.

"Yeah, same. I was also wondering about Santa Claus. I don't know if I'll make it on the nice list this year," I say. "I haven't been the best boy. Someone even told me I had a little bad boy in me. My chance of getting presents is dwindling by the day."

"Something tells me there's enough good in you to keep you on the nice list," she says. "For instance, you want to cook for Gram and that's a pretty big undertaking."

When I question what she means, Maggie begins telling me stories about her grandmother's legendary meals — from chicken cordon bleu and slow cooked roasts to apple bread and home churned ice cream. It makes me a little jealous that, despite having great meals as a kid from what I remember, I didn't get home churned ice cream.

"Okay, well you might have a grandma who makes ice cream for you, but I'm going to wow her with tomahawk steaks and grilled asparagus," I say, perhaps a bit defensively. Trying to quell the hostility in my voice, I add, "And Sawyer is going to knock her socks off with an apple crisp."

"Oh, did I touch a nerve, Mr. Rogers?" she asks.

"Nah. I just didn't get things like that when I was a kid," I say. "I mean, we had ice cream, but it was from a carton from the store, you know?"

Maggie's quiet for a minute and I try to figure out how to redeem myself while I wait for her to come back to me. When I hear rustling in the background, I question what she's doing.

"Um, I'm just making a quick grocery list," she says.

"Okay?" I say it as a question. Maybe this is her norm and I just don't get it, but it seems weird to start making a grocery list this early in the day.

"So I can pick up the ingredients," she says, letting out a yawn, "for homemade ice cream."

Stunned, I forget how to talk. When I finally find my voice again, I have to clear my throat a couple times before words come out.

"You're going to make ice cream to go with dinner?" I'm quiet when I say it. This girl is too much. Not to mention she's younger than me and part of an entire generation of people that others like to consider selfish. She's the furthest thing from that, though.

"Well, we can't have apple crisp and no ice cream, and now that I know you haven't had homemade, I can't let you go another dessert without trying it."

She's extremely matter-of-fact, and I really love it.

"I can't wait," is all I can muster before my alarm clock begins ringing. "I guess that's my cue to get up and make coffee."

"Same," she says. "I'll see you in a couple hours."

"See you soon, indeed."

*****

Sawyer didn't want to go to school, but I made her go anyway. In fact, I compromised by driving her to school and dropping her off after letting her get a coffee drink thing from the Jumping Bean. Before she could ask, I told her no I wasn't going to let her skip and go to Gram's with me.

"Then don't be surprised if I magically end up at the bakery after school instead of at home," she says as she pulls her backpack up her arms.

"Well, if that's the case, then see if Maggie will drop you off at her house because that's probably where I'm going to be."

She rolls her eyes and sticks her tongue out at me before slamming the door.

"You're being grumpy," I yell through the closed window.

Before I pull away, she turns and I see the smile on her face. I know some of the mood is girl stuff related. The bathroom she uses downstairs is a ticking timebomb of makeup, face wash, maxi pads, and tampons. Oh, and there's about three different curling irons and a blow dryer. I can't believe she hasn't blown a fuse yet.

Regardless of all the woman stuff, she's still way less maintenance than her mother ever was and I will take that any day of the week over the messes Hannah would leave behind.

I wave to her as she meets up with a small group of girls who I assume are her cheer friends. They've never been to the house, but some of them look familiar from when I've picked her up from practice and games. We need to remedy that, too. She can't live with me and me never meet her friends.

Slamming on the brakes, I almost drive into the back end of a minivan when I see a kid wrap his arm around her shoulder. I recognize him as one of the football players from the homecoming game. He was the only one who seemed concerned Sawyer was hurt. The way she looks up at him now as they walk into school, though, is more than a just friends look. I don't know if I'm ready for this part.

A horn blows behind me and I realize I'm holding up the drop off line. Lifting my hand to wave to the car behind me, I pull forward and push down all the emotions that just climbed to the surface.

Thankfully, when I get to Gram's, Will is already there and doesn't give me any shit for being behind schedule. Instead, he's sitting on the front porch with Maggie and Gram, visiting over a pot of coffee.

"Mornin' Rick," he yells, lifting his mug as if in salute. "These beautiful young ladies were just sharing with me what a wonderful evening you had yesterday."

Walking up the pathway to the porch, I lift my hat and scratch the top of my head.

"Oh, have they now?" I play along. "And did they also tell you about dinner tomorrow at my house? Because future dinner means way more than past dinner."

Will looks at Gram, feigning shock.

"Of course they did," he deadpans.

Turning my attention to Maggie, her cheeks turn pink and the tips of her ears change a couple shades darker. She shrugs as she takes a sip from her coffee.

"Was it supposed to be a secret?"

Unable to hold in my smile I shake my head.

"Not at all. Now, if you two don't mind me stealing Will, we have a flower bed to dig up," I say.

"Take him. We're done grilling him for information on you anyway," Gram says, standing from her chair. She's dead serious the way she says it, too. I fully believe she would pump Will for info, if for no other reason than to make sure her granddaughter is in good hands.

Maggie covers her face in embarrassment, but I wish she wouldn't. I think it's great Gram is protective of her. Their protection of one another is mutual, and I hope someday when I'm older I have someone to care about me the way they do each other.

Will gets up from his seat and gives Gram a peck on the cheek, then leans down to kiss the top of Maggie's head. With so much always going on with Sawyer and the drama of being married to and divorced from Hannah, I hadn't realized how close he was with so many other people here. Like the art girl in town — Jacelyn — he took her under his wing when she first started out in her shop. He's forever stopping in to help Father Murph with his group of misfits, spending time with them and asking them to help him with projects so they are reminded of their worth.

I guess in a huge way I'm one of Will's projects, too. When I first started the tree farm outside of town, he would show up like magic when I was planting to replace what we lost or sold the previous season. He's one of the big reasons I finally expanded and took on the first landscaping client and began carrying shrubs and flowers. Well, him and Sawyer, because they ganged up on me and she told me she'd cry herself to sleep if I didn't have more plants than just Christmas trees. She was four and obsessed with magnolias. Talk about a shot to the heart.

Before Will and I can wander into the yard and get started with our work, Maggie walks up and wraps her arms around my neck.

"Good morning," she says, then gently presses her lips to mine.

There's an audience, so we cut the kiss short, but she leaves my lips feeling tingly and full.

"You know, I could get used to mornings like this," I say. Rubbing my lips together, I question, "Peppermint lip gloss?"

"Me, too." She kisses me one more time before releasing her arms. "And yes, it's peppermint. I'm trying to get into the spirit of the season."

I laugh loudly.

"But I thought it's still pumpkin spice season."

"Oh, no, good sir. Pumpkin spice season ends Tuesday with Halloween. We're deep into mint preparation," she says, walking away from me. "Stop by the bakery later. I have more of those cookies from the other night that you liked and a couple other test flavors."

I tip my ball cap up and smile broadly at her retreating form, letting her have the last word.

*****

The flower bed in front is all marked out how Sawyer planned it and we've spent most of the morning removing sod. We got the tiller in there around lunchtime and worked the dirt up nicely, mixing in some fertilizer as we went.

Since the first mention of fall flowers, and with it getting late in the season to be planting, I scrambled to find any sort of healthy looking mums. I made sure to give them some TLC at home before bringing them with me today. Once I get a refill on my coffee and shove a sandwich in my mouth, I'll be measuring out where to put the yellow and maroon flowers. I have three for each side of the flower bed along with some other fall blooming plants that will go in the center of the garden. I'm crossing my fingers the dianthus doesn't die and saying a prayer that the asters come back next year since they're not really a late October flower. If they don't, I'll replant them.

If anything happens to any of these flowers, I'll replant them all just to see Maggie and Gram smile.

"It's looking good, Rick. What's going in the beds out back?" Will asks, leaning on his shovel.

Lifting my hat, I wipe the sweat from my forehead not even concerned with the amount of dirt I'm getting on my face. Seeing how filthy I can get is half the fun of the job.

"I want to run it by Sawyer, but I'm thinking if all the women are in agreement, we'll do two of the pollinator beds. One on either side of the tea table and chairs Gram wants out there," I say.

He nods. "Okay, but that's not what I asked."

"I was thinking out loud. I was getting to it," I say, lifting a small scoop of dirt with my shovel and flinging it at Will. "We're definitely planting bee balm, I want to add more asters back there, Hosta, hibiscus, zinnia, coneflower, and I think Sawyer really wanted bleeding hearts."

"What if they don't want two?"

"Then maybe they'll want one big one in a semi-circle so the table and chairs can still be right there surrounded by the flowers," I say. "You don't think this is too much, do you? I'm not a flower guy, I deal with trees, so you know I know less than nothing about what goes together."

Will laughs at me, but he's not mocking me. He's well aware of where my expertise begins and ends. Flowers are not part of my wheelhouse at this point, but I'm trying.

"That's why you have Sawyer. Plus, you should ask Maggie what she thinks would go well together. She's got a good eye for that sort of thing," he says.

"Her taste in floral arrangements is almost as good as her taste in men, right?" I ask rhetorically, a smirk on my face.

Will just shakes his head, laughing, and walks away.

"If you're not careful, you'll fall in love with the girl before you finish the job," he says over his shoulder.

Chapter 17

Maggie

"Oh my god, you're falling in love with him!"

"What? No. Love is a very strong word, Lilah. I wouldn't say that," I say, attempting to diffuse the situation. "I would say that I'm very much enjoying his company and getting to know him better."

In order for her to not see how red my cheeks are, I make sure to keep my head down and continue writing my list until she goes back into the kitchen.

There are cookies to bake. So many cookies. And cupcakes. Fall flavors and winter flavors, and regular flavors. All. The. Flavors. We have a few more events coming up that I'll be at either with the food truck or at a table set up inside, and I want to make sure we have a nice variety. My goal is to have enough cupcakes and cookies on hand for people to put together dessert boxes.

The bell at the door rings as someone enters and, without looking up, I greet them.

"Good afternoon! Welcome to the Bakery on Main. How can we help you today?"

I do a quick double check of my list and raise my head to find Sawyer standing at the counter in front of me.

"Hey, Sawyer," I say, smiling at her for a split second before I realize something is very wrong. "Why were you crying?"

She wipes her cheek but a new tear forms in its absence. I drop my pen and leave the safety and security of my spot behind the counter as she opens her mouth to speak and nothing comes out. Cupping her face, I take a deep breath and she follows suit as if we've done this a hundred times.

"A boy?"

She nods her head vigorously, clenching her eyes shut, and letting out a choked sob as she falls into my arms.

"Do you have ... oh. Never mind," Delilah says as she comes through the door from the kitchen.

I lay my cheek on top of Sawyer's head and gently rub circles on her back, making eye contact with Lilah.

She mouths, "What happened?" and I respond silently, "Stupid boy."

Lilah nods her head in understanding and slides her hand into the display case, pulling out a chocolate cupcake topped with faint orange buttercream and sprinkles shaped like oak leaves. I sign "thank you" to her, one of the few signs I know and use religiously with our hard of hearing customers, as she places the cake in a small cupcake box.

Sawyer's sobs quiet, but she doesn't let go of me. I won't let go until she needs me to. I think we established that when she was here earlier in the week.

"Want to talk about it?"

She nods, sniffs back the boogers, and takes a deep breath as she uncurls herself from my body.

"There's this boy, he's on the football team. We've been talking. You know, texting here and there, hanging out with friends at lunch, he was there the night I sprained my ankle and stayed with me until Dad came to get me. Literally the only guy on the team to be even a little concerned," she says. Settling into her chair at the same table we shared just days ago, she continues. "I'm not super popular. Not the way most of the other cheerleaders are. I'm a major nerd, I love school, I get good grades, and I work hard at it."

I'm waiting patiently for her to get to the part where this guy broke her heart, and trying really hard to not show that patience is a virtue I'm still working on.

"The last week or so he's been pretty hands on with our friendship, if you know what I mean," she says, looking at her hands as she twists her fingers around in her lap, popping a few knuckles. "Nothing horrible. Stupid fifteen-year-old guy behavior. A hand up my shirt, his hand way too high on my thigh when we're sitting together."

I feel myself getting angry. She's obviously uncomfortable with his behavior and getting more agitated as she keeps talking about it.

"You don't have to tell me what happened if you're not comfortable," I say quietly. "Your dad is at my house working. I can take you there if you'd rather talk to him."

Her eyes go wide.

"No! I don't want to tell him. He'd murder this kid," she says.

"He wouldn't, but I can take a wild guess he'd have a conversation with him," I say.

"I just … I just want to talk to you about it. You're a girl. You get it." Taking another deep breath, she says, "But it gets worse."

Oh, dear fucking lord it gets worse.

"He told his friends he was going to get me to sleep with him. Like he wanted to take me out after the homecoming game and then I got hurt, so I didn't go to the party they had after," she says.

"Let me take a wild guess," I say, and she starts shaking her head. I raise my hand to stop her. "Someone said, 'Let's bet on this,' and you found out?"

"Basically," she says. "And since I found out yesterday, I really didn't want to go to school today and deal with anyone. I went anyway because Daddy wouldn't let me stay home and he bribed me with coffee."

I laugh because if there ever was a kid after my own heart, aside from Lilah's children, it's this one. I slide off my chair and crouch on the floor in front of Sawyer. Taking her hands in mine, I smile at her.

"Listen, I might not know you that well yet, but you're a strong young lady. Whoever this guy is, if he thinks it's okay to place bets on something like this and play roulette with your life, he's not worth the tears you've cried," I say. "Did you tell him to fuck off? Because I feel like this would be the best time to tell a dude to fuck off if ever there was one."

She smiles at me, a sad smile but still a smile.

"I did. I took advantage of lunch and let him have it. His friends called me some shitty names, though, and he didn't defend me. Then at dismissal, he kind of broke up with me. All because I won't sleep with him," she says, taking another deep breath. "But it's weird because we weren't officially seeing each other either. There was never a 'will you go out with me?' moment, you know? And … he's not my type. At all. If you get my drift."

My eyes widen slightly, just enough for her to know I understand. I hate this for her. I hate the teen years in general, but this is worse because it's sex and popularity and teenagers. A volatile combination if ever there was one.

"They're all football players who think banging cheerleaders is the height of popularity. One of them is going to end up with chlamydia and spread it around and I am not about that life, Maggie. Honestly, I'd rather wait to lose my virginity with the right person than a person who is interested right now, you know?"

"I absolutely know," I say, though I don't go into the details of how I know. "What are you going to do now?"

Sawyer shrugs and I feel the heaviness of what she's going through lift with her movement. I want to take it and carry it for her for a while and just let her be a kid.

"I should probably talk to my dad about it later, but how do you talk about something like this with an already protective father?"

She bites on her thumbnail. I have a wild idea forming, and it absolutely involves me talking to Maverick about the shit his kid just unloaded on me, but purely as a precaution for him so he knows what he's walking into when they get home.

"I could have looked past all of the stupidity and the bet his friends made if he told me that he just told his friends he was going to sleep with me to get them to leave him alone about it or something."

Pulling her hand away from her mouth, I shake my head.

"Listen, Sawyer, if a guy allows his friends to talk about you like that and he then doesn't even stick up for you he is trash. Throw the whole man away," I say. "You're worth more. You're young, but that's a lesson I want you to learn right now. You. Are. Worth. More."

Sawyer nods her head, fresh tears threatening to fall, and she reaches out to me for another hug.

"Thank you," she whispers when she pulls free from my embrace. "I really wasn't planning on coming here today and falling apart. And I know you're busy, but if you have a break, do you think you can take me home? Or to your house? Dad mentioned he'd be there all day and it's closer than my house."

Standing from my kneeling position, I go in back and grab my keys, letting Lilah know I'm going out for a bit.

"Are you going to tell him?" Delilah asks me quietly so her voice doesn't travel too far.

"I feel obligated. This isn't something I think should be kept from him, and she's already worried about how to talk to him about it," I say, giving her a sideways glance. "If anything were to happen to her because of these boys at school and I knew shit went down but never said anything to him, I would feel responsible."

Lilah offers me a weak smile, then a quick hug and some well wishes for the conversation soon to take place.

119

*****

As I pull onto our road, I carefully approach the subject.

"I know you're unsure about talking to him, but would you be okay with me opening up the conversation for you and your dad? Give him an abridged rundown of what took place?"

Her backpack is at her feet and her hands are clasped in her lap. Sawyer's looking at the floor and she has her thinking face on. It takes almost until we're in the driveway before she gives me the green light, with the caveat I only tell him about the boy and not her lack of interest in boys.

We get out of the car and I wait for her on the driver's side before we trek across the front yard in the leaves to where Maverick and Will stand by the very humble beginnings of a flower bed.

"I really didn't think she was going to have you drive her over," he says when I get close enough to hear him. "Did she tell you she wanted to skip school to help me and I wouldn't let her? I figured she would end up at the bakery again, but honestly assumed she would just have me pick her up instead of cutting into your day."

Does he think this isn't okay? It's absolutely fine that she asked me to bring her to my house, and instead of subjecting her to her dad's scrutiny over the situation, I point to the door and tell her to go ahead in and put her stuff in the kitchen, grab some milk, and settle in with her cupcake to work on homework.

Maverick smiles at the interaction, but I don't think he understands I'm about to cause him some major distress. I worry what the next part of this conversation is going to do to our budding relationship. How could I not worry?

"We need to talk," I say, matter-of-factly, shooting a look at Will that causes him to follow Sawyer into the house.

Maverick's brow wrinkles in concern and I don't love that I'm putting that look on his face. So, taking a deep breath, I lay it all out for him as best I can without going into more detail than he needs from me. If he wants the nitty gritty, he needs to get it from Sawyer. He goes through a range of emotions, many of which are versions of shock and horror and "that motherfucker."

"And she came to you about all of this today?" he questions when I finish speaking. "Was it the kid whose arm was around her this morning?"

Pushing my hands into the pocket of my hoodie, I shrug. I'm not quite sure how to talk without using my hands, but I think this would be a good time to keep the flailing to myself.

"I would assume so, but she didn't tell me that part. Just that she really didn't want to go to school, but did because you didn't want her to miss."

He lifts his ball cap and scratches the top of his head before shoving it back down.

"Look, I know what it's like to be a teenage girl —"

"But you aren't her mother," he cuts me off, and it feels like the worst kind of pain.

I know he didn't mean it any other way. I know he meant it as she has a mom and I don't have to do things like this, but I'll be damned if I let him think that's how this relationship with me is going to go. If I care about him, I'm going to care about her.

"Someone has to be, and if Hannah isn't going to be here for the good stuff, she sure as hell doesn't deserve to be around for the hard times. I might not be Sawyer's mom, but if you ask her, she just might tell you that I'm the closest thing to it right now."

He backs away from me, as if a woman has never stepped up and held her ground against him. He's going to learn a thing or two about me really quick.

"As I was saying, I know what it's like to be a teenage girl. In fact, I'm not that far removed from my teen years and unfortunately the majority of my adulthood has, up to this point, been spent trying to undo the damage those years did to me," I say, taking a step in his direction to close the gap. "So, if what that girl in there needed from me today was for me to act like someone's mother, then sign. Me. Up. She needed someone who wasn't you for a minute."

He narrows his eyes and I see the moment he decides this is going to be our first fight.

"What is that supposed to mean exactly?"

Rolling my eyes, I put my hands on my hips and stare at him.

"Really? You want to do this? Okay. She didn't need you flipping out and hunting down a kid for being a nasty asshole. She needed a woman who was going to listen to her words, all of them, and then be somewhat rational."

"And ... I'm not being rational?"

"I did not say that. What I am saying is, your daughter is your entire world and she knows she is. The last thing she wanted was to come home in tears and try to explain what happened to you before she could figure out just how bad it really is."

He mirrors my stance, hands on hips, and I watch as his face softens. I feel a lot of my own energy drain out of me because this was a lot of emotion for one afternoon, and for the first time in a long while it wasn't because of Gram.

"I understand," he says, finally. "And I'm sorry for saying you aren't her mother."

"Why would you be sorry about that? I'm not," I say, confused.

"I know you aren't," he says, staring at his boot as he crushes a leaf beneath the toe, "but I wish you were."

I meet him where he stands, the toes of my Converse All Stars nudged against his Wolverine work boots, and place my hand over his heart. The honesty tumbles out of me before I stop to think about the words.

"I've never dated a guy with kids, but I'm telling you right now I know if I'm dating you, I'm essentially dating you both. If I'm going to fall in love with you, you bet your ass she's part of that. You understand me?" He nods, laying his hand over mine and gently squeezing my fingers. "Please don't get upset if I step in and give my two cents where a woman's wisdom might fare better than yours. You have an amazing kid in there, Maverick. Isn't it better that she come to me, your not-even-official girlfriend, than to no one?"

Lifting my fingers to his lips, he proceeds to kiss each tip before pulling me to him. It's like I'm in the middle of a dream and it's messy and perfect all at once.

"You want to be my girlfriend?" he asks. "And you're falling in love with me?"

Lightening the mood is exactly what I needed from him. We both needed it.

"That would be very nice. Maybe let's have the second date before we take each other off the market," I say, laughing. "Also, I said 'if I'm going to fall in love with you' not that I already was. Way to put the cart before the horse."

His mouth is a breath away from mine as he says, "What if I said I'm right there with you?"

My eyes crinkle as I smile. I hope we know what we're getting ourselves into.

"Just shut up and kiss me already."

Chapter 18

Maverick

I've never been this spun up over a woman in my life, but I'm not taking that as a bad omen. Maggie is a force and somehow in the last week she's gone from being a stranger to the person I want to wake up beside for the rest of my life. I haven't shared a bed with her yet, but I'd let her choose her side in a heartbeat.

It's weird right?

I'm not sure what it is that has me going to sleep with a smile every night since I met her. If it's because she's down to earth but absolutely going to argue until I see her point, smart but also a complete goofball, kind but respectfully puts me in my place, or because she has my kid's approval, or all of them rolled together.

She makes me a nervous wreck, and it's because I've met my match.

I come into the house for a shower after taking care of a few things in the office, mostly seeing how much we have for supplies for wrapping Christmas trees and what needs to be ordered, and make sure to be quiet since Sawyer is still sleeping. We've only got a couple of weeks before people start planning their trip to the tree farm and she's going to need to be getting up early on Saturdays. I expect it's going to be just as busy this year as it has been in the past, maybe even busier with the addition of a few new attractions. The greenhouses are going up the rest of the way between now and then, and we'll be selling wreaths and have the hot cocoa station set up in one of them. Will usually helps me up front, but he's picked a couple weekends to pull out his suit and play the part of Santa Claus, which is also new this year.

Our operation really isn't big, but if Sawyer has it her way, that's going to change between now and when she graduates high school.

Sitting on the bench by the back door in the mud room, I untie my boots and set them on the mat so they can dry out. I pick up my clipboard with the list of plants I've been working on — an assortment of flowers that we can start with in the greenhouses after we get through winter — and stop in the kitchen to refill my travel mug with coffee.

The steaks have been thawing in the fridge since last night and Sawyer said she was going to wait until this morning to make the apple crisp. We're going to put together a pan of homemade mac and cheese, and a salad, later in the day. I triple check that I have everything for dinner before finally making my way upstairs to my bedroom.

The conversation Maggie and I had yesterday is on replay in my mind as I let the hot water wash over me. I stand in the steam and let it beat on my back as I come even more to terms with the fact she's right. Sawyer really did need someone who wasn't me. I'm proud of her for knowing she could go to Maggie and told her as much when we sat down to talk about what happened at school. But I wish she'd told me she was even talking to this boy in the first place, even if he was just a friend.

Her explanation was that at the time he started paying attention to her she was still living with Hannah and, even though we were seeing each other most days of the week at that time, she didn't want to burden me with a "potential relationship." Not unless it became a real more than just friends situation, she said. I referred to him as a "boyfriend" and she cringed and looked grossed out by the thought. I'm not sure if it's just that boy in particular or more than that, but we'll cross that bridge when we come to it.

After this whole debacle, though, we've come to an agreement that we aren't keeping things like this to ourselves.

Consequently, I've agreed to also not keep things from her about any serious developments with me and Maggie. She put me on the spot about it, too, by telling me she saw our interaction in the yard when she was inside Gram's doing homework. While she might not have come right out and said she saw us kiss, I'm not stupid enough to think she didn't. But, I'm also smart enough to know she was talking about the royal reaming out Maggie gave me.

I smile at the thought of this woman giving me hell for all the world to see.

I get out of the shower, dry off, and find fresh clothes for the day. We're just going to be staying here for the day and having dinner, but I don't want to look like a complete bum. Skipping the comfort of sweats and a hoodie, I opt for worn in jeans and a long sleeve Henley. Swiping a bit of cologne on my neck, I take a look in the mirror before stepping out of the room and make a mental note to schedule a haircut.

125

"Hey, Daddy," Sawyer says from her position on the couch as I come down the stairs. "I like it."

"Like what?" I ask, stopping on the second to last step.

She motions to all of me.

"The look."

"Because I look so different every other day of the week?"

"Yes and no," she says, pausing the movie she's watching. "During the week, you're in jeans and usually a T-shirt, a flannel, looking a little grungy. Today, though, you look like you're ready to impress."

I nod, fully understanding what she's getting at.

"Do you think she's going to like this version of me? I mean, I looked a lot like this when we went to dinner the other night, but I want your opinion. Is it too much for dinner at home?"

"Not at all. She's going to love it," Sawyer says, a look of genuine care on her face. Lowering her voice, she asks, "She's really great, isn't she?"

Leaving my spot on the stairs, I walk over and plop into the recliner perpendicular to the couch and stare at my daughter. We wait to see who breaks eye contact first.

I win.

"She is, Sawyer. I like her. She's not like anyone else I've dated — before or after your mother — and it's refreshing."

I know I don't need to tell her things used to be great in the beginning with Hannah, she knows. But she also knows there were a lot of issues in the relationship we had.

"That doesn't mean it's going to be perfect," I add. "It doesn't mean our relationship is going to take less effort than others, either."

Sawyer bites her lip and pulls her knees up so she's curled on the couch. Grabbing the blanket from the back of the sofa, she covers up and I can tell she's doing all of these little things because she's thinking. About what, I don't know. I hope she shares with me.

"Perfect is kind of boring," she says, finally, after she's done fidgeting. "I don't want a perfect stepmom. I want one who's going to love me and be willing to drop everything if I need her, and willing to tell me I need to wait if she has something else that's more important in that moment."

Leaning forward and balancing my elbows on my knees, I'm not sure what kind of comeback she's expecting.

126

"It's a little early to be talking about stepmoms. I can tell you I'm fairly certain Maggie isn't perfect," I say. Her face falls just slightly until I complete my thought. "But I do think she's perfect for us."

*****

They showed up with food in hand, a small bouquet of flowers for Sawyer, and a box of cookies just because.

Gram walked in and pinched my cheek, then told me I was the most handsome man she's seen in a long time. It was the confidence boost I didn't realize I needed, but absolutely needed in that moment as my nerves had kind of taken over, right down to having a case of sweaty palms.

"I still have to put the macaroni in the oven," I say once Maggie's in the house and has her jacket off. "I lost track of time and haven't gotten as much done as I was hoping to."

Kissing my cheek first, then nuzzling my neck and taking a deep breath, I feel everything she's offering. It's sensual and forgiving. I place my hands on her upper arms and slowly trace my fingers down until my fingers intertwine with hers.

"I'm not worried. This gives me an excuse to spend more time with you," she says. "Show me your kitchen?"

She might as well be asking me to show her the bedroom the way she says it. There's a pleading in her voice that I haven't heard in all the teasing we've done, and I'm willing to take care of all her needs. Just not right now.

I have to remind myself Sawyer and Gram are in the other room. Sawyer stole her away as soon as she made it through the door and my best guess is she took her to the book nook in her bedroom. That's where all her gardening texts live — even I have to ask to borrow them because she has everything catalogued like a library.

Fingers still twined together, I pull Maggie toward the kitchen.

"It's not much, but when we built it, I made sure to design based on current need with the ability to expand if we wanted to down the road," I say, noticing a slight hesitation in her step. I'm not sure what it's about, but just in case, I add, "It was just me, and Sawyer was only here a few nights a week, so the design was really just so there would be enough room for the two of us. We've always said if we add more people to our family, we'll add more rooms. For the time being, it's cozy."

127

I feel her hand relax and there's an understanding passing between us. She was worried Hannah shared this space with me; I would never share this sanctuary with her. The only time Hannah has ever been in my house is if she's invited herself in when picking Sawyer up, and that's rare.

"I like what I've seen so far," Maggie says. "Can I help cook?"

I love that she asks if she can help, as if I would tell her no.

"Can you cook? I know you can bake, but isn't cooking different?" I say, dipping in for a kiss so she knows I'm playing with her.

"Oh, buddy, you forget whose granddaughter I am."

She starts rolling up the sleeves of her flannel shirt, then washes her hands, and promptly waits for instructions.

"Your Gram is a whole mood. I would never ever forget who helped bring you up," I say, smiling and handing her a plate of steaks.

Everything works like a well-oiled machine in the kitchen. It doesn't matter that I'm not used to sharing my cooking space with anyone other than a teenager who sometimes forgets to put her dirty dishes in the sink instead of on the counter. Cooking side-by-side with Maggie is otherworldly. She fits perfectly in every space she occupies.

Including the ones in my heart not taken up by my kid.

"I'm going to go check on Sawyer and Gram. Would you mind grabbing out the rest of the stuff for a salad?" I ask, kissing her temple as I pass through the kitchen behind her.

She doesn't say anything, but as I round the corner to the hallway leading to Sawyer's bedroom, Maggie's already making her way around the room grabbing vegetables.

I rap my knuckle on Sawyer's bedroom door. It's slightly ajar and I push my way in quietly, there's a lamp turned on, and the strands of Christmas lights she hung up almost a year ago light up the room. Snuggled up on the bed is my 15-year-old and my girlfriend's 84-year-old grandmother, looking through gardening magazines.

"When I was about your age, I used to pick wildflowers and sell them on the side of the road. That's how I met Margaret's grandpa. He stopped to buy a bunch of my flowers. Told me he was planning to ask a girl out to watch the sunset at the lake and wanted something to give her," Gram says.

Sawyer covers her mouth as if she's shocked, but I feel like we both see where this story is going.

"Did you sell them to him?" she asks.

Gram's eyes fill with longing as she sees me standing in the doorway listening to their conversation.

"I did. I wasn't going to turn down the chance to have money to help with the house. Things were tight, it was the 1950s and there were a lot of mouths to feed," she says. "So, when he drove off with the flowers, I didn't think anything of it and was just happy to have sold some pretty flowers."

Hanging on her every word, Sawyer asks what happened after that. If that's how they met, how did they finally end up together? I'd like to admit I tell my kid to stop being nosy, but I want to know the answer, too.

A smile creases Gram's cheeks and her eyes crinkle at the edges.

"He started stopping by my little table of flowers regularly. At first it was a couple days after that first time and I asked him if the flowers won this girl over. He told me, no they hadn't, but he wasn't giving up," she says. Sawyer wrinkles her nose. "It was different back then and men tended to think if someone wasn't interested, well then, they just needed to try harder. But, I'm with you Sawyer. I told him if she doesn't want his affections, perhaps he should move on. He said that he just might do that."

I snicker, but cover my mouth because I don't want her to stop sharing.

"Then he was stopping a few times a week. Each time buying a bundle of flowers, but never mentioned another woman," she says, her eyes getting a little misty. "It turns out he was buying the flowers for his mother who had been ill. When he finally told me who he was giving flowers to, I gave him an extra bunch to give her from me. His heart was so big."

Sawyer wraps her hand around Gram's and squeezes.

"He must have loved his mom very much to bring her so many flowers," she says. "Were you able to meet her?"

"Oh, yes. Our time together was brief, but she made sure to let me know how much she appreciated my love for her son. She passed the following summer when I was sixteen, and Jim and I married the summer after that when I was seventeen."

"I can't even imagine being married that young," Sawyer says.

Gram laughs and says she can't either, but she didn't regret it for a moment.

"Sometimes, when the right person comes along, you just don't want to wait to get your life started with them. I wouldn't recommend marrying so young these days. Everyone has too many distractions and they don't take the time to really get to know people well. Not in the beginning anyway," Gram says. "But when I was a teenager? There wasn't much to do but talk to one another. It took me less than a month to know I was in love with Jim. I knew his entire history by Thanksgiving that year, and after that we were ready to start making our own memories together."

I feel like she's talking to me. Maggie slides beside me in the doorway and leans her head on my shoulder.

"I like making memories," she says. Looking up at me, her eyes say a lot more than her mouth does. Whispering she asks, "Was Gram talking about Grandpa?"

I nod.

"Love of her life, that one."

"Yes, he was, Margaret," Gram says. "What are you two doing lurking in the shadows?"

"Dinner will be ready shortly. The macaroni is almost done and the grill is ready for the steaks, so if the two of you are done having your gossip session about dating and would like to join us, we would like that very much," Maggie says, playfully.

"Gossip? Margaret, I do not gossip," Gram says as she and Sawyer slide off the bed and make their way to the door. "I discuss. There's a difference."

Maggie and I step out of the way to let Gram and Sawyer through to the hallway. Then we bring up the rear, following them to the kitchen, her hand fitting perfectly into mine.

Leaning down so only Maggie can hear me, I whisper, "I wish I had been able to meet your grandpa. He sounds like the kind of man I could learn a lot from."

She looks up at me and smiles.

"I don't know about that. You seem to be doing well on your own."

*****

It turns out, as on top of the plans for tonight as I thought I was ... I really wasn't. The apple crisp wasn't made until the steaks were going on the grill. It's just coming out of the oven as Maggie and I finish washing and drying dinner dishes, so we still have plenty of time to sit and visit before dessert.

Sawyer pulls out her plans for the butterfly and pollinator garden and we talk to Gram about having two instead of one large flower bed in the back. The idea is a win for her, but she's also concerned with the vegetable garden we discussed.

"Will and I were thinking about putting it here," I say, pointing to a spot on the aerial photo I printed of her property. "This way it's not too far from the house and it's easy for you to access."

With her approval, we set a plan to begin work on the pollinator gardens starting Monday. Hopefully we aren't too late getting spring bulbs in the ground. I figure if we are, we'll adjust and fix it for her in the spring when we work on the vegetable garden.

"I think if we get this done and the weather is still fairly mild, we might be able to till for the garden. It would just be so the area is clearly marked. Then in April or early May, I'll be back to till it really smooth and Sawyer can come help you plant the vegetables you'd like," I say.

Motioning to Sawyer, as if to say, "That's okay, right?" she immediately jumps at the chance to work in the dirt with Gram. I didn't ever think I would see the day my kid became best friends with a senior citizen, but this is good. I think they could benefit from having each other.

Maggie and I can benefit from them having each other, too. Maybe between her mom helping and Sawyer spending some extra time with Gram, it'll give us a chance to have another date, just the two of us.

While my three favorite ladies get deeper into a discussion about squash and beans, I get out bowls, spoons, and the tub of homemade vanilla ice cream Maggie brought with them. Scooping the last bowl, I use my spoon for a taste test and am instantly curious why we never made ice cream when I was a kid.

"This can't be that difficult to make," I say out loud as I turn to put the ice cream back in the freezer.

"It really isn't," Maggie says from behind me. "I could teach you."

I slowly spin to face her, my spoon still hanging from my mouth, and smile.

"You could teach me?" I question after sliding the spoon from between my lips.

Raising one eyebrow and stepping in close to her, I hear her breath hitch when the energy shifts.

"I feel like you could teach me a lot of things, too," she says, quietly.

"When are we going to have time alone?" I ask, knowing damn well I'm being a little too forward. I brush my fingers along her cheek and push the hair out of her eyes. "I haven't known you long, Maggie, but I want to know you better. It's been a really long time since I felt this strongly about anyone. I'm just afraid I'll scare you away."

She closes her eyes and presses her cheek into my palm. She reaches for my waist and hooks her fingers through the beltloops, pulling me closer to her.

"I'm not going anywhere, Maverick. I've let myself feel too many things for you too quickly to walk away before I see where this leads," she says.

I want to say it. I almost slip and let the words come out of my mouth. It's too soon, though. There's still more to learn about one another before saying it.

"What are you thinking about?"

She's opened her eyes and is watching me as my mind spins.

"I'm thinking I wish you could stay tonight," I say, pressing my lips to hers.

Chapter 19

Maggie

I didn't stay the night. It's been almost another month of seeing him almost daily even though the work at Gram's is done for the time being, and we still have yet to have a sleepover.

A lot of that is because I don't want to leave Gram for an entire night. The rest of it is because we're trying to keep things somewhat kosher since Sawyer lives with Maverick full-time, her mother is proving to be nearly totally useless, and she's so busy with school and helping with the business that she doesn't even want to hang with friends on the weekend. At least, not overnights.

That's not to say we haven't found the time to get to know one another, it just hasn't been like that. Yet.

And now we're heading into a really busy season for Maverick and Sawyer at the tree farm, so there's even less time to spend with him. Plus, Delilah and I are slammed with orders for the upcoming holidays and gift giving, on top of the handful of end-of-year winter weddings we're booked for.

Thanksgiving week is here and I've had Mom stopping at the house daily before I get home so she can visit with Gram. She's been doing better with Sawyer around, but there are still slipups here and there with the occasional wrong name or believing she's in a completely different year.

"Is that sweet girl coming for dinner tomorrow?" Gram asks from the doorway to my bedroom.

I finish putting my eyeliner on before responding. It's Wednesday.

"I wish they were going to come over, Gram, but Maverick said they're going to see his family down in Interlaken. Sawyer's grandparents came and picked her up today so she has a little extra time with them before tree season begins," I say, and don't bother hiding that I'm sad we're not going to spend this first holiday together. I'm not going to let the sadness overwhelm me, though, because I know he sees his family so infrequently. It's important for Sawyer to visit her grandparents and aunt and uncle, as well, and for the rest of the year both businesses are going to be eating into the lives of the family members working. "I'm planning to go over and cook on Saturday so there's food for him and Sawyer throughout the day while they're working. Would you like to come with me?"

"That's not even a question you have to ask. I'd be coming even if you didn't invite me." She smiles and then adds, "Maybe we can find a small tree for us while we're there."

"I love that idea, Gram."

I go back to finishing my makeup and getting ready for the day at the bakery as she wanders down the hall to the kitchen. I hear her fumbling with the coffee pot, but don't think much of it until I walk into the room.

"Are you okay?"

Gram's mug is tipped over and there's coffee dripping from the counter, down the cupboards, and onto the floor. She's tossed a hand towel down to begin soaking up the mess on the linoleum, and has another on the counter and is trying to sop up the liquid around her mug.

"Just a little spill. Not the first time, won't be the last, Rebecca. Is your homework done?"

"Gram, I didn't have any homework," I say, without correcting her. It's easier to divert and reinforce than try to reason with her. This could just be a blip and she'll come back from where she is momentarily. Or I'll be late to work and she'll be coming with me today. "Can I help by wringing out the towels for you and getting them in the wash?"

She sees me, a slightly confused look on her face, and hands me the towels.

"You're so funny, Margaret. Why would you have homework? Unless Delilah is sending home ideas for you to work on," she says, chuckling. "Wouldn't that be something? Not that you don't already spend your time off coming up with new ideas for the bakery as it is."

Kissing her on the temple as I pass her, I step over to the sink and begin rinsing the towels.

"I do love my job, that's for sure," I say, giggling.

Just a blip.

But I'm worried.

So, I ask her to come with me to work. Maybe she can help. Maybe I can ask Will to bring her a coffee and come visit. Maybe, just for today, I won't have to worry about her all day.

And even though she's with me, I still worry about her. In between the timer going off in the kitchen and boxing up orders and greeting people as they come in, I'm texting my mom asking her if I'm doing the right thing. I'm searching for information on living with a person with dementia and dementia related illnesses. My YouTube algorithm is showing me nothing but videos about how to work with seniors dealing with cognitive issues.

Before I know it, it's after lunch. Will stopped in with coffee and some sandwiches for Gram, me, and Lilah on his way out to Maverick's just before noon. Today is when they begin cutting trees for the people who don't want to go out and cut one themselves.

Fisher and the kids came in to get orders to deliver around town and have popped back in to grab more twice, each time with Genevieve and Jaxon sitting to visit with Gram for a few minutes before they were shuffled back out the door with more boxes.

The day is busy enough I shouldn't be able to focus on my concerns, but that just isn't the way this works.

"What kind of pie are we making for Thanksgiving, Margaret?"

She breaks me out of the anxiety I've created for myself just like that. For a moment.

"Your favorite is apple, but what about Maverick and Sawyer. Do you know what they like?"

Gram's got her head bent over a piece of paper, no doubt making a list, and I love that even with so many other things happening to her, she's concerned about us.

"Well, I know for a fact Sawyer loves cheesecake, but I think pumpkin and pecan are also safe bets," I say. Leaving my station behind the counter, I walk to where Gram is sitting and peek over her shoulder at her list. Kissing her on the head, I add, "But Maverick and Sawyer won't be at dinner tomorrow. They're going to see his parents."

Reaching up to pat my hand, Gram points with the tip of her pen at the top of the paper. She's written "For Saturday" there.

"I know, but that doesn't mean we can't still enjoy a feast with them over the weekend. We are going to be there all day, and I want to be sure their opening weekend for trees is a delicious one."

"That sounds like a great idea, Gram. Let me know if we need to run to the store on Friday to get anything," I say, gently squeezing her shoulder.

We share a smile and it's a moment of bliss where I see my grandmother the way I saw her when I was a kid — strong, healthy, loving, and kind.

*****

"Have you ever had a fresh cut Christmas tree?"

"Um, no. I grew up with the Christmas tree coming out of a box in the attic every November. I know it's not as cool as chopping down our own tree in a field, but it worked for us," I say, lifting my beer to my lips.

"We need to remedy that. Immediately."

"I've been drinking and so have you. I don't think now is the best time to go into the woods with an axe."

How is it we aren't spending tomorrow together? I stretch my legs out and put my feet in his lap. As if on cue, he places his free hand on my ankle and mindlessly begins massaging.

"We don't have to do it tonight. That would be crazy. I know my trees, but even I can't pick out a good one in the dark." He takes a sip of his beer and when he swallows, I watch his Adam's apple bob and the dimple in his cheek play peek-a-boo. "But you'll be here this weekend, so I was thinking you could help Sawyer pick one out for the house and then she could help you find one for at Gram's."

I love his dedication to his daughter. I love even more that he's willing to include us in each other's lives. In return, I've made sure to include him and Sawyer in anything and everything I can with my family. We never had a real "we're now a couple" moment; we just fell into life together as if it were the most natural thing in the world.

"How is Gram doing?" he asks, though he sees her several times a week and knows how she is. My face must tell him what I'm thinking. "I know how she's doing most days, but how is she really doing? How are you doing?"

Mom asked Gram if she could stay at the house tonight so she's already at Gram's in the morning to get started on cooking. It was all a ploy, because as soon as she walked in the house tonight, she started asking me what my plans were for the evening. When I told her I didn't have any, she handed me my jacket. It didn't matter to her that I was in sweatpants and a tank top and it's freezing out. Then she told me to go to Maverick's and spend some time with him. She knows I'm getting burned out and needed a little break, so I tell him as much.

"I know Mom is there to help me when she isn't working and Gram's friends are always willing to come spend time with her, but I feel like if I ask for too many favors now, no one will be willing to help when I really need it," I say, but I say it quietly.

"You know that's not true, Maggie. None of us who love you and Gram are going to let you handle this on your own. I know moving in with Gram was a little bit of a way for you to have independence and a lot about being there to support Gram," he says. He doesn't know my heart stuttered at the word he used. "This isn't something you need to do alone."

It feels like it is, though. My mom still has a few years before she can retire. I can't ask her to take on more when I can easily take care of Gram and work and try to have a relationship. But I should. I should be able to talk to her about this and ask her to cut her hours at work. I will.

"I need you to know something," I say, shifting in my spot on his couch. "I don't know how to do any of this. Take care of an elderly woman, be a responsible adult, have a grown-up relationship. It feels like it will all implode and come falling down."

He stares at me. He's looking at me, not through me, and I don't know what to think or what he could be thinking. I'm hoping I don't screw this up.

"I don't want my life to ever go back to the way it was before you came crashing into it with your trees and landscaping and big heart and amazing kid." I get up from the couch and start pacing in front of him. "Eventually, I'm going to mess this up, aren't I? Or someone is going to mess it up for me."

His smile tells me I'm crazy, but he doesn't say it. He doesn't even move. Just sits on the couch and watches me as I try to catch my breath, my hands on my hips and my chest heaving.

"Margaret."

He says my name as if it's the most important word in his entire vocabulary. If I were against him I would have felt the rumble in his chest beneath my palms.

He motions me closer to him, crooking his index finger asking me to come near.

And when I do, he sets his beer on the coffee table beside him, then reaches for my hips. Pulling me into his orbit, closer and closer until I'm left with no other option than to straddle his legs and climb onto his lap.

"Nobody calls me Margaret," I whisper, bringing my mouth near his ear.

"Nobody?"

"Okay, one somebody, but other than her it's only been used for when I'm in trouble," I say, keeping my voice even.

"Well, then, it seems to have gotten your attention, just like it was supposed to," he whispers back, pulling my earlobe with his teeth. "I wouldn't say you're in trouble, though."

Letting out a sigh, I slide my hands up his chest until they rest at the base of his neck. My fingers find the longer hairs he hasn't had time to go get trimmed and softly tug. When he drops his head back, a small moan releasing from his lips, I shift my hips.

I know exactly what I'm doing. I haven't done it in a few years, but I haven't forgotten how to make someone feel good. Making Maverick feel good is all I want to do tonight.

"Maybe you are in trouble," he says, resting his head on the back of the couch, his hooded eyes looking directly into the center of my being.

Leaning against his chest, I drop my arms behind his head so I'm level with his stubbly chin. The roughness tickles my lips as I kiss my way across his jaw. Flicking my tongue against the soft skin beneath his ear, he lifts his hips ever so slightly in response. I can feel him through the material of his jeans. It's just enough to touch all the best spots and cause the heat in my abdomen to begin unfurling.

Slipping my hands back down his body, I find the hem of his thermal shirt as his mouth connects to mine. His tongue searches for mine and I press my fingers into the warm skin beneath his shirt, walking them up his chest, feeling each muscle as I push the fabric higher on his body.

Maverick takes control of the moment. Reaching behind him, he grasps the collar of his shirt and tugs it above his head. In a single movement, it lands on the couch beside us and I'm graced with the beauty of his naked chest and defined body beneath me.

"I like that," I say, touching a spot on his chest.

I trace the tree of life tattoo with my index finger, getting lost for a moment in the detail when I notice the date and initials holding up the roots.

"She kept me grounded when things were difficult," he says, his voice hoarse. "Sawyer was only a week old when I got it."

"It's perfect," I say, placing a kiss on the ink, then looking in his eyes. "So are you."

The energy shifts and I no longer feel like we need to go and get this done. Suddenly, it's not like the first time needs to just hurry up and happen already. I want it to last all night. I want it to last forever. His fingers find the small of my back, tracing my spine, slowly up and slowly down until his other hand joins in and together they drag my tank up my belly, caressing the sides of my fabric-clad breasts, and finally over my head.

Wrapping his arms around me, Maverick leans forward causing me to reach out and hold onto him as he stands from the couch. Hitching my legs on his hips, I smile down at him and kiss his mouth gently.

"Take me to bed, Maverick," I say.

"Yes, ma'am," he responds, taking steps toward the stairs that lead to his bedroom.

We make it to the landing on the second floor before he slides me down his body. Placing my feet on the floor, I attempt to get my bearings before he leans in and kisses me. He presses his body against mine and gently pushes me backward down the hall, but his skin never loses contact with mine.

I come to a full stop when my back reaches the bedroom door.

"When I open this door, I want you to know you're the first woman to be in this bed with me," he says, and I feel the floor drop out from beneath me. "And if I have it my way, you'll be the last."

Turning the knob, the door opens against our weight. I don't take the time to look around the dimly lit space. I let him lead and when the backs of my knees touch the mattress, I shimmy out of my sweatpants and kick them off to the side. Looking in his eyes, I reach out and find the button on his jeans. Popping it through the hole, my fingers clasp the zipper pull and slowly push it down over the straining fabric. His breathing quickens so I take my time. His head drops forward, his forehead touching mine, and I watch as he closes his eyes against the sensation.

His fingers dig into my hips as I slip mine into his waistband until his jeans give way and drop to the floor.

This is the furthest we've gone. Up to this point we've had amazing make out sessions and spent time getting to know one another. But now, here we are standing in our underwear in his bedroom and I can't remember what I'm supposed to do next.

Maverick's touch brings me back to him. His hand against my cheek as the other one glides across my skin to find the clasp of my bra is all I need to be present again. I gasp the moment his mouth touches the bare skin of my nipple, my eyes flutter closed and he lowers me to the bed. Each press of his tongue causes my back to arch. A nip of his teeth releases a moan from deep within me.

My hands are in his hair, but my legs search for him, pulling his body between them so I can feel him everywhere. My hips lift as I try to get him closer and he responds by pushing himself against me.

"I need you," I say, unsure if it was out loud or just wishful thinking.

He kisses along my breastbone as his hands find my underwear. Standing at the edge of the bed, he slowly pulls them down my legs and off my feet. Hooking his thumbs in the band of his boxers, he looks at me, quirking an eyebrow.

"Please," I say, pleading just enough to make him move faster.

But still he teases. It's the longest undressing of my life, but when his body is bare and he's climbing back between my legs I can't wait to savor every fucking moment of him.

Trailing his tongue from my belly button up between my breasts, I shiver at the sensation and shift my bottom trying to bring him closer to me. He grips my wrists in each of his hands and cautiously pushes them above my head, holding them against the comforter.

"Is this okay?" he asks, hovering above me.

I barely squeak out a yes when his lips crash against mine. Offering me a lesson in giving and taking from one another, he places his chest to mine and drags his hips higher until I feel him. Losing the ability to think straight, I wrap my legs around his thighs in an attempt to have any part of him brush against my clit.

"Condom," he says.

"Uh huh," I respond, but lift my head to steal another kiss from him.

The head of his cock presses into my swollen skin as he breaks away and I can't control the moan escaping my throat. The smirk tells me everything I need to know — that little maneuver was far from accidental.

He leaves me breathless and reaches into the top drawer of the bedside table. My eyes follow the line of his body, from his broad shoulders down to his muscular thighs and everything in between. Unwrapping the condom, he turns back just in time to catch me checking out all he has to offer.

"You like what you see?" he asks, but I just nod unable to tear my eyes away from his hands as he expertly rolls the latex down the length of his shaft. When I look up, the smirk has reappeared and, goodness, if I don't love the way it lights up his entire soul. Quietly, he asks, "Still okay?"

"I couldn't be better if I tried. But I am getting a little cold."

"I think I can help with that," he says, climbing back between my legs. One hand rests on either side of my head as he kneels on the bed over me. "You're beautiful, Maggie. I'm so lucky to have you in my life."

When his lips meet mine and parts them, deepening the kiss and filling me with more emotions than I could have predicted, he gently presses his hips into me. Rocking slowly, I feel every inch as he enters me for the first time. My head falls away from him and my back arches when I try to pull him deeper.

There's a desperate need to touch him.

Grasping his back, my hands slide up toward his shoulders tracing the muscles built from years of physical labor. Slowly, I drag my fingertips down until I feel the curve of his ass and grip it gently, encouraging him to find a faster rhythm.

He lifts up onto his knees and suddenly I feel the buildup of an orgasm I haven't experienced before. Maverick is relentless as he pumps his body into mine, bringing us both to the precipice as we prepare to fall over into the blissful abyss.

The tidal wave of sensation overtakes me and my body pulses around his as he continues to draw the orgasm from me. Then his breathing changes and he's telling me he's going to come.

"Please," I breathe out.

His mouth is on mine as he deliberately pumps his hips and finds that sweet, built-up release.

We lay together, him still firmly seated inside me, as I trail my fingers up and down his spine and he catches his breath. My heart is racing from the action, but there's more happening in there than just a workout.

So. Much. More.

Chapter 20

Maverick

I never want to get out of this bed.

Maggie's hand is curled up on the center of my chest and everything feels right. I don't know if it's because I'm older now and know what I want or not, but never once did I feel this level of comfort when I was with Hannah. Should I be comparing how I feel now with Maggie versus how I felt with my ex-wife a decade ago? No, probably not … because there is no comparison.

Wrapping my fingers around her hand, I pull it to my lips and place a gentle kiss to her knuckles. When she climbed into the bed last night and snuggled up to me, I wasn't sure how long she was going to stay. Then she fell asleep, and I did, too. It's the first time I've shared a bed with anyone all night since Hannah and I split up.

It's the first time I've wanted to share this space with anyone since the day Sawyer and I moved into the house.

Laying on her stomach beside me, Maggie is facing the window where the sun has just begun brightening the horizon. Her breathing is steady and rhythmic; I'm certain she's not awake yet. I'm not worried that she isn't, except I know she's planning to be back home early to help her mom start the food for later today. I'll have to head to my parents' house at some point this morning, but I have plenty of time to get ready.

Filled with emotion, I kiss her fingers again. What happens now? How do we navigate this when Sawyer is home and she's got to be home at night with Gram? We haven't had conversations about the future. This is still new for both of us. Neither of us have been in a long-term relationship in nearly a decade, which is the biggest reason we have been moving slowly.

I just didn't expect to feel the way I do so soon. I have enjoyed every second of getting to know Maggie, but I didn't plan on my heart rate rising every time I saw her walking my way or each time her name lights up my phone.

"I just might be falling in love with you Margaret Regina Florence Southard," I say in the quiet of the room.

I make every effort to let her sleep a little longer and slip out from beneath the covers. Kissing her bare shoulder, I make sure the blankets are tucked in close to keep her warm, then grab my hoodie from the chair in the corner and sneak out of the room.

Coffee to get the day started, check the weather, scroll the newsfeed. That's how my day usually starts. Even with Maggie here, I'm going to stick to the routine, especially since I'm sure she will want coffee when she gets out of bed.

Looking out the back window over the farm, I witness the beauty of the day as the sun rises high enough behind me to make the trees look like they're on fire. Pouring a mug of coffee for myself and then a second one for her, my mind wanders to places that include exactly this scenario every single morning before I head down to the trailer and she goes to the bakery. I'm so lost in thought I don't hear her pad quietly down the stairs and to the kitchen. I don't hear her until she's close enough to wrap her arms around my waist and lean her head against my back.

"Your heart is beating really fast," she says, concerned.

"It does that a lot lately," I respond, lifting my mug to my lips to blow some of the heat from the liquid.

"Have you had it checked out?" she questions, slipping her hand beneath my sweatshirt to place it over my heart. I set my left hand on top of hers, separated only by the fabric, and feel myself fall a little bit more.

"I have not. It's only been happening recently. Usually set off by someone being nearby," I say, then take a sip of my coffee.

Coming around to face me, Maggie drops her hand to my waist but keeps it under my shirt and adds the other one before she speaks. A curious look crosses her face.

"I make your heart beat faster?" she asks, coyly.

"You do. All the time."

"That's probably the sweetest, most innocent thing anyone has ever said to me," she says. "You're sure it's not anxiety or a panic attack or anything like that?"

I let out a loud laugh and pull her closer to me with my free hand.

"I'm absolutely positive. You, of all people, don't make me anxious. If anything, you make the world feel more calm," I say, setting my coffee beside me on the counter.

She reaches up and, curling her fingers into her palm, touches my cheek with the backs of her fingers. There's a softness in her eyes. I can't keep my mouth from finding hers and slowly caress her lower lip with my tongue. My hands slide up to cup her face, my fingers tangling up in her messy bed hair. Maggie drops her arms and then a shiver runs through me as her hands trace lines up my back beneath my shirt, gentle at first before giving way to the urgency we both feel.

Sensing her bravery, I let her lead me to the kitchen table. Placing her hands on my shoulders and applying the subtlest pressure, she makes me sit in a chair that hadn't been put back in place last night.

"Where are your pants?" I question, not really caring as she comes to stand between my legs.

Her smile lifts just one side of her mouth. An eyebrow quirk tells me she had no intention of needing pants when she came downstairs this morning. Trailing my fingers up the outside of her bare legs, I let them explore. Pushing her shirt — which is actually one of my flannel shirts from a pile of clean laundry in the bedroom — up her abdomen, I kiss her belly. The soft flesh of her ass fitting perfectly in my hands, I pull her into me. Her thigh brushes the erection straining against the material of my sweats and I let out a low groan, which works to encourage her to begin unbuttoning her top.

Every button makes me harder.

The chill in the room causes her nipples to pebble and I grab her around the waist, pulling her into me until she needs to move her legs and straddle my lap just so I can get a taste. First flicking the tip of my tongue against the tender flesh, then gently biting, as my thumb and index finger carefully squeeze and knead the other. Maggie presses her hips against me harder as her breathing becomes unsteady.

Her hand on the back of my head encourages me to continue my assault on her breasts.

"Your pants," she says.

"My pants, what?"

"They're in the way."

"They are? What are they in the way of?"

I lift my face to look directly into her baby blue eyes and there is nothing but pure lust shining back at me. What comes out from between her lips should shock me, but it doesn't. It only makes me want her more.

145

"Your cock being in my pussy."

"Such a dirty mouth."

"You love my dirty mouth," she sasses back.

"Damn right I do," I say before kissing her again.

Lifting my hips with her still on my lap, I slide the fabric of my pants down over the crest of my ass. When she lifts up on her toes, they slip down the front of me, the elastic band releasing my erection. Maggie hesitates before reaching between us and stroking me, stopping briefly when she reaches the head of my penis to brush her thumb against the most sensitive areas.

"I don't have anything down here," I say through gritted teeth, hating that I could ruin what's about to happen.

With her free hand, Maggie plucks a foil packet from her shirt pocket.

"I might have considered that," she whispers, then presses the condom against my chest while she continues working me with her hand.

Making quick work of opening the package, I roll the rubber down my length as Maggie lifts and situates herself above me. Slowly lowering herself onto my cock, I let her set the pace and hold her hips to guide her as she rides me.

The pressure quickly begins to build and with each movement, she feels tighter around me. Grinding on my lap, looking for her release, I lift up to meet her and she gasps at the sensation. This might only be our second time together, but already I know she's close.

Placing her hand between us, I watch as Maggie's middle finger finds her clit and she begins massaging herself to completion.

"That is ... so hot," I say, breathlessly.

I don't even care that I sound like a guy seeing, for the first time, a woman get herself off. It's the first time I'm seeing Maggie do it, and knowing I'm balls deep inside her while she's massaging that little bundle of nerves is the thing that pushes me over the edge.

"I'm gonna come," I grit out.

She doesn't say anything, but her mouth falls open as I begin pulsing within her and her pussy clenches my cock. A throaty moan finds its way out of her as she moves her hand and rocks her hips against mine, teasing out every last drop of our orgasms.

Maggie leans against my chest as I wrap her up in my arms. I kiss the top of her head and rub small circles on her back.

I feel her sigh.
I feel her gather my hoodie in her hands.
I feel her still surrounding my body.
"I think I might be falling in love with you, too."

*****

My drive to Interlaken is uneventful, with one exception being I have thought about her the entire way here and nearly ran a stop sign in my hometown as a result.

We didn't talk about her admission. We didn't discuss that she was obviously awake when I said the same thing before getting out of bed this morning. Instead, she climbed off my lap with shaky legs and led me upstairs to my bathroom where we helped each other clean up before we were forced to leave the house and try to get on with our days separately.

And that's the part that's killing me.

I didn't want to leave her, despite both of us having plans and knowing we weren't spending the holiday together. It makes it that much more difficult to not be with her when I pull up the long driveway to my parents' house and Sawyer comes bounding out the door to see me, and her face falls when she realizes it's just me. It doesn't matter we both knew the plan all along.

"She's doing food and all that with her family, but when we get home tonight maybe we can swing by and take her and Gram some of the fudge Gigi said you guys made last night," I say before she even opens her mouth.

"Promise?"

"Cross my heart, Pumpkin." I snatch her up into a bear hug and kiss the top of her head. "And for the record, she and Gram are missing us, too. Maggie said Gram asked a couple times why we weren't coming to dinner."

That causes my little girl's smile to make an appearance.

"Gram is the best surrogate great-grandmother," Sawyer says, wrapping her arm around my waist and walking to the house with me. Before veering off toward the barn, she says, "She's got so many amazing ideas for gardens. I can't wait to work on her flower beds in the spring and have her experience to guide me."

I take notice that she's talking more and more like an adult these days instead of a teenager. I'm the last person to want my kid to grow up too fast, but it is also kind of nice to have more conversations like this with big words and meaning.

When I walk into my childhood home, I'm hit with a feeling of entering a time capsule that has been randomly updated throughout the years. My senior portrait, along with Bentley's and Harper's, line one wall in the living room. There are family pictures dating back to when I was five and the other two were babies. Dad still has our Little League trophies and Harper's gymnastics ribbons on a bookshelf.

But then there's electronic gadgets galore, they've hung a television on the wall, and swapped out the furniture recently, which are things I never thought I would see happen. The old adage "if it ain't broke, don't fix it" was like a family motto back in the day, so I'm just going to let myself believe the TV kicked it and the decades old couch broke.

"I see you looking at it. Don't ask," Harper says from the doorway. "Or do. It's up to you."

"Story?"

"Bentley's girlfriend broke up with him, so he decided to do some remodeling for Mom and Dad." She shrugs and takes a sip of her drink as if that's really all the explanation needed, which where Bentley is concerned it really is. "He did a really good job picking out the furniture by himself. I wouldn't have gone with the brick red upholstery myself, but it definitely fits the rest of the décor."

"Especially this time of year," Mom says coming up behind Harper. "I still don't understand why they broke up though."

"The rumor is she's poly and he can't get on board with that," Harper says, nonchalantly.

"Poly? What the hell is that?" Mom asks, which I'm grateful for because I didn't want to.

Rolling her eyes, Harper explains, "Polyamorous, Mom. It means she wants to be in a relationship with him and at least one other person, and that person would also be in a relationship with Bentley. It's not really my ideal situation, but if it works for her, awesome."

I can't help myself and snort out a laugh. Between her explanation and Mom's dumbfounded expression, this is gearing up to be a fantastic day together.

"So, uh, how do you know all these details, Harp?"

"Duh. I read his text messages."

With that, I check to make sure my phone is securely in my pocket. I've kept Maggie and Gram a little bit of a secret and I don't want my baby sister snooping in my phone reading some of our not-so-PG conversations.

"Fabulous," I say. "Well, on that note, I'm going to the barn to see Dad. Sawyer headed out there when I came in the house, so I'm just going to assume that's where the less insane family members are."

As I brush past my mom, I kiss her cheek and wish her a happy holiday then I also wish her good luck in dealing with my sister as I saunter out of the house.

Do I feel bad for Bentley? Absolutely. No one likes a break up, and it sounds like his situation was pretty unique. He'll talk to me about it when he's ready. In the meantime, I'll be sure to harass him about his furniture shopping. But, knowing Bentley, he'll remind me of all the reasons it's worth it to spend the money instead of save it. Honestly? It doesn't bother me. Mom and Dad were due for something new and since he's living back at home, why not let him pitch in and help decorate.

I pop open the door to the barn, which really is a lie as far as barns go. When Dad first started the business when I was a baby it was a simple lean-to. Over the years it has been enclosed, torn down, and rebuilt into an elaborate event space. It's not huge by any means, but there is plenty of room for families to sit and visit or wait for others in their group. Mom makes sure there's coffee and hot chocolate, they have treats … basically it's a lot of what Sawyer and I are trying to do with our expansion. The only difference is I don't have the capital — yet — to build a barn, so the greenhouses will do for this year. The wheels in my head start spinning and when I walk up to my daughter, I know I have to ask her now or risk losing the nerve to proceed.

"What do you think about asking Maggie and Delilah if they can set up the food truck at the house for the weekends we're doing trees?"

"Who's Maggie and Delilah?" Bentley asks, a perplexed look on his face, until he breaks into a smile and I know he's heard about them.

"Maggie is Dad's girlfriend, Delilah is her best friend, and," she says turning her attention from her uncle back to me, "I think that's a brilliant idea. Have you talked to Maggie about it?"

Shaking my head, I step toward the coffee maker and pour myself a cup. Before I can answer, Sawyer is distracted by her cell phone. She's in her own world suddenly and rather than respond I walk toward my father and shake his hand.

"How are the trees?" I ask.

"It was a good year. Hopefully people want real trees this season," he says.

Every year he worries the artificial tree companies are going to put him out of business, but there's just something about a real tree. It's the smell of pine, asking the earth to borrow a piece of her for a little while, utilizing the wood after the holiday if we can. I don't think he's ever going to go out of business unless Bentley and Harper show no interest in taking over when he and Mom are ready to retire.

"How's business?" he asks.

He wasn't too keen on us starting up a landscaping branch, but we needed to grow. Sawyer and I needed something that was our passion.

"It's been really good. We've stayed busy through the fall. Sawyer is working on a big project with Maggie's grandmother, so that's been exciting for her," I say. "Will helped us get the greenhouses up before that last cold snap, so we'll have better shelter now for people who come out for trees."

Bentley and Dad exchange a look I can't read and I don't really care to ask, so when my father tells me how proud he is of me and Sawyer for making this jump into something new I'm unsure how to react.

"Maggie talked to Delilah and they both said yes. Since she's planning to be at the house this weekend to feed us anyway, she sees no reason not to bring the truck," Sawyer says, looking at her phone.

"What?" I stare at Sawyer. "You already asked her?"

"Yes? It's a great idea. I didn't want to let you think about it too long because you would have talked yourself out of it. I asked. She said yes. Now we can also post it on social media and send it to the newspaper," she says.

"Who are you and what did you do with my teenager?"

She rolls her eyes and puts her hands on her hips.

"Ah, there you are," I tease. "I guess we'll have to make sure to do those things you said we can do. Know anyone who can help me with that?"

Bentley snickers, knowing full well my daughter just got herself an extra job since I don't love the Internet or social media. The only reason I have it is because of Sugar Shack Landscaping and even then, I rarely share information there. It's an afterthought.

150

"I'll take care of it, old man. I know technology scares you," she says, looking at her phone again and smiling. She glances in my direction and I raise my eyebrow. "Um, she's really excited about helping out and sent me a list of flavors to choose from."

"Can I choose a couple?"

"Me too!" Bentley joins in.

We gather around Sawyer, looking over her shoulder at a list of cupcake and cookie choices as if we're seeing pictures of a newborn baby. My brother chooses chocolate cake with cherry cream cheese frosting. My pick is a cinnamon swirl cupcake with vanilla buttercream and caramel drizzle. Dad opts for vanilla with chocolate buttercream and crushed Oreos. Sawyer, getting into the spirit of the holiday season, decides to go with chocolate cake and peppermint frosting with crushed mints on top.

"Sawyer, you coming with me to check the trees?" my dad says as he walks toward the door. My kid never wastes a chance to go out and check over the fields with her grandpa, and she skirts past him out the door as he turns back to me. "That was difficult. She really makes all those flavors on that list?"

"Every day. Not the same ones every day, but there's rarely a day she isn't creating something brand new to mix in with the normal chocolate and vanilla. She has an entire menu of bakery items. Her s'mores cookies are pretty fantastic."

"She sounds like a keeper, Rick."

He doesn't give me a chance to respond before he wanders out the door and climbs on one of the 4-wheelers we use out in the grove. He fires it up and pulls out, Sawyer right behind him on another ATV.

"He's not wrong," Bentley says from the chair he's slid out from the table closest to me. "Sawyer's been talking our ears off about her since she got to the house."

I feel my neck start burning, and I know he can see my reaction.

"The kid is already attached, so just ... be careful."

It's strange to hear my kid brother warning me about letting someone in, but he knows the history with Hannah better than anyone else in the family and how broken our relationship was. How broken it continues to be.

"I've tried to be, but," I pause, looking into my empty cup and swallowing hard, "but it's hard to not let her get so attached when I am, too."

He nods in agreement.

"I know. I could tell," he says. "I would give you some line of bullshit about getting to know her and really know how you feel before you take it too far, but I know you and you are the epitome of careful. You'd never let someone in if there was potential for Sawyer to get hurt in the mix."

After tossing my cup in the trash, I turn to face him and shove my hands in my jacket pockets. I don't want to admit to him that I'm so far gone about this woman that I've wanted to get back in the truck and head home since shortly after I arrived.

"Harper told me about your girlfriend," I say. It's not intentionally to get him off the subject of Maggie, Sawyer, and my relationships with them, but it's not not intentional either. I know he'll talk about something else if I bring it up, so I take the opportunity to change topics. "I like the new couch. It was a good choice."

"Harper has a big mouth," he says. "It sucks, though. I really liked her. The couch and new television were a good way to heal my broken heart, don't you think?"

I smile and nod because there's no way I'm going to disagree with him. It isn't often he finds someone he meshes well enough with to have a romantic relationship with them. For him to find that and then this to happen? He's in a fragile state right now.

"So, when do we get to meet the amazing Miss Maggie?"

"Maybe soon. We'll see what Christmas and the new year bring," I say, knowing I'm going to have to talk to Maggie about the remaining holidays for this year and try to figure out how we're going to work them. It's just Christmas and New Year's Eve, but I don't know what Hannah's plans are for spending time with Sawyer or if Maggie has standing plans with her family. Since the divorce, I haven't been in a serious relationship up to now, and definitely never thought about having one through the holiday season. "It's possible all the Christmas cheer will drive her away."

"A little bit of Christmas magic goes a long way," he says, quietly. "Hell, we've been living the winter wonderland life since the days we were born and we still believe in the magic. I can't imagine if she's the right woman for you she won't fall in love with all of this along with you and Sawyer."

*****

Sawyer comes crashing through the door into the kitchen filled with excitement.

"We found the one! Grandpa and I found the tree," she exclaims.

Every year since she could walk, Sawyer and my dad have picked out the tree for the Interlaken house. Most years it's been on Thanksgiving, and if not that day, then the day before or after if someone is able to get her to my parents' house. This year is no different and I knew they were going out hunting for the perfect evergreen when they took off on the ATVs earlier.

While they were playing in the trees, Bentley, Harper, and I took to the kitchen and helped Mom get the rest of the food on for dinner. We may have taken the liberty to start working on the cookies and brownies Mom likes to have on hand for the families that will arrive early tomorrow to choose their Christmas trees. With my own business doing so well now, I won't be able to come back down to help with that part of it, so I'm trying to pitch in where I can in case Harper or Bentley aren't able to bake with her next week or the week after.

"Did you already cut it?" Bentley questions.

"Nah, we came back to get the truck first. Grandpa marked it, though, so we don't lose it."

Coming in behind her, my dad says, "It would be difficult to lose it. I think she picked the biggest one out there just like she does every year."

He taps Sawyer playfully under her chin and she gives him a look of deep adoration.

"I learned from the best," she says, complimenting him.

It's still early enough in the day, we opt to sit and eat first. Bentley makes the executive decision that we'll leave the dishes and go out as a family after dinner to cut the tree and bring it back.

"Then we can have dessert," he says, eyeing Sawyer. "I heard there's cheesecake."

"Two flavors actually."

"Be still my heart, sweet Sawyer Mae. You are by far my favorite niece," Bentley says, clutching his chest.

She rolls her eyes, but laughs just the same.

"That's because I'm the only one," she says. Reaching for a stack of plates from my outstretched hands, Sawyer looks me straight in the eyes and says, "He's ridiculous."

"I taught him well, Pumpkin. He had to deal with me for years before you came along."

"Yeah, well, hopefully it doesn't take too long before this family gets someone new to pick on," she says. The words are just barely audible as she works her way around the table setting out the dinnerware, but when I catch her eye, she acts bashful. She knows I heard it, and I want to tell her we'll make Maggie part of the family someday, but it's still way too soon to be talking out loud like that. It's barely been two months since we met. I want to take my time this time. This also isn't a conversation I want to have at a holiday dinner with my siblings and parents.

I'm grateful when dinner — which is really just a late lunch so we can have the excuse to have dessert twice — is had without any incident. No one presses me for more information about Maggie. Bentley doesn't get upset about his girlfriend situation. Harper talks non-stop about her work as a social worker in a nearby long-term residential home.

"I love it there, but my training has always led me to work with the elderly. I mean, I had to start somewhere so working with pediatrics has been great," she says between mouthfuls of mashed potatoes. "It's only been a couple years, but my heart can't handle it anymore for the time being."

"I can understand how that would weigh on you. Are you looking for something else?" Mom asks.

Harper swallows and takes a sip of her water. She wipes her mouth on her napkin. Then she sheepishly looks my way.

"I'm actually in the process of interviewing at a nursing facility close to Ricky. It's not right in Brockport, so I absolutely will not cramp his style, but it's close enough that I won't feel like I'm completely alone," she says.

A nursing facility?

"Like a nursing home?" Sawyer questions.

My sister nods.

"Is it a good one? Do they actually care about the people living there?"

Harper tips her head to the side, and I see her brain trying to figure out what Sawyer is getting at. I'm way ahead of her.

"I'm just curious. The last time I even visited a nursing home was when I was in second grade in Girl Scouts and that was to sing Christmas carols. My scope of knowledge is pretty small," she says, searching for words to get the attention off herself.

Harper smiles, and it's one of understanding, which I think puts us all at ease and I take a deep breath. Again, we're skirting around a conversation I don't want to have with my parents right now.

"It's one of the best homes in the area and has a small nurse-to-patient ratio. I would be working directly with family members of the dementia residents on a ten-bed unit," she says.

Her excitement is felt through the room and I'm happy for my sister finding a job she feels she's going to love, though we all are aware it won't be without its hardships and low points. She begins talking about how she's going to need to explore the area for an apartment since she doesn't want to commute from Interlaken to Pittsford every day.

"Spencerport is right between Brockport and Pittsford," I say without stopping to think. "That way you're not too far from work, but you're not too close to me. Ew."

"Punk."

"Snot."

"That's enough, you two," Dad says, trying to stifle a laugh.

Harper shoves her hand in the air toward the middle of the table and I reach out to grab it, shaking it on a deal.

"Promise not to be overbearing?" she asks, raising an eyebrow.

"Promise to call or text before showing up at my house?" I respond.

"Deal."

"Good. Settled. Start searching for places with apartments available and let me know when you need me to go look at them with you," I say.

"Love you," she says quietly.

"Love you back."

*****

Sawyer has slowly drifted off to sleep on the drive back home. After spending yesterday and all of today with my parents, brother, and sister, she's exhausted. Regardless, I knew it was going to be difficult for her to get in the truck and not really know when she's going to get to go back down to the homestead, as we took to calling it when she was just a baby. It's usually difficult for me, too.

But I have a woman at home waiting for me.

Well, not at my home, but at a home and I'm planning to stop and see her because I miss her mouth. I miss her.

It's hardly been twelve hours since we left my house. It feels like it's been days.

When I pull into the driveway and park the truck behind her car, I don't miss the rustling of the curtain in the kitchen window. Even though she knew I was coming over on my way home, I didn't give her a solid timeframe. I was vaguely aware that it was going on ten at night, but still my need to see her won out over going home. Texting to let her know I didn't want to stop by and wake her or Gram if they were already in bed wasn't a viable option.

I park the truck and let it sit, idling. Not waking Sawyer, I reach into the seat behind me for the bag Mom sent with us that has extra cheesecake and some of the brownies we made for the weekend visitors. She doesn't even budge when I open my door and the interior lights come on, so I take that as I've made the right decision and will deal with the consequences later.

By the time I've silently closed the driver's door, Maggie is waiting for me at the door to the breezeway. Wrapped up in an old quilt, her hair in a messy bun, and an exhausted look on her face, but she greets me with a smile before kissing me. That kiss holds so many emotions and when I break away from her lips, I see there's a bit of sorrow.

"What happened?" I ask, reaching up to tuck a stray strand of hair behind her right ear. "You look like you've been crying."

When she wipes her cheek with the fabric of the blanket, I know I was correct.

"Gram had a rough day. It's nothing we can't handle. I promise," she says before changing the subject. "Where's Sawyer? Did she stay down at the lake with your parents?"

I give her a get out of jail free pass and let her know the kid is passed out in the car after a very full day with her aunt and uncle.

"We brought home some extra dessert. I would wake her, but I'm more afraid of that wrath than letting her sleep and be mad she missed seeing you tonight," I say, lifting the bag of food. "I'm not going to keep you. If Gram is resting comfortably now, I think you should try to get some sleep, too. We're going to have a busy weekend."

Maggie touches my face and pulls me closer to tenderly kiss my lips.

"You're the best thing that's happened to me in a long time, Maverick," she whispers into the sliver of space between us. "I'll see you bright and early tomorrow. Goodnight."

Pressing my forehead against hers, I whisper my "goodnight" in response and then turn to go home to an empty bed that still smells like the woman I'm madly in love with.

M.L. Pennock

Chapter 21

Maggie

Watching him back out of the driveway was hard. So hard. If it weren't for Sawyer already being asleep in the truck, I would have had him come in for a while and she could have just snuggled up on the couch or in my room to rest.

But instead, I stand in the cold darkness until his taillights are gone and the road is swathed in black again. Only then do I turn out the lights, lock the doors, and quietly go back to my bedroom to work on some new ideas for the bakery and food truck.

I should follow his directions, though, and get some sleep. Tomorrow, I need to be up extra early to go get the food truck so we can have treats for Maverick's customers. Thankfully it was something Delilah and I had talked about in passing with Sawyer, so we were already planning for extra cookies and cupcakes this week in case he asked. And if we hadn't gotten the request to come out to the farm, nothing would have gone to waste. Now that the holiday season has officially started, we know if shoppers in town don't buy up everything we have in stock, Murph will take a bunch for his guys and Will is always receptive to taking extras to the Veterans hospital.

Lilah messaged me earlier to say she and Genevieve will be at the shop early to help me load and then they'll be there for the day. Saturday, Gen might come out to the farm with me, but that's still up in the air. After I'm done at Sugar Shack I'll be going back to the bakery to whip up the cookies and cupcakes I'll need for the next day. This is going to be my life until Christmas.

Sitting on my bed, I feel my head bob forward as I catch myself falling asleep. It's time to call it a night. Placing my drawing pad and pencil on the desk, I check my phone to find a new message from Maverick. It was sent right around the time he left the house. I immediately hope he wasn't texting while he was driving. It's not safe.

I haven't always been like this. That thought never would have crossed my mind a few years ago.

I missed you like crazy today. Sleep well.

My second thought is how much I miss him, too.

I send a quick reply, at the off-chance he's awake and will see it. A tiny part of me wants him to already be sleeping since he has to get up as early as I do. A bigger part wishes he was still awake because I'd love to hear his voice right now. I'd love to tell him everything that happened today and how Gram might be joining me at the farm every day I'm out there.

We can talk about it tomorrow.

There's plenty of time.

But what if there isn't?

Nope, I'm not thinking like that. It was just a difficult day. She got a little more confused than normal. She wasn't angry, just ... upset. It took us all off guard since she's been having such good days. She didn't know who Mom was. She kept asking when Grandpa would be home for dinner. It was 1962 for her today. But the day was also busier than normal, and there where people here who she's not used to seeing on a regular basis. We didn't consider the obstacles we put in her place.

He hasn't texted back, and that's okay because the flood of tears blurs my vision. If he were to call, I wouldn't be able to speak through the sobs.

*****

I fell asleep crying, my phone clutched in my hand, and when I wake up there's a missed call from my mom and a voice message. I'm not even fully awake and coherent, but I listen anyway.

"Hey baby girl, we need to talk about Gram. I'm worried. I mean, we've both been worried, but I'm calling you at four in the morning and that's another level of worry. I know you and Gram are going out to Maverick's for the day, but call me when you have a chance. ... I love you."

I save the message. The tone of her voice hits deep inside me and I opt to call her before even getting out of bed.

She picks up on the second ring.

"Mags."

"Mom."

"I haven't slept."

"I cried myself to sleep."

"Are you okay?" she asks, her voice softening even more. "She hasn't been that bad before?"

Shaking my head, I respond. "No. Yesterday was the worst I've seen her, but it's been so few and far between lately. She was doing really well."

"Her doctor told us it could be like this. We aren't going to lose her all at once. She knows, too, and I think she's doing her best to not have us worry," she says. There's a lengthy pause and I'm unsure what to say, so I wait. I know there's more on her mind, more words she's trying to find a way to say to me. "Do you think it would be worth looking into having a health aide to come be with her when you're at work? Someone who can visit with her and keep her safe on the rough days? I can't be there all day every day, but that's going to change. We can't expect more from her friends, and I want them to be her friends not her caregivers."

"What do you mean it's going to change? Mom, you still have like two years of work," I say, wide awake now.

She's quiet, and I don't press for information.

"We can talk about that part later. I don't want to make any changes she isn't comfortable with. So, if we consider a health aide or someone like that, we'll sit and talk about it with her. Does that sound okay?"

"I think it's better than the alternatives, which are not talking to her about it at all and just hiring someone or putting her in a nursing home … which I think we both know is out of the question right now."

Glancing at the clock I notice the still early hour. It's dark out and I don't want to leave the warmth of my blankets, but I need to get up and moving.

"I'm sorry you've had to do this on your own," she says, regret lacing her statement.

"There's nothing to be sorry about, Mom. When I decided to move over here, we didn't know she was starting down this path. We didn't know. It had no bearing on my decision," I say. "I need you to understand that nothing would have changed my mind. Can we agree, though, that if she continues to decline, we keep her at home as long as possible? I honestly think that's the one thing she's going to want most. This is her home, the one she shared with Grandpa, the one she brought her kids home to, all of it."

Hearing her sniffle through the phoneline I know I hit a nerve. It needs to be talked about.

"Are you going to be okay? I know this is difficult. Not just for me and you, but it's going to be difficult to adjust to the changes as things progress," I say. I don't even comprehend how I'm coherent at this point. I didn't sleep well and there's no caffeine in my system yet.

"I'll be okay. Promise. I need to talk to your uncles about all of this, too. They are beside themselves after yesterday."

The three uncles. I always joked about them being the Three Wise Men when I first learned that story, but as I've gotten older they've become more like the Three Stooges. My mom is the youngest. Watching them all together makes me wish I wasn't an only child and I'm positive I want more than one child when that time comes.

I'm not sure how that conversation will go, though, since they're all extremely headstrong. That concerns me. Maybe the only saving grace is none of them live locally. Their opinion and recommendations can be taken under advisement, but they shouldn't be the final say if they're rarely here. The aunts might be a problem, but we'll deal with that when we get there.

"Do you want me to come be part of that conversation?" I ask, but it's more rhetorical than not. She knows I'm not going to do well with it if they start trying to make decisions that affect Gram without them taking into consideration that Mom and I are her primary helpers. And "helpers" at this point is being used loosely; Gram still runs the show.

"You and Gram are at the tree farm all weekend. Everyone else will only be here until Sunday morning," she says. The statement is more her trying to work through the logistics of when and where than to get my thoughts on the matter. "Can we try to do dinner tonight or tomorrow?"

"Yes. Talk to them and figure out what they want to do. Gram and I will be at Maverick's until four today doing the truck, and then we were going to eat with him and Sawyer. I'm afraid if we came to your house after it would be too much for her," I say. My concern is apparent and I know we both want to keep things as chill as we can for Gram. "I don't think this initial conversation has to include Gram too much. It's just to figure out where the uncles heads are at and get their thoughts on what's happening, right?"

"That's my intention, yes," she says, sounding more and more awake.

I uncurl myself from the blankets, pulling on sweatpants so I can talk and wander to the kitchen to start the coffee.

We talk while I finish waking up, making the plan to have an early dinner tomorrow night with everyone. Then over coffee while Gram watches her shows with Dad, Mom and I will talk to the uncles about what's going on.

"Good. It's a plan then," she says. "I'll let you go so you can get yourself ready for the day. Is Gram awake yet?"

I glance down the hallway toward her door that's set slightly ajar. Her bedside lamp is on and I hear shuffling, so tell Mom she's up and I'll call her if anything needs her attention.

Refilling my mug, I go back to my bedroom and get ready for a chilly day in the food truck. When I emerge, Gram is in the kitchen with a cup of coffee. She looks like she's prepared for a blizzard with a turtleneck under a sweater and her flannel lined jeans. As she finishes tying her sherpa lined boots, she glances up at me.

"It's going to be cold, Margaret. We live in New York and it's November."

Smirking, I nod in her direction, but do a mental check of what I'm wearing. Leggings under jeans, a T-shirt under a Bakery on Main hoodie, two pairs of socks, and I have a winter hat in my hand. I think I'm good.

"I'm layered like a wedding cake, Gram. And if we get colder than we can handle, we can go in the house. I've got food ready to make at Maverick's so he and Sawyer have lunch, so we'll be in and out of the house anyway," I say as I pull my boots on. "Let's go sell some cupcakes."

*****

Watching him work with the community is another level of erotic I didn't know I needed. More than once during the day Gram catches me staring at him from my space in the parking area near his office. In the months we've known one another and all the time we've spent together, this is the first I've seen where he "works."

Maverick explained to me that the trailer was the house he bought with the property when his ex was pregnant with Sawyer. I'm not sure if he didn't tell me that sooner because he was afraid I might react poorly, or just what his reasoning was. Maybe there wasn't a reason and it just wasn't one of those things that was important. It just kind of slipped out this morning when Gram and I pulled up into the small gravel lot.

Honestly? I don't care. It doesn't bother me. It makes no difference to our relationship that this house that is now his workspace is where she lived with him.

"Whatcha thinkin' 'bout?" Sawyer asks, bounding up to the window of the food truck.

"How freaking adorable you are in your overalls and Carhartt helping your daddy load trees for your customers," I say without thinking first and am so grateful my brain didn't say what I was actually thinking.

It makes her laugh. The giggle is exactly the sound I needed to clear my head.

"Feeling cute, might cut some trees down later," she says. Her eyes widen, "Ooooh, do you think Dad would be opposed to us making shirts to sell?"

Now it's my turn to laugh. Laugh and write down what she said in my notebook.

"Not if we ask him together. He can't say no to both of us."

"You're my favorite, Maggie. I love you," she says, the words slipping from her mouth so easily there's no way she doesn't actually feel that way.

"Love you, too, kiddo. Looks like there are more people pulling up," I say, pointing toward the driveway leading up to the parking area.

Sawyer runs off to greet her new customers and I don't miss the pure, unadulterated joy on her face when a boy gets out of the car followed by two other younger kids and two adults. Glancing in Maverick's direction, there's an emotion on his face I can place, but only because I saw it when I talked to him about the last boy. This one feels different, this is friend energy, and I'm not saying that because I have a good idea about Sawyer's preference. I'm not so sure her dad does, but that's not my place to tell him.

When Maverick pulls his eyes away and sees me watching him, he offers a strained smile before meandering over to see me.

"Stop." It's a directive from me and not to be argued with. "We don't know the situation. Let her be fifteen."

"I know."

"I know you know, but you've got your hackles up and need to relax your shoulders. You still have another hour of working out here and don't need to spend it being moody," I say.

"Am I being moody?" he questions, his jaw ticking slightly as he clenches his teeth while watching Sawyer and her mystery boy walk toward the posted map of where they're cutting today.

"You're getting there, and neither of us can leave our posts for me to go get you out of a bad mood right now, so knock it off."

His head whips around to look at me, his ears already pink from the cold grow a deeper shade of red.

"After we close?"

"After we eat dinner, I take Gram home, drop the truck at the bakery, and come back?" It's a question, but only because that's a lot of extra between now and me getting back to his house. He narrows his eyes at me like he's mulling it over. I sweeten the pot. "I'll ask Mom if she can come stay with Gram for a few hours. I can't sleep over, but I'll be back tomorrow, mid-morning."

His smile makes me a little weak in the knees. I'm a strong-willed woman but Maverick Rogers brings out a different side of me that no one else ever has.

Before he walks back over to help a family who just came back to the trailer with a tree they need wrapped, he crooks his finger at me with a silent request to lean out of the window. He steps up onto the stool we have for short people and presses his lips to mine.

"I'm glad you're here," he says, his mouth a whisper away from mine.

"There's no place I'd rather be."

*****

With Gram safely at home, Mom and the uncles there visiting, I bail on family time. When they aren't home often this is a good excuse to give them time to catch up. Before I left to come back to Maverick's they already had cell phones out with pictures of my cousins and their kids, giving her additional updates that weren't provided on Thanksgiving because of her obvious distress. I was asked why I didn't want to stay to hang with them, but thankfully my mom came to my rescue. She knows where I'll be, but as far as they know I'm just out having a normal 20-something Friday night life.

"Go Fish," I say.

Normal, yes. For an under-30 in a college town, not so much.

165

Sawyer pulls a card and throws her final match on the table, taking all the quarters from the middle as she hollers about her amazing card playing skills. Maverick and I share a look, laughing along with her, before he announces bedtime.

"It's still so early!"

"And we all need to be up early tomorrow. You're miserable when you're tired and cold. You're going to have no choice but to be cold, but you do have a choice in being tired or not," Maverick says, his negotiating skills top notch after years of this argument, I'm sure.

"Fair enough, but I'm reading for twenty minutes before I turn the light off." Gathering all of her winnings into a weathered coin purse that barely holds all the money she took from us tonight, she smirks, adding, "I'll be listening to music with headphones, too."

My mouth falls open slightly. Maverick stammers, but doesn't find words. We both know what she's insinuating, and when she doubles over, cackling at our reaction, I have to stop myself from high fiving her for her quick wit.

"Please, you're adults. You think I don't know what adults do?"

"Bed. Now," Maverick says, his ability to not crack waning.

"I love you, Daddy," Sawyer says, walking around the table to kiss him on the cheek. Stepping next to me, she kisses my cheek as well, "I love you, Maggie. Goodnight."

"Goodnight. Love you, too," Maverick and I say at the same time as she skips off to her bedroom.

He sighs deeply once we hear her bedroom door close, picking up his mug of coffee and draining the last bit from the bottom.

"She's going to give me grey hair before I'm ready for it. Not just a couple here and there, but my whole fucking head. Are all teenage girls like this?"

I side-eye him, pursing my lips as I think how to respond and just wing it.

"Not all. But the ones who have a good support system and feel comfortable with their adults seem to be okay with being themselves. I would almost bet she's pretty similar when she's with friends she trusts," I say.

"She told you she loves you. That's new."

"It is, but she says what she feels … and I love her, too. Your daughter is pretty amazing."

He looks at me, reaching up to tuck my hair behind my ear.

"So are you. I know this is a lot — dating a guy who's older and has a kid. I can say for certain we both needed you in our lives, though."

"You're not that much older. Seven years isn't a huge gap," I argue quietly, leaning toward him. I don't want him to ever think age is anything but a number for us.

"Older-ish then," he rebuts, meeting me where I'm at and connecting our mouths. He pulls my bottom lip between his, giving me more control. Cradling my face in his hands, Maverick removes his mouth, placing his forehead against mine, and says, "How long do I have you tonight?"

Fisting his shirt and rubbing the soft fabric with my thumbs, I bite my lip before answering. I don't have nearly as much time as I wish I did.

"An hour or so." I look up at him trying to get an idea as to what he's thinking. He hides his thoughts well, not always allowing them to show in his expressions, but the hunger in his eyes tells me my hour is going to be filled with nothing but his touches, kisses, and caresses.

"Bed?" he questions, and I stand as if it was a command.

He reaches for my hand as I begin stepping away, but stands and lets me lead him quietly up the stairs, turning lights off along the way. I'm grateful we aren't sneaking around behind his daughter's back, but I'm worried about how this will look to her when I'm not here in the morning. I tell him as much once we're behind the closed door of his bedroom.

"We don't have to do anything tonight. I just want you close," he says, and the vulnerability is enough to shatter my heart. We're moving faster than I ever thought I would, but moments like this make my brain stutter and hope we never slow down.

The bed compresses beneath him as he lays down on his side. I slip the flannel shirt off that I wore over a strappy tank and set it in the chair with his collection of hoodies and sweatpants. It looks at home there and makes me stop to create a memory of it before I crawl my way up to him from the foot of the bed and curl into his side, my head resting on his chest.

Maverick's fingers trace circles on my back, putting my body at ease without realizing how much tension I was carrying.

"What happened with Gram yesterday?" he asks in the quiet.

And my breath hitches. I wasn't expecting the tears to start. I was planning for a sexy night with my boyfriend, but I'm so tired.

"Things are changing. Slowly, but they're still changing. My mom wants to talk about home health aides and I'm afraid my uncles will suggest moving her out of the house," I say, my tears wetting his shirt because they fall faster than I can wipe them away. "We agreed that isn't going to happen unless necessary. There's a family dinner tomorrow to talk to all of them. They don't live here. They don't know what every day is like, that it's different every day, and I don't want them making decisions or trying to make decisions based solely on one long weekend of Gram being overwhelmed."

He keeps rubbing my back. Never once stopping the motion.

"Today was a good day. I hope they're able to see she's still okay at home."

"She was phenomenal today. Being here was good for her," he says. "I've never seen so many people know one person outside of weddings and funerals. You grandmother is pretty legendary and we didn't even know it."

That earns a chuckle from me. I guess being one of the only houses in the area to always give out full sized candy bars at Halloween has its perks.

"It's more than that, you know? I heard stories from people closer to her age who remember her from when they were kids. They literally described her as an angel, Maggie," he says, catching me off guard with the use of my name. "I had no idea she worked at a wildlife rehabilitation center."

"It was my favorite place to be when I was a kid." Just being with her was my favorite place, we could have been anywhere.

"It makes sense now why she looked so sad when we took down the tree out back. I hate that we needed to remove that piece of history for her, but once it was down, we saw it was more of a safety risk than anything else if it stayed," he says. "I want her to be able to stay in her house, and I'm glad we've been able to make it safer for her."

I don't miss the way he brings us back on topic.

"My sister is a social worker. She specializes in dementia."

I lift my head from his chest and stare at him.

"I didn't say anything because ..." he trails off to collect his thoughts. "Because I didn't want to overstep, she's been working in pediatrics for the last few years so I figured she was sticking to that, and because until yesterday she was still working in the Finger Lakes and not closer to Rochester."

I still don't say anything as I try to wrap my head around how his sister being closer will affect him, us, Sawyer, the whole dynamic.

"She's looking for an apartment in Spencerport?" he says it as a question, and I watch the unease in his eyes as he attempts to gauge where my thoughts are.

Instead of words, I push my body up onto his and bury my head in the crook of his shoulder as best I can. We're in a weird position but I just need him to hold all of me. His arms wrap snugly around me.

"Sawyer and I didn't tell her what's going on with Gram, but if I think she can help and you want me to, I'll talk to her," he says, each word softly imprinting on my heart.

"I love you so much, Maverick," I say, not caring that it's new, not giving my brain and mouth time to censor my heart.

"I love you, too," he whispers back, his arms tightening around me as his fingers begin tracing little circles once more on my skin through my shirt.

Chapter 22

Maverick

My head is tangled up with thoughts of Maggie and Gram and Harper … and how to talk to Harper about Maggie and Gram. I'm thankful for the slow start to work this morning because I've spent more time than I'm proud to admit typing out, deleting, and typing out again a text to my little sister.

I should just call her. That would be the smartest thing to do. And I will. Later.

Maggie and Genevieve pulled in around ten this morning and even with the few cars we had at the time, they've stayed consistently busy. Sawyer's idea to put the info on our social media was smart. The Bakery on Main is getting business from people who never would have known they exist because they've all come from closer to Rochester. It's not hurting my business, either.

I've kept myself by the office, enjoying the view of my girl in her element. Girls, actually, since Sawyer keeps jumping in to help when we don't have anyone needing us to wrap and load their tree.

It's nice to see my daughter hang out with my girlfriend and be making a new friend herself.

My head is turned when I hear the giggling getting closer.

"Daddy, why did you name the tree farm 'Sugar Shack'?" Sawyer asks, her arm looped through Genevieve's. Both girls are sporting huge smiles and rosy cheeks. Gen is younger, but not by much, and her background has given her reason to grow up faster than necessary. Maggie's told me how she and her brother came to Brockport after being in foster care on Long Island, and I'm happy to see her having the chance to be a kid. "Dad?"

"Right," I say, pulling myself from my thoughts. "Uh, well, you know how from the upstairs window you can see all those maples lining the edge of the farm? They kind of separate us from the other side of town."

They both look at me expectantly.

"That explains nothing, Mr. Rogers," Gen says, then tucks her lips between her teeth when she realizes what she said. I wait a beat, knowing what's coming because it's not the first time it's happened. Her face cracks ever so slightly, laughter spilling out, "I loved your show when I was little."

I gently pop her under the chin, smiling because it's funny and was definitely something my dad dealt with over the years.

"I wish I had sweaters as cool as him," I say. "The trees, though. The plan was to eventually buy the lot behind us so we can tap trees for syrup. I used to help a neighbor do his when I was a kid. We just haven't gotten that far. We started building the landscaping aspect and that's that."

One thing I haven't made my kid privy to is that Sugar Shack Landscaping does, in fact, own the wooded lot filled with maples. I bought it when she turned double digits, and it's been sitting there doing its thing for all these years.

Sawyer's face contorts. Her thinking face. I wish I had someone to help, or someone who needed a ride out to find a tree, because she's coming up with an idea and I have trouble telling her no when those ideas are good.

"So ... you're saying we could be making our own maple syrup? And you kept this from me my entire life?"

"As if it was on purpose. You never asked about the name. If you want to get into syrup production, let's talk about it. That's another huge undertaking and we're already doing greenhouses," I counter. "That is not a yes to any question you're thinking about asking, by the way."

"Fair enough. We'll talk about it later," she says, turning on her heel and dragging Genevieve back toward the food truck, though Gen goes willingly, looking a bit starry eyed.

They're back to smiling and laughing almost immediately, so I don't feel too bad about anything. And why should I feel bad? Because I bought a ton of land and haven't done anything with it or because I didn't let my tiny business partner know? I pull my bottom lip into my mouth, falling deeper into thoughts about sap and tapping and more work and if I can keep up with it all.

The feeling of someone touching my back snaps me back to reality. I smell coffee and twist my head to find the source. Maggie stands close enough to kiss, but holds a mug out to me. I want to kiss her more than I want the coffee, but I'm cold and could use the heat to warm me from the inside.

She has other ideas and as I reach for the mug, she pulls it closer to her.

"Tease," I say.

She lifts a perfectly shaped eyebrow, then takes a sip.

"Not. I'm testing it to make sure it's not too hot."

"May I?" I ask, stepping further into her personal bubble to wipe the small amount of liquid from her lip. She closes her eyes, the air leaving her lungs, as the sensation of my fingers on her mouth works its way into her brain. A low moan reaches my ears. My cheek against hers, I whisper, "You shouldn't do that or we might need to leave someone else in charge for twenty minutes."

It's not my imagination that her legs wobble. I pull the mug of coffee from her hand, kiss her cheek where my days-worth of stubble brushed her tender skin, and wink as I step away adjusting my hardening cock.

She catches the motion, her face turning pink from more than the chilly air.

"Now who's the tease?"

Sipping my coffee, I smile. "Still you, but we'll take care of it later."

The "we" is intentional. I need her alone tonight. I don't know how that's going to happen since Sawyer is home and Maggie has the family dinner to talk about Gram's health.

As if she reads my mind, she says, "Come to dinner tonight?"

I don't know how going to dinner will resolve any of the current issue, but I agree.

"This two houses thing is starting to suck," I say. I lower my voice, unsure about saying it out loud but needing to say it regardless.

"It could be worse. We could be a hundred miles apart and rarely see one another. That would really suck."

I'll give her that. She's right. I'm thankful it's just a short drive, but I'm starting to hate going to bed alone every night. She's spent one entire night with me and I'm already getting needy about having her here all the time. Maggie is definitely the only one who has made me want to move faster. I can't keep my mind from jumping to what happens to our living situations when things get more serious. Though we've gotten extremely serious in the last few weeks, houses is not a conversation we've even broached. Me saying what I'm saying about it not being awesome is the first either of us has mentioned it.

Taking the last sip of my coffee, I hand the mug back to her. Once it's in her hands, I slide my fingers along either side of her neck, pulling her closer, and kiss her like she's my last breath. There's no pretense. No hesitation. No lust. It's purely because I am falling so fucking hard in love with her that I know when she walks away to go back to work thirty feet from where I'm standing, I'm going to miss her.

As our lips part, she pulls in a deep breath. Her eyes remain closed, but her kiss-plumped mouth reveals a fulfilled smile.

"More," she says without opening her eyes. Her hands glide up the front of my jacket, reaching for the zipper and sliding it back down so she can step into the warmth with me. I pull her more snugly to me, and give her what she requests. The sound of the mug clattering on the not yet frozen ground barely registers in my brain as something to be concerned about.

Wrapping her arms around my waist and pulling away, Maggie leans her forehead against my chest to catch her breath.

"I will never get tired of this," she says.

"Tired of what?"

"All of this. You. Watching you work your business. The way being here makes me feel," she says, finally looking up at me. "I should get back to work before I get too honest."

For just a moment I'm curious what she means, until I hear someone whistle. Not a whistle like they're trying to get someone's attention, but the type I would have made if I was single and out at a bar looking for something more than alcohol. The look on Maggie's face tells me I'm not wrong in my assessment, but then she's up on her toes peeking over my shoulder and smiling.

"Well now, look what the weekend brought out of hiding!" she squeals.

I don't have a chance to turn before she's darting around me and throwing herself into some other man's arms. My anger immediately flares, and I can't excuse it. I won't. She's my girlfriend and hugging some other guy I've never met. This isn't how I saw the day going.

"Why would you catcall me?" she says, laughing.

At least she's laughing.

Until she glances in my direction and sees my face.

He pulls her into another hug. I'm too pissed to see it's not a possessive touch and she knows.

"Maverick." She says my name like it's a whole sentence. I swallow hard, unsure if I'm swallowing my pride or bile because seeing her in someone's arms that aren't mine makes me want to gag a little. She says a little louder, a little more stern, "Maverick."

Snapping out of it, I look at her.

"This is Alex. He's a friend of mine," she says, narrowing her eyes at me as if to tell me to knock my shit off and behave.

Alex reaches his hand out to me, untangling Maggie's arm from around him and stepping toward me.

"It's nice to meet you," he says, but I'm not sure he actually feels that way considering I still have my hackles up. But, I place my hand in his and give it a firm shake. "I'm assuming Maggie hasn't talked about me at all judging by your face."

He looks to Maggie for confirmation. She shakes her head.

"Been a little busy between things going on with Gram and, um, falling fast for this guy," she replies, pointing at me. I feel slightly better. Slightly.

He has the audacity to smile at me, squeeze my hand one more time and let go.

"I'll fill him in," he says, winking at Maggie. Before I can lose it, he says, "We went on one date a couple years ago. She's not my type and I'm not her type but I made a forever friend that night. Your woman is amazing and I'm thrilled to see her so happy."

"I'm so ... confused," I say, not even sugarcoating it. "She's not your type?"

I would have thought Maggie was most guys' type.

"I'm a music adjunct at the college," he says, as if that explains it. He looks at Maggie for help. "She likes more rugged guys and she told me I was too pretty to date."

My eyebrow shoots up in question, my face talking before I can think. Then I see it. She's in jeans and flannel and wearing one of my old Carhartt jackets and a knit cap. Alex stands there, freezing his ass off, in a pair of slacks, a button-down shirt, and a tie. Clean shaven, tall, and skinny to boot.

They are night and day.

"You're gonna get real cold out there," I say. "And she's right. You're way too pretty for her."

He offers me a genuine smile and I take a deep breath to will my body back into a state of calm. It's not easy, though. Mostly because I know he knows her better than I do and I don't like that.

"That's okay. I'm not planning to stay that long. You have precut trees? I'm looking for something small for my apartment," he says, pivoting right into conversation I can be comfortable with.

Nodding, I tell him we do and I can show him what's available.

"I'm going back to work," Maggie says, quietly. Stepping up to me, she chastely kisses me before looking deep into my eyes. There's nothing but love for me shining back and my face relaxes. "Play nicely. I love you."

She emphasizes the "you" as if she knows I needed the confirmation.

"I love you, too. If she's not busy, would you send Sawyer out? I need her to ride through the lot and make sure no one is lost or needs a hand."

"Absolutely," she says. Turning to Alex, she gives him a quick hug. This one doesn't affect me like the first one, thankfully. "Call me and we'll do coffee. I'll bring you up to speed on everything going on."

Watching their interaction knowing now what I didn't know ten minutes ago? There's nothing there at all but a good friendship. Since Maggie doesn't talk about friends other than Delilah and Fisher, I'm just going to allow myself to feel grateful she has more than me and Sawyer and Lilah and Fish.

When she walks back over to the food truck, I motion to Alex for him to follow me. There are precut pines behind the office. Not many, but enough in case someone doesn't want to cut their own.

"So, how'd you two meet?" he asks.

I start touching trees, the biggest ones first. I'm unsure about this conversation, especially without her here. I take the bait though.

"Homecoming at the high school. She had the food truck there and I was there with plants and small trees from the landscaping side of things. How's this one for size?" I say, pointing to a four-foot-tall blue spruce.

"That's perfect," he says. "Right time, right place for you two, huh?"

I hadn't thought about it like that.

"We didn't really get to meet that night. It was more in passing. My daughter ended up hurt and we needed to leave early," I say. "I don't know why I'm telling you this. Isn't this the kind of thing you'd want to talk to her about?"

"I like learning about people." Alex shrugs. "And I know her already. This gives me a chance to start getting to know you."

Grabbing the tree from its stand I begin walking toward the wrapping station.

"Fair enough." I start pushing the tree through the baler. Feeling gutsy, I ask, "Want to know what happened next?"

*****

Never in my wildest dreams would I think hanging out with a guy my girlfriend dated briefly before me would be enjoyable. However, Alex is nothing to be afraid of. We were both pretty amused with one another. He looked me up and down, and I think I saw him nod his approval when he was saying goodbye to Maggie before he left the farm, his little tree strapped to the top of a Chevy Equinox.

Maggie, Genevieve, and Sawyer hunted me down when it was time to close up. I wasn't surprised when Sawyer asked if she could go back to the bakery with Maggie. The two of them have gotten really close since the first time Sawyer showed up at the bakery and I'm starting to feel that Christmas feeling — you know, the magic — so I'm rolling with all of it. Especially after the way I reacted to the unknown with Alex today.

"Is it okay if I go to Gen's for the night?" Sawyer asks.

I tip my head, as if I couldn't have possibly heard her correctly. My kid isn't the kind to ask to sleep at friend's houses. Not that she's never had a sleepover. It's just uncommon. I look to Maggie for help because I don't know Delilah and Fisher all that well. They've been customers, but we haven't spent time together doing couple things.

Maggie smiles.

"Genevieve already checked with her mom, her mom is my best friend, and they're just going to watch movies and eat pizza. Probably homemade because Fisher is home from the restaurant tonight," she says, reading all my thoughts. "And if she needs you, you're a phone call or text message away. Will it make the decision easier if I say her house is pretty much the midpoint between Gram's and here?"

I hear what she's not saying. Let them go be teenagers. My daughter is practically dancing with anticipation, pleading with her eyes for me to say yes.

"Go pack your bag, don't forget your charger, and try not to stay up all night. You're miserable when you don't sleep," I say.

Sawyer throws her arms around my neck, kissing my cheek as she pulls away, "Thank you, Daddy."

Genevieve looks shyly between me and Maggie as Sawyer runs up to the house to get her things together for the night. It would feel way more awkward if Maggie wasn't standing here with us, but I still feel out of place.

"See? I told you it would be okay," Maggie says, looking at Gen and pulling her into her side for a hug.

"Were you worried I would say no?" I ask the two of them.

Genevieve bites her lip, contemplating.

"I wasn't sure. I ..." she takes a deep breath. "I don't have a ton of friends and I've had a lot of fun hanging out with Sawyer since Aunt Maggie introduced us."

I nod, absolutely understanding what she means.

"Between the two of us, I wasn't sure if I was going to say yes. Your Aunt Maggie is pretty convincing, though," I say, winking at Maggie. "Let's head in to get the rest of this day finished so you girls can go enjoy your evening, shall we?"

Maggie and Genevieve turn and I step between them, an arm around each of their shoulders. I'm well aware Gen had some rough years, so I'm cautious, but I trust Maggie to tell me if I'm overthinking. The three of us walk back over to the food truck and make quick work of closing up. As the two of them drive toward the house, I step into the office making sure I have everything I might need for the night.

Locking up, I watch from the small porch as Maggie and Gen walk into the house through the back door that leads to the kitchen. Everything about it feels right. Maggie and a teenager. Maggie and my teenager. Maggie and my teenager's friends. Just ... Maggie.

Chapter 23

Maggie

"I don't understand why you think she needs to go to a facility!"

I'm pissed. Everyone in this kitchen knows it. Everyone in Brockport might know it since I refuse to "calm down." Don't my uncles know better than to tell a woman to calm down? Fuck that.

"None of you live here. You've had three days of seeing her condition. Only one of those days was rough," I say vehemently. "When one of you chooses to leave your life and come live with us to help out, then I think your opinion will carry more weight. I don't see any of you doing that."

Four sets of eyes are on me. Dad and Gram are in the other room, trying desperately to avoid the train wreck in the kitchen. Maverick stands in the doorway to the breezeway, as if he's there to keep any of them from storming off when I get to be too much. If they don't want to listen to me and Mom, I will absolutely become too much.

"You're young and can't do this," Uncle Phil says. They've chosen him to speak for all three of them and I hate it. "Don't you want to have your own life? Taking care of your elderly grandmother is not how normal 27-year-olds want to spend their time."

"I do have my own life. She's a huge part of it," I say. "You aren't taking her away from me."

I feel the sting of the tears gathering behind my eyes and burning my nose before I ever let them fall. They don't understand how important she is to me.

"Maggie," Uncle Phil says, gathering my hands in his. "Mags, look at me."

I blink, tears landing on my jean-clad thighs though I try to will myself to not cry. I can't look weak. It'll give them even more reason to take her away. Against my gut, I look at him.

"Our intention is not to take her away. I agree with you and Becky that we should keep her at home. I think it was wrong for anyone to rush to the conclusion that Gram needs to leave the house," he says. He's being levelheaded, but the other two look irritated with what Phil is saying. "What

179

would you suggest we do in the meantime? Your mom still has a couple years of work, and you're right — the rest of us don't live close to home."

I bite my lip and steal a glance at Maverick. I know he talked to his sister earlier. Harper has ideas. My eyes plead with him to speak up and in this moment, when I watch him uncross his feet, push off the doorframe, and step toward the table, I realize the connection we have is stronger than either of us realized or, possibly, understood.

"Can I interject?" he says. His tone is polite, but also stern. It's his dad voice, and even though this is the worst time to think about what it does to me, my body doesn't care. "We might have a solution. Going to a nursing home is out of the question. Maggie and Becky are the ones who are here with Gram all the time and neither of them are ready to make that drastic a change. Can we all agree on that?"

A chorus of "yeses" meets my ears.

"My sister is a social worker and by some twist of fate she works with the elderly community. Specifically, those with dementia related illnesses. I think Gram is falling into that category. Even if it's not classified as Alzheimer's, she's got plenty of confusion and having someone who works with this give us some suggestions would be helpful," he says. "Would you all be content with having Harper come visit Gram and see what's actually going on and offer some advice?"

Uncle Phil turns to look at Maverick, then back at me.

"Why didn't you lead with that?" he asks me.

"Because they didn't want to hear it," I say pointing to my other two uncles. "They act like it's fine to just push her off on to someone else, but they won't be here to handle the fallout if that happens and she doesn't adjust well. It'll be me and Mom."

"Ignore them. They're assholes," Phil says, glaring at his brothers. Twisting to look at Maverick again, "When might Harper be able to come see her?"

I throw my arms around Uncle Phil and hug him until he starts pretending he can't breathe. Whispering, "Thank you," I pull away and go hug my mom. I need a mom hug. She's mumbling that everything is going to be okay as Maverick and Phil talk details.

"Hey, what's up?"

I hear her voice over speakerphone. We've never met and a part of me feels guilty for asking for help without having even been able to see her face-to-face. I've seen pictures of Maverick's brother and sister because he's the kind of guy who has family pictures on walls and shelves. I'm not sure who he does it for — him or Sawyer — but I have definitely appreciated the stories he shares when noticing me noticing a photo he has out.

Not intentionally, I zone out while Maverick and everyone else talk to Harper. They all know my position. Harper also knows where Maverick and Sawyer stand on the matter, but the uncles don't need to be aware of their opinion right now. Confident I don't need to sit here and listen to everything since Maverick and I will rehash it all later, I leave the room and find Dad asleep in one recliner. Gram is busy looking over a crossword, her shows are on the TV even though she's not paying attention. It's background noise for comfort.

"They figure out what they're doing with me yet?" she asks, looking up from her puzzle. "Do I need to whack my two youngest boys with a wooden spoon?"

The smile we share is lighthearted, but I do let her know the spoon might not be a bad idea.

"Figured as much," she says. "They're not getting rid of me that easily."

"We wouldn't dream of trying, Mom," Uncle Phil says from the doorway. "How do you feel about meeting Rick's sister? She thinks she might be able to help."

Gram looks at me and then back to her firstborn.

"Help with what?" she asks, skepticism alive and well.

"Making sure when Maggie or Becky can't be here that you're safe. It's to prevent a need for something more drastic, in case you have a moment of forgetfulness," he says.

She squints her eyes at him, questioning if there's a motive without actually asking.

"She's not going to make me move into a home with a bunch of old people?"

Chuckling, Phil attempts to keep the conversation light. The entire evening has been too heavy and I'm exhausted from the weight of it all.

"Old people smell funny. We're going to do everything we can to make sure you're okay at home unless a bigger need arises," he says, walking into the room and kneeling beside Gram's chair. Lowering his voice, he continues. "Mom, we just want you to be safe."

Nodding, she agrees to meeting Harper.

181

"Plus, it's good to have family who can help. If Maverick is as interested in her," she says, pausing to nod in my direction, "as he seems to be, it's probably smart to get to know his family before we have to start planning a wedding or a baby shower."

I gasp, covering my face to hide the amused smile, and under my breath say, "Oh my God. Gram, it's a little soon to be thinking about weddings and babies."

But I don't let on that I have absolutely had those thoughts cross my mind. The look she gives me tells me she knows, though. She always knows.

"It's never too soon to let someone love you the way you deserve to be loved," she says, reaching for my hand. "Let him love you."

*****

Mom and Uncle Phil are staying with Gram tonight. Dad and the rest of the uncles are going back to Mom and Dad's since they both have early flights out tomorrow and need to get their things together. I hug everyone before they leave, but I don't expect the apologies from Uncle Brett and Uncle Mark before they let go of me.

"You don't need to," I say, trying to stop them.

"But we do," Mark says, looking at Brett and having a silent conversation. "We shouldn't have come in and tried to argue with you and your mother about this. You're right. You are the ones who are here to handle the daily life with Gram."

My chest tightens. For my entire life I've just been Little Maggie, the baby of the family, the grandchild who shouldn't have an opinion because I'm the youngest one of all my cousins. His comments make me feel a little vindicated for my earlier behavior. It was justified. It's behavior I will never apologize for because I will defend my grandmother's right to make decisions for herself until the day she can't any more. I know my mom feels the same way, but through all of this I've been worried her brothers will get in her head and change her mind.

But, just like with making decisions about the landscaping we're having Maverick and Will do, she deserves to call the shots.

"Thank you. Thank you for trusting me and Mom to do what we think is best for Gram," I say to Brett and Mark. "It hasn't been easy so far, but it hasn't been so difficult we can't continue providing the best environment to keep her safe, you know?"

They nod their agreement.

"When the hell did you grow up, Mags?" Mark asks, a touch forlorn. "Weren't you a little girl playing with makeup and experimenting in the kitchen last time we saw you?"

"I'm just taller now. I still play with makeup and experiment in the kitchen. And I'm a huge advocate for not fucking with my family."

Brett laughs. "So we've been made privy of. At any rate, Maggie, we're both glad Gram has you in her corner. Call or text if you need anything, please? Anything."

I nod, pulling them each in for one more hug before they gather their coats and leave for the evening. Despite the sticky situation and the concern I had that they would try to pull something, I'm glad they were here for the conversation. Family meetings are never fun when it's intervention-type gatherings, but we made progress.

I feel him enter the room before he ever makes a noise, my body relaxing after holding tension all evening. His hands on my shoulders and his chest pressed against my back, Maverick places a kiss to my neck, just below my earlobe.

"Are you ready to go home? Gram said I was to, and I quote, take you like a bride on her wedding day," he says, dropping another kiss to my neck. "Your gram is my favorite grandparent, by the way."

I palm my face, wondering aloud where her filter is.

"She knows you need a break after dealing with your uncles. They're nice guys, but a bit hardheaded," he says, slowly turning me around to look at him. "Must be a family trait."

"Definitely a family trait. You sure you want to be part of this insanity?"

"Absofuckinglutely."

*****

The house is so quiet when we get back to Maverick's that I'm unsure how to … be. I'm so used to us spending time with Sawyer that not having her home is strange. It's rare she's even gone for the day on a weekend. Her mother hasn't bothered to reach out since she moved in with her dad full time.

It happened without my realizing it, but in a way I've staked a claim on Sawyer as my kid. I am well aware she isn't and that I still need to be careful not to overstep. But, for all intents and purposes, I'll go to bat for her any time of day if she needs me.

Setting my bag on the table, I kick my shoes off and leave them by the door. Unzipping my coat, I hang it on one of the hooks above the shoes. There's a heaviness in my chest that I can't explain, even as Maverick moves to settle behind me. He wraps his arms around my abdomen, splaying his fingers over my belly and pulling me tighter to him.

"Everything is going to work out, Maggie. We're all here, supporting you and Gram, and your mom. We know there's plenty of things to consider and Harper will help," he says, sensing the overwhelm and all the things I'm thinking about.

Relaxing my shoulders, I try to believe him. I also want to stop worrying, even if just for tonight.

Turning in his embrace, I snuggle into his chest, my arms automatically tucking under his and wrapping around his waist. I feel safe here, with him.

"How has this happened?" I question.

"How has what happened?"

"You, me, us ... how has this moved so quickly but been so everything I needed?"

He tips my chin up. Placing a chaste kiss to my lips and then staring into my eyes, his brows furrow.

"I think, sometimes, when things are right the timeline gets thrown away. I don't need to wait forever to know you're an amazing co-parent and partner. I don't need a years-long courtship to know I'll love you for the rest of my days," he says.

There's no perfect way to respond. I press up on my tiptoes and kiss him. Letting go of me long enough to move his hands to my face, Maverick cups my jaw, deepening the kiss as his tongue finds mine. My fingers find the muscles in his back, formed from years of hard labor cutting trees and digging holes. I trace each vertebra down until I reach his belt and follow it around to his hips, twisting my fingers through loops on either side of his abdomen, and I pull him closer to me.

I swallow down the groan released from between his lips and his teeth gently nip at mine.

"We have the house to ourselves," he says.

Not waiting for a response, he reaches for my thighs and lifts me up to straddle his waist. I hold tight, hooking my feet together behind him, as he takes careful steps toward the living room. I don't question him not taking me to the bed. My brain is done asking things for the day. I just want to feel him against me with nothing between us.

Maverick never once lets go of me as he kneels on the couch and lays me down, his body following and pressing me deeper into the velvety fabric. My thighs fall open and his hips join with mine, our clothes in the way and preventing each movement from getting us closer to a release we both are desperately in search of. I break away from his mouth long enough to pull the hem of my T-shirt up and remove the fabric, tossing it to the floor. Grasping the bottom of his shirt, I do the same to him. A sigh escapes when his warm skin makes contact with mine and he envelops me in his arms.

His hands still between me and the couch, his fingers finding the strap to my bra and expertly unhooking it, pulling it from my arms. It joins the shirts on the floor, the black lace standing out against the plain T's. My nipples pebble at his touch, the calluses on his thumbs scratching the sensitive skin in all the best ways, causing my back to arch in an attempt to get closer still.

Trailing my fingers along his shoulders, I gently drag my nails up the back of his neck and into his hair, prompting him to slowly begin kissing a path down my body. Closing my eyes, I let myself feel all of what he's doing to me. His fingers find the button on my jeans and soon I hear him say, "Lift." My hips obey the command and he slides the fabric down my legs, pulling them off along with my underwear and socks, leaving me stark naked.

"You're so fucking beautiful, Maggie," he says, and I open my eyes just enough to watch as he slowly removes his pants, leaving just his boxers in place despite how his cock strains against the fabric.

I don't let myself react when he doesn't move to remove the rest of his clothes. I remain silent as he drops to his knees between my feet. His hands reach for the underside of my thighs and, as if we've rehearsed this dance a thousand times, I bend my legs to offer him full access.

Leaning into me, he nips my bottom lip, then quickly deepens the kiss before he leaves me wanting more and is cautiously trailing his tongue down my belly once again. His tongue is the first thing I feel, flattened against the most sensitive parts of me, and my hips lift off the couch. The feeling of his stubbled jaw is foreign on the tender skin of my inner thighs, this is the first time with him and, as his lips latch onto my clit, I pray it isn't the last time. He lingers, finding pleasure in exploring every crease and crevice, making sure I'm thoroughly loved.

I detonate at his touch as he presses two digits deep into me, falling apart around his fingers as my hands grip his hair.

"So beautiful," he mumbles, his tongue continuing its gentle assault as my orgasm crests and I begin coming down from the high.

My feet fight to push his boxers away from his legs, the need to feel him inside me stronger now than ever. Lifting up on his knees, I'm granted my wish as he shoves the fabric away, kicking it into the pile we've left on the floor. Maverick dips his head, catching my nipple in his mouth. Sucking hard, carefully biting the nub, and then flicking it with his tongue distracts me from the feel of his cock at my entrance.

He slips easily into me, a groan emanating from his gorgeous mouth as he pushes in to the hilt. I encourage him to move, pressing my hips up into him, begging for his release.

"You feel too good," he says, a look of concentration causing his brow to wrinkle. "I won't last long once I start moving."

I thrust my hips into him again and, on a sharp intake of breath, he meets me where I am as we both chase the orgasm we're trying to delay. With hooded eyes, he finds his rhythm, and with each movement he pushes us closer to the precipice.

"Let go," I encourage him as my body begins to quake around him, pulling him deeper into me.

Wrapping my arms under his shoulders, I hold tight to him while he uses his elbows for leverage to thrust harder … once. Twice. Three times and he stills while I relish the feeling of his cock pulsing inside me, filling me.

Breathlessly he places his forehead against mine, his eyes closed, a look of pure contentment in his features. Gently kissing his lips, I tighten my core, gaining another groan of pleasure from him before the sensitivity kills the pleasure and he can't handle the grip I have on him. He deepens the kiss, his tongue sliding along mine, knowing it's the distraction I need as he pulls out of me.

"Shit."

My eyes remain closed as his whispered comment reaches my ears. I feel the satisfied smile on my lips as I quietly respond, "That was so good."

"There's a reason it was so good," he says.

He shifts and the warmth of his body leaves the shared space. As I close my thighs, the trickle of fluid clues me in and my eyes fly open. "Oh, shit."

He stands before me, bare. All of him. And at the exact same moment he begins to worry, I'm hit with the realization that this wasn't planned. We've been diligent about protection.

"It's okay," I say, reaching for his T-shirt the wipe myself off before anything gets on the couch. "It's going to be okay."

Grabbing my underwear as I stand up, I quickly pull them on.

"Maverick, it's going to be fine." I say, more to calm myself than anything else. He's not hearing me. Instead, he's scrubbing his hands down his face, then chewing on his thumbnail, staring at the floor.

"I'm so sorry, Maggie," he says, but he isn't listening.

"Maverick, look at me." He doesn't. "Maverick. I'm not mad." Still nothing. "Rick."

His head whips up and the fear in his eyes is heartbreaking. I've never, not once, called him anything but Maverick.

"We've never talked about this," he says, motioning to his lower body. "I'm so sorry."

"For what? I was an equal participant."

"We're always careful. It's just a given. We have sex, we use condoms. We've never talked about other birth control or even not using condoms," he says, stepping into my orbit. Placing his hands on either side of my face, his forehead against mine, I hope my calm surrounds him and gives him some relief. "How can you be so relaxed about this? How are you not panicking?"

I don't know. Truly, I have no idea. But I feel absolutely nothing but love — for him, for me, for us.

"Maverick," I say his name again. This time he looks in my eyes the first time. "Whatever happens, happens. Maybe we caught me at the perfect time in my cycle for nothing to happen. Maybe we didn't. I'll have to check a calendar and report back with how much we need to freak out. But freaking out right now? Not going to change anything."

He pulls me into his arms, holding me snugly against his chest. Pressing my ear to his heart, I listen as it slows to normal, and hold onto him until he's ready to let go.

Please, don't ever let go, I say to myself.

Chapter 24

Maverick

FEBRUARY

I didn't make a New Year's resolution because I don't believe in them. What I did do was have a long conversation with my kid about how hard it is to be an adult, a single parent, and kind of lonely. I didn't realize how absolutely true those last words were until Maggie was sick for about a week right after the new year.

We were thankful the big winter season for both of us was over for the moment. But then we were staring down the pike at another one — maple season for me and Valentine's Day for her. If I thought her keeping her distance to keep Sawyer and me healthy was brutal, the fact I hardly saw her leading up to the holiday every single person I know hates was worse. Because we aren't single and I missed her. We've barely had time to sit and watch a movie let alone anything else. Sawyer picks on us because we fall asleep as soon as the movie starts and are becoming "boring and old."

I miss her. And she's minutes away. I don't need anything exciting with her. Just being with her is exciting, even if all we do is take a nap.

"This bucket is full. We might need to invest in one of those tube systems and the barrels for next year," Sawyer says. "We're going to have to get this boiling as soon as we get back. I'm worried the season is going to end early this year."

I barely hear her, lost in my own thoughts as I pour another bucket of sweet water into the barrel on the trailer hitched to the ATV.

"Okay," I say, watching as the warm Saturday sun continues rising over our home in the distance.

"Are you?" she asks, and I know I look confused. "Okay? Are you okay? You're not acting like yourself. What's going on?"

Sawyer turned sixteen last week — my Valentine's Day baby — and ever since then I've been more off my game. My dad game, the boyfriend game, the business game. Everything just feels ... difficult. Our conversation back in January doesn't help, because the more I think about being here with just Sawyer, the more I miss Maggie every night. I watch her car pull away or I leave her at Gram's and wish it was different. It will be one day, but we've been stuck waiting it out.

At Christmas, Becky dropped the bomb that she was taking early retirement in order to be with Gram more. We were all a little relieved, because even with Harper's assistance, we still were having trouble figuring out how to manage everything. Gram would spend days at the farm with me, or at the bakery with Maggie and Delilah, but it wasn't fair to her to keep her away from home for so many exhausting hours. Not that she ever complained. It was the exact opposite. She's dug right in helping tap trees and enjoyed the hell out of helping bake cookies for the holiday rush the girls experienced. Gram doesn't see it as work like a lot of people might. It's a labor of love.

Becky's done working as of Friday, the retirement party is on Saturday, and on Sunday we'll figure out the rest. One week until we start planning for the next step.

"Yeah. Yeah, I'm okay. There's just a lot on my mind," I say, playing it off like it's nothing for me to zone out deep in thought while in the middle of working.

"Are Maggie and Gram coming over for dinner tomorrow? They hosted last Sunday, so it's our turn," she says.

"They'll be here around three," I say, hanging the empty bucket back on the tree it came from. The drips are slower, but the sap is still just as sweet. "I'll pull the taps next week. Let Mother Nature do her work. For our first year, I don't think we should keep them in right up to the end. I'd rather take what we have and be thankful for the learning curve."

I brush my gloved hand down the trunk of the maple, giving silent gratitude to nature for giving me and Sawyer a chance to expand. We're doing a lot of that. In the last year we've branched out more with the landscaping, added the greenhouses, and now this. None of it would be possible if it weren't for my kid. She's been my reason for so many years.

"Hey, Pumpkin, you about ready to call it a day out here?"

She carries the last bucket over, lifting and expertly dumping it into the barrel.

"I think so. Is Will coming to help boil?"

"He's already at the house. Texted and said he was starting a pot of coffee and checking the fire," I say, climbing into my seat of the ATV while she rehangs her bucket. "It's a good thing we've had a mild winter and were able to get a shack built in time. I really didn't want to remodel the kitchen in the house from all the steam we're creating."

She rolls her eyes at me, something she's been doing more. Things have been hard for her since the holidays. Hannah hasn't been around. She showed up one day with the things Sawyer left at her apartment and dropped them at the porch. The new boyfriend must have a big enough bank account to keep her happy and she didn't renew her lease. Unfortunately, or maybe it is fortunate, that also means she's opted out of seeing our daughter on a regular basis. Not that she was putting in any effort before, but giving up the option to have Sawyer and spend time with her has seemingly caused a hurt in my baby I can't fix. She's seeing her mom for who she is, and it's giving her a good idea of why things never were going to last for us.

It's also shown Maggie how bad I was at choosing partners in the past and on more than one occasion she's questioned what I saw in Hannah. She wasn't being critical, just curious because they are complete opposites. Knowing all the details about Sawyer's stuff showing up at the house randomly, though, ticked her off to a point I didn't think Maggie was capable of. If anything, her knowledge of the history between me and Hannah and how Hannah seems to have abandoned her job as a mother has given Maggie more of a reason to dig her heels in harder to make sure my daughter knows she's loved unconditionally.

That final conversation I had with Hannah, when she appeared while Sawyer was at school, comes back to get me again.

"I should have loved you better," she says. "I should have been more like her."

Standing on the porch, Hannah at the bottom of the steps, a garbage bag filled with our child's things hanging from her fist, I look down at her. Considering how angry and mean I could be, I take a breath and a long sip of my coffee before letting my mouth run.

"But, that's the thing, Hannah," I say, stopping short to make sure I get it right and she understands all the words. "You never would have been able to love me like she does because you are nothing like her. She's never wanted to change me. She's never not wanted my daughter. You gave up on everything because we were never what you wanted."

She drops the bag on the ground, zero remorse, and lets me know how right I am when she turns and walks back to her still running car, gets in, and backs away. It's the only time she's willingly let me have the last word.

"Hello. Earth to Maverick Rogers."

"Huh?" I turn my head, Sawyer sitting beside me ready to head back to the house. I apologize the best I can with a look, because "I'm sorry" only goes so far. "What?"

"You were … not here. I don't know what's up, but you're starting to worry me. Want to talk about it?"

Turning the key, the engine starts and I slowly begin pulling away from the grove of trees.

"Not really," I say. I want to keep the hurt from her. I know I can't protect her forever, but if I can keep her from knowing her mother never bothered to ask me how she is, I will. Sawyer didn't even question how her things ended up at our house. I quietly emptied the bag, put her makeup in the bathroom and tossed the clothes in the washer.

She didn't have to ask. She knew.

"Thinking about Maggie? She's been so tired lately. I think keeping up with Gram and the bakery and starting to fill the calendar with food truck events is getting to be too much," she says, genuinely concerned. "They've got so much business even when it's slow, I think it might be beneficial if they hired someone. Even part-time would help. Gen is trying to help more at the bakery so Lilah and Mags can work on the bigger stuff. It's really admirable."

She lets a tiny sigh escape when she finishes her proclamation, and I chance a glance in her direction. The pink of her cheeks deeper than from the cold.

"Are you crushing on Delilah's daughter, Sawyer?" I ask, a lilt to my voice. It's a serious question, though, because I've seen their interactions. They're adorable together, but since Christmas it has felt like more than friends. I haven't prodded, but I also haven't been blind to them snuggled up together watching movies on the weekend. My brain apparently wants to tackle all the tough subjects today. "I like Genevieve. She's a nice girl."

Sawyer doesn't say anything, just watches the world slowly go by as we drive back to the house. Once we hit the clearing, she speaks quietly.

"You aren't disappointed?"

"Disappointed? About what?"

"That I like girls. Mom never acted like it was okay — she always made it seem like gay people are less than," she says, staring at her muddy boots. "So, I tried to like the guys, but I just don't feel anything. Some of them make great friends, but they don't make me feel the way I feel around Genevieve."

I stop the ATV and get out. I walk around to her side and wait for her to look up at me. My heart shatters when she does because there are a thousand reasons in her tears that make me hate her mother even more.

Pulling my gloves off, I wrap her face in my warm hands and wipe the tears as each new one threatens to trace its way down her cheeks.

"You. Will *never*. Ever. Be a disappointment. If Hannah made you think you were less than because you're not into dudes, fuck her." I've never been so crass about my ex-wife when talking to our kid, but I'm done. Sawyer closes her eyes tightly, clamping her lips shut to keep the sobbing at bay. I don't stop, though, because I love my child more than I love the idea of keeping peace with a woman who used us and left. "Her concept of love is deluded because it begins and ends with a dollar sign. Does Gen make you feel like you can take on the world? Do you support her in all the cool things she's doing? Yes? Good. That's where love starts. It's got nothing to do with what's between your legs or hers."

She nods, her cheeks smooshing between my hands, and I brush the last few tears away.

"Thank you for trusting me enough and letting me in, Sawyer. I don't know how other dads do it ... not knowing their kids," I say, pulling her into me. "You're one of my most favorite people on this planet."

"You're one of mine, too," she says. "Maggie is running neck-and-neck with you though. Some days she's more my favorite."

I pull away, a mock horrified expression on my face. "You wound me, child. You'd choose my girlfriend over me?"

"Um, in a heartbeat depending on the conversation or situation."

"What conversations am I not helpful with?" My curiosity will kill me in the end, I'm sure, but I'm interested. "Hmm?"

"Okay, I'm going to play this game and you're going to lose," she says, laughing. Her eyes sparkle as the unshed tears dissipate with her joy. "My last period was really heavy and I was bleeding through a regular tampon every hour. Can you make sure to add super tampons to the grocery list?"

My mouth opens, and closes, and I understand.

"Got it," I say, walking back to the driver's side of the ATV so we can get to the house. Pulling away, I add, "I'm glad we've got Maggie. Just so you know, though, I have no problem buying whatever tampons you need."

"And this is why I chose you," she says, quietly, looking my way. "Thank you for letting me be me, Dad."

"I don't want you any other way, Pumpkin."

I smile at Sawyer, hold up my fist, and she bumps it. We've run the gamut of emotions on this short drive and I'm ready for a glass of something strong while everything sinks in.

*****

"We've got a good boil going. We can either add more now or finish this batch before worrying about the barrels you just brought up," Will says as I park the ATV between the house and sugar shack.

I don't know how I lived my whole life without a Will before moving out here. With the exception of my own dad helping in the beginning, I wasn't expecting anyone here to step up and befriend me as quickly as Will did. The difference in our ages is nothing more than numbers and I appreciate his generosity. When Hannah and I split, he kept me sane when I couldn't see Sawyer as often as I wanted.

"If there's room, might as well top it off, right?" I say, though it comes out as a question. We're learning how to do this together.

We work in quiet solitude, draining off what we can from the sap we just carried in, and stirring the lightly golden liquid.

"How are things going with Gram and Maggie?" he asks out of the blue.

Even growing up in a small community myself, I'm still surprised by how connected people in Brockport are.

"Oh, you know. They're going," I say, walking over to a table that holds a thermos he brought out from the house. I pour a fresh cup of coffee, but when I look in his direction, I catch him staring at me with concern. "They're good, Will. Don't go getting worried about things. They're good. Maggie's just overwhelmed and Gram is trying really hard to make things not seem so complicated. Becky is officially retired at the end of this week, though, so we'll figure it all out."

Knowing he's been around for a majority of Maggie's life is comforting. I know I can go to him if I need to talk to a dad figure about our relationship without going to her actual father.

"What's got her overwhelmed these days? She doesn't usually get like that," he says.

"I know. From what Sawyer was saying things are really busy at the bakery, so that's one thing. Then Gram's health and waiting for Becky's retirement to start so she can spend more time with Gram instead of us dragging her to the bakery and out here to the farm, even though Gram loves being helpful," I say, putting my mug to my mouth. "Plus, she was sick right after Christmas and hasn't really bounced back to full capacity yet. She's just exhausted. But, Maggie's passionate about the bakery and really making a push to get the food truck aspect rolling this year."

"She needs to rest. Take her on vacation," he says, as if it's that easy. Who would cover for her at the bakery? It's just her and Delilah, and Genevieve when she can be there. "Don't overthink it. Just mention it to her."

I nod my agreement; I'll mention a vacation to her. Maybe we can take Sawyer and hit the Adirondacks for a long weekend over February break next week. Or plan for something more extravagant for Sawyer's spring break.

"Your brain's working overtime," Will says.

"Just trying to figure out when we'd be able to take a vacation and where she and Sawyer might want to go."

"You aren't going to like what I'm about to say," he says, clicking his tongue and pulling his ball cap down over his eyes to shade them from the blinding sun. "But, maybe leave Sawyer at home. It's not like she doesn't have enough extra family around here to keep her busy and safe. You and Maggie would do well to have some time just the two of you."

I've never wanted to leave my kid for more than a weekend, and that was with my parents when Hannah and I were still in our "not a disaster" phase of the relationship. Hell, I never even left her with her mother without balking at the idea once we were separated and I was getting less time with her.

"Just consider it and talk to Maggie," he says, knowing full well I'm getting back into my head again about the whole thing.

My response is a hushed, "yup," as I get back to work, hoping the hours pass quickly.

Chapter 25

Maggie

I spent a solid week right after Christmas in bed, and not the way I like to be in bed. Considering the timing and then a super light period, I took a dozen pregnancy tests.

Negative.

I was relieved.

Mostly.

I haven't said anything to Maverick about them, though, because I don't want him to sit in his thoughts about how careless we were and I don't want to keep feeling whatever it is I'm feeling about not seeing a second pink line. He also didn't ask about the possibility of being pregnant, and the fact I'm working myself to exhaustion every day, I think he's almost afraid to ask.

Letting out a yawn as I stand in line at the Jumping Bean, I read through the specials again. The person behind me doesn't pay attention to the fact I haven't moved up and bumps into me.

"Hey, be careful," I say, turning to speak to them. "Personal space is a thing."

"Is it now? I'll try to be mindful of that," he says, laughing.

I narrow my eyes at him. He mocks me with the same look.

"Alex, you're not funny. I'm tired and need caffeine," I say to my friend. "Be kind."

He pulls me into a snug hug and kisses the top of my head.

"Sorry, Mags. You look like you need the coffee," he says, gently pushing me forward in line. "Get food, too. My treat."

"Seems like a fair price to pay for picking on me. Scone? I'll share with you."

As we make our way to the counter, Brian, the owner, waves a hello. We've gotten to know one another throughout the years since he opened the coffeehouse. When Delilah and I opened the bakery a few doors down, he was instrumental in helping us get off the ground. Literally. He'd show up with a carafe of coffee and a box of snacks on days we were in the bakery figuring out the logistics of the space.

"What can I get you?" Brian's brother, Tommy, asks. "And don't get mad at me if I mess it up because I'm not even supposed to be working here today."

"Good thing our order is simple. Two black coffees and a chocolate chip scone," Alex orders for us.

"You two are my favorite customers. Thank you," he says, steepling his hands beneath his chin and turning from the counter to fill our cups.

Alex and I stand in silence as we wait, reaching for our cups like we practiced it when Tommy holds them out. The scone comes out next and we make our way to a table near the window.

Sitting down across from me, Alex releases a sigh.

"I know you're dating Maverick, but I was wondering if you might want to be my date for a wedding. It's my cousin's wedding and if I show up alone it's going to be a shit show," he says in a rush. "Also, it's out of town so it would require staying overnight and I know that's a big ask for you."

My mouth opens, but nothing comes out. This isn't something I can make a snap decision about.

"Can I think on it?" I ask.

"Yes, absolutely. Talk to Maverick about it, too, because I don't want to step on any toes. I just ... I'm probably the only cousin left who is single. Everyone is starting to wonder what's wrong with me."

He laughs when he says it, but I know how much that hurts. I'm the last one, too.

"How are things aside from being single?" I ask, cautiously taking a sip of my coffee.

"They're good," he says, refusing to make eye contact.

"Liar. Tell me the truth." I'm too tired for social graces and he's too good a friend to let him get away with being dishonest.

"You have so much going on with Gram, I don't want to unload on you," he says. "But, aside from a lack of love, I'm not sure if I want to stay at the college as an adjunct. Having my master's degree is great and I love teaching, but I feel like there's more I should be doing."

This isn't anything new. We've had this discussion before. Typically, it ends with him sad because he's "just" a music teacher and he didn't follow his dreams of having a band. This feels heavier.

"And ..." I press, knowing there's something rattling around he isn't vocalizing.

"And I think I should go back for my doctorate in music theory. Maybe. I haven't figured out exactly which program I want to pursue, but it's a start."

Without stopping to think I say, "Do it. Follow your heart, Alex."

Breaking the scone, I offer him half and we sit with our thoughts — mine wondering how Maverick will react when I tell him Alex wants me to accompany him to his cousin's wedding and his figuring out his future.

"Okay," he says, seemingly out of the blue, and I furrow my brows in confusion. "Okay, I'll do it. I'm going to start with Eastman and see if I can get in."

Realization dawns and a smile forms on my lips.

"I am so proud of you. This is a big step, but you can do it." I stand, walking to his side of the table, and lean in to hug him. His body relaxes, the rigidity slipping away. "This is going to be amazing."

As I'm pressing a kiss to Alex's cheek, my arms still wrapped around his neck, the sound of someone clearing their throat behind me registers. But, I don't really pay attention to it because people clear their throats all the time. I disregard it and pull back from Alex, fully prepared to sit down and delve deeper into his thoughts about going back to school.

Until I hear, "This is interesting."

And suddenly I hate the sound of people clearing their throat.

"I wonder what my daughter would think if she knew my replacement was hanging all over some guy in public who isn't her dad?"

She's never even met me, not really. She knows who I am because Sawyer shared the information, not because she cared to know me. The number of times I've interacted with Hannah can be counted on one hand, but this brief interaction she's witnessed between me and one of my best friends is going to put my relationship with Maverick in jeopardy. I can feel it. She's got a small handbag hanging over her forearm and her cell phone out like she's ready to text someone. She's excited she might have caught me doing something wrong; it radiates off her.

"Mags?" Alex says, attempting to get my attention. I shake my head in a gesture that hopefully conveys this is fine and I'll handle it.

I feel exactly zero percent fine, though.

"Hannah," I say in lieu of "hello," thinking I can smooth this over before she grabs at straws to twist together a story to suit her needs. "What brings you to town?"

She watches me, waiting for a bigger reaction, I'm sure. The problem is, she's not my enemy. She's not my competition. She's nothing to me. Sadly, she doesn't seem to realize that.

"I had business to tend to, which doesn't concern you," she says, vitriol dripping with each word spoken.

"Then why are we talking and why would you go to great lengths to tell me you're here?" It's a genuine question. We aren't friends and the only things we have in common, that I can tell, are her ex-husband and their daughter. I'm not stupid enough to think she made her presence known for any reason other than she thinks I'm in the middle of something I shouldn't be.

Her mouth quirks up in a half-smile.

"Also, it's hard to be the replacement for someone who didn't put in any effort to be around in the first place."

Her smile dissipates. Alex let's out a nervous laugh. And, me? I'm not going to let her intimidate me after bailing on Sawyer.

"Do you want me to call Maverick myself and tell him I'm having coffee with my friend? Or do you want to try to sneak a picture and send it to him? Either way, he's going to believe me. I don't keep secrets from him and he knows Alex, so if you're going to snap that photo, make sure it's a good one so I can print a copy."

I turn around and sit back down in my seat, pick up my coffee, and take a long sip while I will my nerves to settle. I don't like confrontation. I don't like when I turn into an asshole.

"Wow, aren't you a sweetheart," she says, snark rolling off her forked tongue.

"Please leave. You're good at that."

Hannah brings out the confrontation loving asshole in me. I'm not sure what else she expects to happen, so when she continues to stand near our table, Alex looking from me to her and back waiting for someone to say or do something, I just wait for her to disappear.

From the coffeeshop.

From my hometown.

From our lives.

I just wait.

*****

"Should we schedule ourselves for more event things during the week?" I ask Delilah during our weekly powwow. I walked in with my brain working faster than my mouth, but my mouth eventually caught up and I haven't let her get a word in edgewise. "I don't want to look for more if we can't keep up with demand. We're busy all the time, but are there certain items in demand? Can cupcakes be in demand? Help me out here."

She narrows her eyes and purses her lips before responding and that makes me think I should just keep talking, but I'm not going to. I refrain. Which is really difficult because after the shit with Hannah this morning, I am like a firecracker ready to go off.

Delilah closes her notebook and places her bright pink pen on top as she contemplates what she's going to say.

And I wait, uncomfortably, in the quiet of her home kitchen while all the emotions begin to seep into my body.

"What happened?" Two simple words. One simple ask. She rolls her eyes when I don't respond right away. "You've been talking since you walked through the door. I hardly got a hello and you can't stay still in that chair. What is going on that's got you all riled up?"

"That's a loaded question."

"It doesn't have to be. Break it down for me."

I sit quietly clicking my pen, pushing my hair off my face, crossing and uncrossing my legs, and am completely incapable of figuring out the starting point for this conversation. There is no starting point, just a place to jump off and bounce around from.

She sees me struggling. As long as we've been friends, I'm still not used to letting her see me as anything but happy. But, if she weren't a true friend she wouldn't be sitting here telling me it's okay to talk about my problems.

"Just break it down, Maggie," she says, encouragingly in a tone of voice I've heard her use time and again to help calm her kids when they're trying to process hard things.

So, I do. I tell her about Hannah at the coffee shop and Hannah dropping Sawyer's stuff at the house. I confide in her about the almost whoops at the holidays and how I was not prepared for the barrage of feelings about that. I break down about Gram and my mom and how even with Mom being around more because she's not going to be working, I still feel so overwhelmed all the time. I break down about Gram mixing people up more, occasionally losing control of her functions, but still insisting on doing her hair each morning the same way she's done it for fifty years. I talk a blue streak about Harper and all the help she's given us because we're all so fucking clueless, and how grateful Mom and I are that my boyfriend's family is willing to step up and lend a helping hand even though they hardly know us.

"I mean, with the exception of Harper, none of them know us, but still. I've heard him on the phone with his parents, and they're ready to come hang out with Gram if we need them. I don't know what that's like, Lilah. My own uncles are far enough away they can't or won't offer, and here's Maverick's mom and dad saying, 'Just let us lock up and we'll be there in two hours'." I drop my face into my hands as the exhaustion hits after giving words to everything I've kept inside. "I have family, but it's like, holy shit, this is what family is supposed to do."

When I lift my head, she's smiling at me and my brain is so all over the place, I'm not sure if it's her "I understand" smile or her "You're finally understanding" smile or her "God, you're stupid" smile.

"I think the thing keeping me sane is Sawyer. She's a kid, and Maverick makes sure she still gets to act like a kid, and he acts like a kid, and … Lilah, before them I don't remember the last time I really acted like a kid. Had fun. Did something just because it brought me joy," I say. "With the exception of going into work and getting to create every day, I stopped doing other things that brought me joy."

She nods in agreement, her smile softening and it's definitely her "you're finally understanding" smile.

"That's why Fish and I stopped working non-stop when the kids moved home. That's why family dinners with Gen and Jax are so important to us and if there's a school event we both always try to go," she says. "Do not lose yourself in an effort to help others find themselves. That's not your job."

"I think I need to have a conversation with my mom."

"I think you do, too."

Tapping my pen against my notebook.

"Do you think she'll panic if I tell her I think we should move Gram to her house? After all my insistence on keeping her at her home for as long as we can? I've taken on more than I can handle and it's been purely so others didn't have to. I don't want to see my parents have to stop living their lives, but it would be lovely to be able to live mine, too."

There's the "I understand" smile and I know I'm making the right choice by talking to Delilah about everything happening, especially since it all feels like it's happening too fast.

"Mags, I think if you talk to your mom and Gram, they're going to understand and work with you to figure it all out. Gram has been in your corner since you were born. If you're getting burned out, she already knows it. She's not going to want you to burn out because of her."

My entire body feels limp, as if a rag doll took over my limbs, and I slouch back in the chair. Delilah leans forward, placing her hand on my knee.

"If you need someone there with you and Rick can't be, I can have that conversation with your mom and Gram with you. You don't need to do any of this alone," she says, and it's as if she's been talking to Maverick since he also insists that I'm not in this by myself.

I've already decided I'm going to do it alone. Unfortunately. Or maybe fortunately. It will give us three women a chance to really figure things out. I'm perfectly capable of talking to my mom and grandmother about life. We always have been able to have hard talks, and we're good at it. Maybe that's why this is so difficult — I'm slowly losing one of my best friends and there's nothing we can do about it, so I've tried to have control over what I can control.

"Thank you for helping me figure out my life," I say quietly.

"I'm always here to help. It's not like you haven't done the same for me."

And with that, we spend the remainder of the afternoon sorting out business, making sure we aren't overloading ourselves, and discussing the very real need of hiring on at least one extra helping hand.

*****

"I cannot believe you!"

That's what I got the moment I walked into the kitchen at Maverick's house after unearthing all my emotions about Gram during my planning meeting with Delilah. Cannot catch a break today.

"Is Mercury in retrograde again?" Maverick asks, entering the kitchen completely unaware of what's happening.

"I thought you loved my dad. I thought you loved me! How could you?" Sawyer says, tears streaking down her face.

Maverick holds his hands up and stops, triangulating our little group, his eyes flitting from my face to Sawyer's. His eyebrows pinch together as he looks back to me, hoping to find an answer.

"What did she say to you?"

"Oh, so you're not even going to deny it?"

"Sawyer, there's nothing to deny because there's nothing that occurred," I say, trying to keep my voice even. Like Delilah just did with me, I tell myself.

Maverick, still confused but trying to let me handle it, places a kiss on my cheek and maneuvers around us to get to the stove. Dinner smells delicious and my stomach reminds me that I haven't eaten since the scone I shared with Alex.

"Well apparently something happened because she wouldn't have texted me otherwise," she says, wiping tears from her face. "She hasn't bothered to text for anything else."

There's a conversation without words happening between me and Maverick, and when he finally clues himself in and things click, he asks Sawyer for her phone.

"It's my phone."

"Now. You know the rules," he says in a tone I haven't heard.

She begrudgingly pulls the device from her back pocket and slaps it into the palm of his hand.

My brain works overtime, trying to figure out why if her mother hasn't contacted her — even for her birthday — she would believe a damn thing that woman says.

"'Saw your new mom kissing some guy at the coffee shop'," Maverick reads from the phone. He glances in my direction, his eyebrow raised, before going back to reading. "'Your dad really knows how to pick 'em, huh?'"

He opens his mouth to say something and chooses to close it. I'm not even aware of what's happening anymore. He and Sawyer have become so much more to me than just "my boyfriend and his kid." I stand there dumbstruck as he pulls Sawyer out of the kitchen, carefully leading her to her bedroom, and I wait.

I wait even though everything in me is screaming to grab my bag and leave before he can break my heart. I wait because, if he thinks for one second I'll give him up without a fight, he's going to need to get his head on straight. When he emerges from the back of the house what feels like hours later, he's clearly distraught.

There's no point waiting longer for him to speak, and I pull the bandage off.

"I don't know what she hoped to accomplish, but that text message about seeing me at the Jumping Bean with Alex — it was Alex, Maverick, who I haven't ever had romantic feelings for so why the fuck would I start now when I'm in love with you? — and she made it sound as though she caught me making out with him," I say, exasperated. "Either you can trust me it's a lie and listen to the truth, or believe your ex-wife and I'll just grab my toothbrush real quick and leave."

And I'm back to waiting for him to say something. Anything.

"I know she's not the most trustworthy, but if she didn't see that, what did she see?" he asks, and even if he doesn't intend to sound like he's accusing me of anything, that's exactly how it comes out. I'm grateful he wants my version, and even though I know I've done nothing wrong, I still feel like I'm going to throw up over the fact Hannah worked her magic on Sawyer and it's working on Maverick, too.

Taking a deep breath, I pull a hair tie from my pocket and shove my hair up into a messy bun. This is a conversation for an updo. Before I let my mouth run, I hear a distant squeak of a door hinge.

"What she saw was me kissing my friend on the cheek as I congratulated him," I say, making sure to speak loudly so Sawyer can hear me from where I'm sure she's listening in her bedroom with the door ajar. "Alex has been stuck, not loving his job at the college but not sure what else he wants to do. He decided to go back for his doctorate instead of living on pennies from playing gigs at the local bars and being an adjunct. It's a big deal for him."

I stop and realize my chest is heaving because I've been talking without taking breaks for air.

"I hate her," I say a little quieter when he doesn't say anything. "I don't hate people, Maverick, but I hate her."

My bottom lip quivers and I try to pull it back, biting it to keep it from showing how mad I am. When I let the dam break, it's going to be a barrage of pissed off tears, not sad ones.

"Look at what she's doing to Sawyer. Don't you see it?" I ask, my voice even and the words calculated. Maybe if I just keep talking, he'll understand. "It is one thing to have words with me, but a completely different thing to mess with a kid who I love like I've known her her entire life. How dare she. How dare she play with her own child's head just because she's mad that you're happy. She knows exactly what she saw at the coffeehouse and she knows exactly what she was doing when she worded that text the way she did. It doesn't take a rocket scientist to figure that out."

I'm not sure what I expect, but he hasn't moved closer to me. He hasn't spoken. I said my peace. He's capable of participating in this conversation, and he isn't. Hannah got what she wanted — Maverick and Sawyer questioning my faithfulness — and that's more than I can handle tonight.

Grabbing my bag, I walk out the door.

He doesn't stop me.

Chapter 26

Maverick

"Sawyer. We need to talk," I say as soon as the door closes.

I can't go after her. Not yet. She said what needed to be said and I stood there, feeling overwhelmed and unable to comfort her. I don't know how to after being blindsided by Sawyer's accusation. Now I have to have a really parental conversation with my daughter, something I've done before but not to this degree. Hannah has never caused an issue like this before.

When Sawyer doesn't come out to the kitchen immediately, I say it again only much, much louder. I'm no fool. She stood right there in the doorway and listened to what Maggie had to say. She's obviously going to be worried that I'm mad. Unfortunately, she should be because I am.

"I know you heard me, now get out here."

It's too late to drink coffee, not the right situation to have alcohol, and I'm not a tea drinker. I pull a Mason jar from the cupboard and fill it full from the tap, then chug it. My mouth is so dry it feels like I'll choke on my words before they have a chance to form.

Sawyer slowly creeps out to the kitchen. Facing the sink, I don't see her, but I can feel her there and I know she can feel the anger radiating off me. I'm not sure who I'm mad at more — myself for not immediately telling Maggie I believe her, Hannah for putting our daughter in the middle of something that isn't even anything, or Sawyer for reacting instead of asking questions first. Hannah is in first place, but I'm a close second, I think. Sawyer is a teenager, and though she's a really intelligent kid, she's still only a kid and I can't expect her to be able to break it all down and digest the information without getting her emotions involved. Not when her mother is such a hot button topic.

That doesn't excuse the behavior toward Maggie, though.

"Jumping to conclusions should be a board game, not something we do with people we care about. Get your head on straight where your mother is concerned," I say, turning away from the sink to lean against the counter. My parenting style has never been tough love. I don't like the idea of it and it's not how I was raised. But, I'm not going to mince words with her that the behavior isn't okay with me. Her eyes are red-rimmed, but as much as I feel for my kid, this needs to be dealt with with more than a hug and telling her things will be okay. I don't know if they'll be okay. "We just talked about how little she has to do with you and now you're going to believe her word over a woman who has dropped everything for you when you need her? That's not what family does."

Placing her hands over her face, I watch her shoulders shudder with silent sobs. The worst part is wanting to hug her but knowing she needs to get it out. As much as it sucks, she needs a good cry, and she needs to know why she's upset.

"I know. I know Maggie loves me and I don't know why I would believe Mom and I hate myself for being this way," she says, drawing in a ragged breath. Her voice rising, she continues, "Don't you think I hate doing things to make her like me? Do you really think I enjoy pandering for her attention?"

"So why do it?"

I used to do it, too. I tried for so long to do things that would make Hannah love me and I just couldn't anymore. I was exhausted from losing myself to keep her happy. She's part of the reason I didn't move forward with the maple trees. I didn't let myself get too into landscaping until she left me because she always argued that I worked too much as it was. She fought with me that I didn't give her enough attention instead of her trying to be part of the growth with me.

"I don't know. Maybe deep down I think she'll like me if I'm just like her."

"Hannah doesn't even like herself, Pumpkin. Don't reduce yourself to her level when you've always been so far above it. You are so much better than her."

The itch to hug her begs to be scratched, but I know she has more to say first. Hopefully, it's a way to rectify the situation with my girlfriend.

"Maggie is going to hate me."

"Maggie is going to hate me more. I let her walk out without a fight," I say, smiling sadly. "Next to you, I think she's the best thing that's ever happened to me."

"I am so sorry I'm fucking things up for you," she says as fresh tears make tracks down her cheeks.

"You're not, though. We're learning lessons together. And now we're going to have to work to win her back."

We stare at one another, each trying to figure out how to fix what we broke. I know couples go through things worse than this and can come through okay on the other side. I don't want to just be okay, though, because I can't imagine a life without Maggie in it.

"Our apology is going to have to be pretty epic," I say. I run my hands through my hair and lock my fingers at the back of my neck. Taking a deep breath, I slowly exhale, hoping it will help calm the pain in my chest. "I really don't want to lose Maggie because of your mother. I refused to open up to anyone before Mags came into our lives, Sawyer. I can't lose her when she's the only partner who's ever felt right for me."

I'm not sure how Sawyer feels about my honesty. I don't want to overstep the boundaries about relationships with my kid, but I also need her to know that regardless of the short amount of time Maggie and I have been together, she's definitely become the one I want to spend forever with. I see that for us. To give her up now? It's not something I can fathom.

"You know, Mom wasn't completely wrong with what she said in her text," Sawyer says. Seeing my shocked expression, she smiles. Not a big, happy one, but a small one that makes my heart hurt for her as much as it's hurting for me. "Maggie is my new mom and you do know how to pick them. She's perfect for us. I just hope she takes us back."

"Me too, Pumpkin. Me too."

Chapter 27

Maggie

Sitting in the chair beside her bed, I pull the flimsy hospital blanket up over my shoulders and try to get comfortable. We've been here all night, but she's just been moved to a room in the last hour. Mom and I are taking shifts.

Releasing a sigh, I look at Gram, content and mildly sedated.

"I promised I wouldn't let them take you out of your house, but you're making me feel like a fool," I whisper in the dim light.

Maverick let me walk out nearly a week ago, he didn't come after me, and instead of reaching out to him, I've allowed myself to get all up in my head. I didn't pay attention when I heard her open her bedroom door after going in to rest yesterday afternoon. My brain didn't register that she was moving around the kitchen, but why would it? She's always in the kitchen. She's just not been this confused before.

"You're not a fool, Margaret," she says, slowly turning her head my way. Her eyes aren't even open, and her voice is so low I strain to hear her words. "Maybe it's time we make another plan."

She's banged up from the fall, but we're fortunate nothing is broken. How I didn't hear her leave the kitchen is beyond my comprehension. She swore the steps from the kitchen to the breezeway weren't there before. And she isn't wrong, but she was in the wrong year again. Yesterday, she was heading out to check the vegetable garden in 1959 when there was a ramp instead of stairs. When she and Grandpa first built the house, he wanted them to be able to push the baby buggy into the house in case their babies were sleeping in it, instead of disturbing them. The ramp came out and the stairs went in the early 70s. I only know about the design change because Mom told me after we got to the hospital and we were able to get Gram to tell us what happened.

"I talked to Lilah about plans the other day. I'm afraid I can't do everything that you need, and I'm failing you. Astronomical failure now that you've gotten hurt," I say, reaching my fingers out to caress the papery skin on her hand.

She grips my fingers, a slight squeeze.

"You aren't failing, me or anyone else. My mind is failing us, my body is old," she says, taking a ragged breath. "Rebecca and I have had a conversation similar to you and your friend. Your parents are ready to move me in when we need them to."

"Are you sure?" I ask, my voice catching. I don't want her to change her mind because I can't handle life. I don't want her to take herself away from home because of me.

"It's not like I'm going very far. Plus, Harper is helping with extra details," she says.

Harper. My boyfriend's sister. Is he still my boyfriend? Are we still together after this?

"I'm glad we've got Harper," I say, swallowing my sadness. "What will happen with the house?"

I notice her blinking has slowed, her breathing shallow and steady, and before she can answer, she's softly snoring. Our hands are still clasped and without giving it a second thought, I pull out my phone and take a picture. Someday, I won't have this with her and I want to remember it. Checking my messages, there's nothing new from anyone important.

Hearing soft footfalls enter the room, I turn just as a cup of coffee is being set on the hospital table beside me.

"I thought maybe you could use a pick me up," Mom says. I open my mouth to argue that she's supposed to be home and in bed, but she raises her hand, effectively shutting me down. I know when I won't win. "Neither of us planned to go home and stay home tonight, so don't start an argument."

I whisper "thank you" and carefully remove my hand from Gram's.

"At least she's resting. But she woke briefly," I say, taking a cautious sip of my coffee.

"Did you have a good talk?" Mom says, a half-smile lifting the corner of her mouth.

"You probably overheard a majority of it," I say, "but, yes. She was lucid so I think it was productive."

We sit in hospital-grade silence, sipping our coffees and watching Gram breathe as she rests easily for the time being.

"Nothing is going to happen to the house," Mom says out of the blue. "She's already put the deed in your name. You just need to sign the paperwork to actually take ownership. She wanted it done without you knowing because she was afraid you would fight her on it. So, whatever happens with the house is your decision. Keep it and live there, sell it and buy something else, move in with Rick and have it as an income stream. It's all up to you."

She's right. I would have fought about it. I don't say that, though, nor am I going to take for granted that she did this for me. She did it for me. She's making sure I have a home that isn't my parents' house.

"I wish I could say more than just 'thank you' but I don't know what else I could say." Wiping my face to clear the exhaustion and the few small tears that have snuck out, I try to come up with the words to properly show my appreciation … and I can't. "I don't even know if moving in with Maverick is an option, but I'm glad I have a place to call home."

She cocks an eyebrow in my direction and takes another sip from her cup. She's asking questions without asking them and I lean into my mom as a confidant.

"We had a fight," I say. Picking at the opening in my cup lid, I say, "His ex made some nasty assumptions and put Sawyer in the middle. She accused me of cheating on her dad, I accused him of taking Hannah's side, and when I walked out, he didn't come after me."

"You haven't talked to him since?"

"Nope. Not so much as a text message," I say, looking at her sadly. "I thought I saw him drive by the bakery the other day, but if it was him he didn't stop and come in."

"Oh, baby girl."

I won't let myself cry more. I've already cried my tears about this and I just need to figure out if it's fixable. The last thing I want is for Sawyer to think I would ever do something like that to her dad … or her. I have known from the moment we got involved that Maverick and Sawyer are a package deal. My involvement with them will not replace her mother, but I can certainly attempt to be a good substitute.

Mom places her hand on my knee and pats it. It reminds me of all the times I needed to be reminded I was loved as a child. Hardheaded I might be, but my emotions frequently got the best of me, and we'd all be fools to think that's not still the case.

"Maybe he's trying to figure out how to handle the situation. It can't be easy for him, either, with a teenager and an ex-wife in the mix," she says. "Give him time."

213

"It's been five days."

Her eyes widen, but she recovers quickly.

"Don't give him too much more time. It would probably do you both some good to have time together without Sawyer, too," she says. I look at her, my brain immediately wondering how that would work if we are actually breaking up. "You know, if that's an option still."

Biting my thumbnail, I stay quiet and take the time to snuggle in and consider the possibilities.

*****

Waking up in a hospital recliner that leaves very much to be desired, the first thing I notice is the sun streaming through the window. It's deceiving because I know it's actually cold outside, but the sun makes it feel like there could be a break from it and perhaps some springlike weather. False spring. I'd rather have false spring than consistently grey winter, so I guess I'll take it.

"Morning, sleepyhead."

Mom hands me a muffin and a fresh cup of coffee.

"Thanks. I can't remember if I even ate yesterday," I say, taking a bite of the orange cranberry bread. "Have you talked to the uncles about what happened?"

My heart tells me they aren't going to blame me for her fall. My head is giving a different story.

"I did. They're all worried about how you're reacting to it. They know how much you have tried to keep Gram safe and don't want you to feel like you've done anything wrong."

I nod. In the weeks since they were home for the big family discussion, Uncle Phil has gotten the other two to come around more to my perspective on things. I just don't want them to second guess anything.

"The good thing is we've all agreed on Gram coming to stay at our house and no one is willing to pick a fight with me. The advantage of being the baby sister, even if I am a grown up now," she says. "Plus, having Harper involved gives us more leeway."

They want formalities and strategy, and Harper can give them that. I just want her safe and somewhere that isn't unfamiliar.

"Any idea when we can abscond with Gram and sleep in real beds?" I ask quietly as Gram begins to stir in the bed.

"Abscond?" she questions me with a raised eyebrow and a smirk.

"I was doing crosswords before you came back last night."

"Noted," she replies. "Not sure on the absconding. We need to wait for the doctor to come in, but between you and me, I'd like it if they kept her one more night. It'll give us time to figure out logistics for moving her to the house with me and Daddy."

"He's not coming to see her, is he?"

My dad doesn't love hospitals, and I can't blame him. I don't particularly care for them myself, but this is Gram. You'd think he would at least pop in for a few minutes.

"Probably not. It brings back too many memories for him."

I sigh, resignedly, and drop the subject. I don't want to talk about all the bad things that happen in hospitals, anyway. Gram cautiously opens her eyes, giving me a small smile. She's been awake for a few minutes now, but let Mom and I have this time.

Kissing her on the forehead, Mom wishes her a good morning. This is harder on my mom than she's letting on, but we're going to figure it out. We'll figure it all out. Just us girls.

Within minutes a man in a button-down dress shirt and slacks enters the room. If the stethoscope hanging around his neck wasn't a dead giveaway that he was the physician, the badge claiming "DOCTOR" in bold, red letters clipped to his pocket would be. He takes time to introduce himself, but I don't recognize his name. I do what I can to not end up at the hospital, you know?

"You're a tough woman, Norma. Do you want to go home today or think you need an extra day with us?" he asks, settling himself on the edge of her bed. Sliding the stethoscope from his collar, he begins his exam, listening intently to her back.

"If all the doctors are as handsome as you, I'll stay," she says, chuckling despite Mom and I giving obviously mortified looks.

He smiles, moving the diaphragm of his stethoscope from her back to her chest. Satisfied with her lungs and heart, he pops the ear tips out and pats her on the arm. Carefully placing his fingers on her wrist, he tips his arm so he can watch the time as he checks her pulse.

"I'm not sure if they're all as handsome as me, but I do think it would be best to keep you for an extra day."

"Any particular reason?" Mom asks.

"She took a pretty nasty spill, and though I don't see anything that would require her to stay, I am worried about the bruising on her leg," he says, standing from his seat beside Gram on the bed. "My biggest concern is the possibility of blood clots, so I want to be proactive given her age and the memory issues you brought up last night."

Mom and I both nod. Those are solid reasons and we can't argue with him.

"So, we'll keep her today for observation, and then tomorrow get her ready to go home," he says. Turning to Gram, he gives her a thumbs up, and asks, "Sound good to you?"

"Perfect," she says.

*****

With things settled at the hospital, I allowed myself to be convinced to leave for a while. I stopped at the house only long enough to throw myself through a seven-minute shower, put my hair up in a messy bun, and pull on clean clothes. Then I went to the bakery.

My biceps start hurting after the first five minutes of mixing and kneading. I've decided to branch out — with Lilah's blessing — and try my hand at cinnamon rolls. I know Brian and Tommy have theirs at the coffeeshop, but I needed something new. This is going to be a weekly special, and I'm pouring everything into it today. It takes my mind off things that shouldn't matter and keep them from taking over.

I'm midway through rolling out a batch of dough when Delilah sidles up next to me and holds her phone in front of my face. I don't even have to ask what it is. I recognize Sawyer's handwriting right away.

"Are these her plans for Gram's house?" Delilah asks. "The girl has talent."

"Yeah, she does," I respond, but that's all I can say. I don't want to get into it. I don't want to hear how Gen has talked to Sawyer about what happened and that she and Maverick know they were assholes. What I want is an apology from both of them because I deserve one. It's been nearly a week and nothing from either of them. "I need the butter."

"Please."

I take a deep breath so I don't scream.

"I need the butter, please."

"You need to talk to them," she says, handing me the container and my cinnamon brown sugar mix. "You know they're sorry. Talk to them."

I stop in the middle of spreading butter on the dough and stare at her.

"And would you just talk to Fisher had he accused you of cheating on him? In a very public place? Knowing full well you know half the fucking county and it would have gotten back to him?" I say, holding back tears. When she says nothing, I answer for her, "I didn't think so. So why should I make the first move?"

She doesn't step out of my way, so I work around her.

"Because you're hurting and it's going to affect a lot more than your relationships with Rick and Sawyer," she says, cryptically.

I can plug-and-play her thoughts, though. It's going to mess up my relationship with Genevieve because Gen and Sawyer are dating. It's already messed up keeping Gram in her own house because I was too in my head about a guy and she got hurt. It's just going to screw me up in general because I'm never going to want to put myself out there for anyone ever again. There's a reason I didn't go on many dates before meeting Maverick.

Looking at her phone again, and then at me, Delilah says in a hushed voice, "Just think about it. I'll support you no matter your decision, but I think it would be worthwhile to let them explain their side."

"Thanks. I'll take it into consideration," I say, swiping my forearm across my face.

I don't have the energy for any of this today. I just want to hide away in my work and have people leave me alone.

When I start spreading the filling, she walks away.

Conversation over.

M.L. Pennock

Chapter 28

Maverick

It's been a week since she left. I haven't reached out, though I've started and deleted a hundred text messages. I haven't dialed her number, despite my finger hovering over her name in my call log. I've driven past the bakery more in the last few days than I care to admit, always with the excuse that I need to go to town for something.

I don't know how to apologize, even though she's done nothing wrong. I'm punishing myself for my ex-wife's stupidity. In turn, I'm probably — likely — punishing Maggie, too. It's wrong of me to not talk to her, and I'm going to remedy that as soon as I can. As soon as I have things in place. What those things are, I haven't got a clue.

"Hey Rick, how's it going?" Will asks coming into the sugar shack. I wave a response as I top off a small bottle of deep amber liquid gold. "How's Gram doing? I heard she was in the hospital, but I haven't been up to visit yet."

Slipping out of my hand, that bottle no longer exists as it lands on the gravel, the top breaking off and the maple syrup flowing like water into the ground.

"What did you say?" I ask, thinking I must have heard him wrong.

He looks at me like I have multiple heads, a question playing in his eyes. That question is, "What the fuck, Rick?"

Instead, he says, "Gram has been in the hospital since last night. How did you not know?"

"Maggie and I had a fight."

I keep it simple for my sake.

"You best correct it." His eyes aren't filled with compassion — the kind of expression I'm used to from Will — but rather it's his "I'm not messing with you, get yourself together" look.

"I'm going to." I take a quick look at him as I continue picking up the glass shards on the ground. He hasn't budged, still standing with his arms crossed over his chest, his hat pulled low. He's waiting for me to explain, so I try my best. "It was a week ago. Hannah started some shit, got Sawyer in the middle. I haven't talked to her since she walked out, but I don't think it's a breakup."

Will scratches the scruff on his chin thoughtfully.

"It might be a breakup. It sounds like it could have been a break up," he says, matter-of-factly. Lifting his hat and scratching the top of his head, he continues, "If she didn't do anything wrong, what are you waiting for? You're a fool if you think she's going to come back all on her own."

"I know. I've just been scared to. I think I'm more afraid of going to her and Maggie saying we're through than living in limbo."

"You should talk to her instead of being stubborn … and if she takes you back maybe consider that mini vacation without Sawyer that we talked about, Stupid Head."

I give him a "yes, sir" because at this point there is no other way to respond. He's an authority on Maggie, and I'm still learning how to love her the best way I can along with figuring out how to love myself. But the truth is, I don't want to talk about what's going on with Maggie, or Hannah, or tell him that his assessment of me being stupid is probably spot on. I'm grateful he doesn't mince words with me, because I don't want shit sugarcoated.

"What happened with Gram?" I ask to clear the silence, dropping a handful of glass in the garbage bin.

"Becky said she fell down the stairs from the kitchen. I guess she was heading out to the backyard to check the garden," he says.

Without me asking for help, he begins working on bottling what's left of the syrup so we can stock the pantry. There really isn't enough to sell, so this year is our trial-and-error year. We've burned some sap, we've had some crystalize, and we've had some that turns out perfect. I definitely should have researched this endeavor more before agreeing to the task, but Sawyer and Maggie were so excited to try our hands at maple syrup. The research has been on the fly and we really haven't done that bad at it.

"There isn't a garden in the back yet." We're still in the planning phases for the garden. Sawyer is using this entire week off school for break to design and prep what she thinks Gram might like for the flowers and vegetable patch. It's literally a bare back yard that's brown and sad without any snow coverage because everything has melted. False spring is what we all call it.

Will looks at me as he caps the jug in his hand and sadly says, "To quote Maggie, 'She was in the wrong year.' Simple as that."

"It's never as simple as it sounds. Is she getting worse?" I ask him the questions I should be asking Maggie, and I feel my heart squeeze in my chest because I miss her.

With the last jar capped, we carry the bottles to the house. There's fresh coffee and chocolate chip cookies in there and it's warm, so maybe he won't want to kill me for my behavior if I feed him.

"I wouldn't say she's getting worse, but things are getting more difficult," he says, pulling his cap off and settling in at the table.

The jars are lined up on the counter and I leave them be for the moment, knowing I need to reorganize the cupboard to fit them all or take them to the basement and put them up on the shelves for our overflow. Setting the plate of cookies in front of him that Sawyer left out cooling he gets a giddy smile on his face. Maybe he'll accept it as a peace offering, I tell myself as I pour two mugs of coffee.

"So, things are getting more difficult. What does that mean? Maggie isn't going to be able to handle it much longer. She loves Gram with her entire being, but she needs someone to take over the daily activity," I say. There are only so many days in a week that Gram is going to want to come hang with me at the office before my season gets busy, and Maggie and Lilah have a growing business that requires their attention. They can't always have Gram at the bakery. "With Becky retiring, I know she's stepping up, and she should be. It's her mom. And the uncles should get involved more, too."

Will chuckles. "Gee, Rick, tell me how you really feel," he snickers again, lifting his mug to his mouth. "I don't disagree with you at all, though. Maggie has a huge heart and wants to save everyone, from puppies to grumpy tree farmers, you know? But she bites off more than she can chew a lot."

"Ouch. That hurts. I'm not a project."

"You absolutely are a project, but in a good way. She's brought you out of your shell. She's been great for your daughter. She's got you both involved in things you wouldn't normally care about. Mags is good for you, but she's put more on her plate than she can eat," he says. He points to a spot behind me and says, "Just ask that one. She knows."

Before I can turn around, Sawyer joins us at the table, notebook in hand.

"Genevieve says Maggie cried all week. At work. At her house. At Gram's. She's exhausted. I wish I could take back everything that happened and tell Mom to fuck off," she says, the word rolling off her tongue without hesitation.

"Language. But I agree."

"I miss her," Sawyer whispers. "I don't want to make her more mad at me, though. So I haven't called or texted her. I'm just afraid I'm going to mess it up more."

"We're messing it up more by not going to her, Pumpkin."

We sit quietly, drinking coffee and eating cookies, and I know we're all thinking about ways to fix what I broke.

"They're moving Gram to Becky's house, if that helps with your plans for how to grovel and get her back," Will says.

"I don't know if it will help, but it won't hurt if I'm going to take her away for a weekend," I say. "That would greatly reduce the level of worry."

"Am I staying home alone if you're going away?"

"Probably not," I say, having put zero thought into that part of the plan. The plan that will only work if Maggie doesn't hate me. "We can talk to Fisher and Delilah about you staying with them or, depending on where we go, I could see if Grandma and Grandpa want you for a weekend."

She nods, agreeable with either option, but would likely prefer staying with her girlfriend for the weekend.

"Do her parents know you and Gen are seeing each other?" I ask, forgetting Will is sitting with us and I potentially just outed my own child before she was ready. I'm hovering in new territory and still getting used to the terrain. Parenting is not for the faint of heart.

"They do," she says, looking to Will, who gives her a smile.

"And things are good there?" I ask.

"They are a thousand percent supportive of her and me and us. When we told Lilah and Fisher we were dating, Lilah laughed and was like, 'Do you really think I didn't know?' and then she hugged us," Sawyer says, smiling.

"I bet it felt really good to have a mom accept you for you," I say, not thinking about what I'm saying.

"Maggie does accept me," she responds, her voice barely above a whisper. "We need to get her back, Dad."

222

Just like that we begin putting ideas on paper. The three of us work though the plans for Gram's garden, because even though things might be up in the air about the house now that Gram is moving, she still hired me to do the landscaping. The vegetable garden, the flower beds, the tea table and chairs are all drawn in Sawyer's notebook. The tinted pencils come out and she adds pops of color to the sketch until I can practically smell the lavender and rosemary.

"It's perfect. I think it's perfect. Hopefully Gram likes it, too," I say as Sawyer pulls her phone out and snaps a picture.

"I'll let you know if she thinks it's good enough," she says, getting up from the table and walking away with her eyes glued to the screen, typing furiously.

My coffee has gotten cold, but I drink it anyway. Will glances my way and raises an eyebrow.

"What just happened?" he asks.

Clearing my throat, I respond, "That was my kid fixing my broken heart."

"She sent it to Maggie?"

"More than likely. Or she sent it to Lilah who will show it to Maggie," I say. "And there's always the possibility she sent it to Becky who will show it to Gram who will tell Maggie and if that's the way it happens, Maggie will either show up here within the next few hours or call."

Will nods his head slowly as he tries to follow the thought pattern.

"Women are a lot of work," he says. "Maybe that's why I've stayed single."

We get up from the table to head back outside and I clap him on the shoulder.

"A lot of work, yes, but I'm learning that the right ones are worth every exasperating moment."

*****

When no one shows up by early afternoon and my phone hasn't rung, I'm not sure what to think. I was hopeful Maggie would call me, but I should know better. By dinner, I was a wreck and Sawyer told me we need to stop being stupid and go to Maggie.

We drive by the house, but the lights are off and her car isn't in the driveway. We make our way out to the hospital, but visiting hours are over and we didn't see Maggie's car in any of the lots we checked. Finally, I drive by the bakery after hours once the sun has long since set and, though the lights in the front of the store are turned off, I can see a faint glow in the back shining through. Her car isn't out front, so I check the back lot, and sure enough Maggie's still at work.

"Gen said she's been working all sorts of weird hours," Sawyer says from the passenger seat.

I swing into the space beside her, and cut the engine.

"What are we doing here? She's not going to want to talk to me and I can't just walk in there because the doors are locked," I say.

"You think she actually locks the back door when she's here working?"

I turn and stare at my kid.

"She better lock that door. It's not safe to be in a building alone at night. Anything could happen."

"Right. Yes. I agree. Just checking." She smiles and I narrow my eyes at her. "Just checking."

"You're up to something," I say, reaching for the handle and pushing the door open. "I don't like it. I feel like you know something."

"Gen might have told me Maggie doesn't usually lock the back until she leaves, but you never know. She might have today," she says, shrugging nonchalantly.

Closing the door, I don't wait for Sawyer to get out of the truck before I'm at the back door of the bakery, pulling it open without meeting resistance. By the time I'm through the door, Sawyer is on my heels.

"Why would you not lock the damn door when you're here alone?" I hear come out of my mouth before the words register in my brain. Sawyer runs into my back since I stopped moving so quickly when I laid eyes on Maggie.

Her apron is coated in flour and frosting, a dusting of cocoa on one cheek, and her dirty blonde hair is on top of her head in the sexiest messy bun. Shock forms on her face a second before she realizes who said it and then I see an expression I never want to see again. Not on her. The mix of anger and devastation as she slams down the bowl in her hands on the counter kills me.

Hands on her hips, she stares me dead in the eyes and says, "Who says I'm here alone?"

I fumble for words, having not thought this through at all. She absolutely could be there with someone.

"Your car is the only one in the bakery parking spots," I say, stuttering through the words.

"Am I not allowed to work alone? In the quiet? I can't get it right lately. I'm not supposed to have coffee with other people and now I can't work alone," she fires. "Which is it? Am I allowed to be around people or no? Do I need your permission?"

Looking to the space beside me, Sawyer might as well be taking notes the way she's tuned into the conversation. I'm overcome with a feeling of defeat. As if this short interaction is going to seal my fate with this woman. I don't like it and I'm silent as I try to figure out what to say next. What can I say to fix it when I know "sorry" isn't enough?

"I need an answer from you, Maverick. I haven't slept much. I haven't eaten a whole lot. I've cried more over you than every other guy I ever liked combined. So be honest with me," she says. "Is this the kind of relationship where I need your permission before I do something with a friend? Do I need your 'yes' prior to enjoying coffee with another person? And do I actually need your permission to work all hours of the night, sometimes alone, because I have big dreams, too?"

"No," I say. It's the easiest 'no' I have ever given and I give it to her while I'm on the brink of tears. I don't want to be the reason she loses herself or doesn't chase her future. "You never have to ask my permission. I trust you and never should have let Hannah's manipulation allow that trust to waver. Not for a minute."

Looking to Sawyer thoughtfully and then back to Maggie, I continue, "I should have let Sawyer have her tantrum and heard the entire story first. I know what kind of person my ex-wife is and what she did to you, and to Sawyer, is one of the biggest reasons she's my ex."

Switching from me to Sawyer, Maggie addresses my teenager. Part of me wants to defend my kid, but I can't. She knows what she did. She knows what her mother did. We've had all of those conversations.

"And what about you? Do I need your permission to have guy friends while I'm with your dad? Or to work crazy hours? Does it matter as long as I show up for you? Because, Sawyer, I've showed up a lot in the few months we've been together," she says, pointing between the three of us. Her cheeks are flaming red, and I feel the heaviness of how this has been weighing on her for days. "I know I'm not perfect, but I fucking show up, and if me doing that for you isn't enough, say so. I can try harder or I can walk away, but you have to tell me which it is because I'm not a mind reader."

It takes less than a heartbeat for my daughter to fall apart, hurling herself across the room and into Maggie's arms, burying her face in her apron and saying over and over, "I'm sorry. I'm so sorry."

Stepping toward the girls, I wrap them both up in my arms, holding my entire world together as best I can, because they are everything to me. My entire world is crying in the kitchen of the Bakery on Main and, somehow, it works for us. It feels like it had to happen this way.

She wouldn't have come to us.

We had to come to her.

*****

"You're going to be famous someday for these cookies," Sawyer says, taking another creation from the cooling rack.

"Famous in a small town, maybe, but I don't need anything more than this," Maggie says, breaking her own cookie in half and handing me a piece.

"What's this one going to be called?" I ask, despite having an idea. It's got marshmallow, chocolate, graham cracker, espresso powder, and toffee in it. It's got to be a new version of her s'mores cookie, but the coffee and toffee are throwing me off. I flash her a knowing smile anyway.

"The Breakup," she deadpans. Then she shrugs. My jaw drops and I laugh. Rolling her eyes, she says, "You had to see that coming."

"Did not, but it's a perfect name. Just enough coffee flavor to not be overpowering, mixes well with heartache and misery. That should be the description," I say, tossing the rest in my mouth and brushing the crumbs from my hands into the sink. "When is Gram coming home?"

Once the tears stopped and we all caught our breath, we had the family conversation we needed to about expectations — what I expect from my kid and my relationship with Maggie, what Maggie wants from me and Sawyer, and what Sawyer needs from us — which brought us around finally to talking about Gram's fall and impending move to Becky's house.

"Supposed to be tomorrow. It gave my mom and dad time to set up a temporary spot for Gram in my old bedroom since it's downstairs. It's not that she can't do stairs, you know? But the name of the game is safety," she says as she and Sawyer start filling packages with cookies.

I don't know if she likes watching me work, but I can say for certain I love being involved when she's in her element. I'm glad I was here to taste test tomorrow's special, even if I'm the reason it was created.

"Is Aunt Harper coming to help get her settled?" Sawyer asks.

"She is. She's going to meet us at the house and walk us through anything else we could do to keep Gram comfortable while she's healing, which is really amazing of her. I don't know if that's part of her job, but we're grateful."

Having a sister who has an in with the elderly is proving beneficial. I sent her a text message after Will told me Gram fell and, after she lit into me for being an idiot, she told me she was calling Becky to find out what she could do to help. Just like Maggie, though, I don't know if that is part of her job … or if it's just because my sister is like the rest of us and has a huge heart.

"Can we still make her gardens even if she isn't living there?" Sawyer asks. I know this has been bugging her. She doesn't want to have promised Gram something special and then have her not get to enjoy it. "I mean, we could do it on a smaller scale if that's easier, but I don't want to not do the project for her."

Maggie and I look at each other. We haven't had a chance to talk about the house or her living there alone with Gram gone since the information is so new, so I feel like the gardens are up in the air. Pursing her lips, I watch Maggie's brain start spinning.

"We're going to go forward with that project. Even if Gram isn't living there, she won't be far away and would love to come sit and enjoy what you're creating for her," she says. "Once the weather breaks and we get some warmth for you to get working, maybe we can have Mom bring her over to oversee the project?"

Sawyer's smile is all the encouragement we need to make that happen, but her look quickly changes.

"But what's going to happen with the house if Gram isn't living there?"

Pulling another pan from the oven, I carefully commit to memory every one of Maggie's movements unafraid of the fact I'm staring at her in front of my teenager until her question hits my brain.

"Uh, yeah. You live there, but it's Gram's," I say. Chuckling, I wink at her and add, "She's going to be one hell of a landlord. Better make sure it's rent controlled so she doesn't try to charge too much."

"I don't need to worry about that. The house is mine."

"She gave you the house?" I ask incredulously.

"It was going to be mine all along. Her fall just sped things up. She doesn't want me to worry about where to go or what to do. I can live there alone. I can get a roommate. I can sell it if I want to. Or, if the opportunity arises, I can move out and rent it to someone else as an income property."

Flabbergasted, I just stare at her for a beat.

"You've put a lot of thought into this."

"Not me," she says, removing cookies from the pan. "Mom and Gram. They had it planned out all along."

Sawyer and I both let out a laugh.

"Of course they did," I say. Pushing off the counter I'm leaning against, I walk over and wrap my arms around Maggie from behind, pulling her tight to my chest so I can kiss her temple and whisper, "I love you. I love the life we're going to build together. And I love that you love us enough to not kick me to the curb."

"Oh my God, never. I would have had to start all over with a new man. No sense in throwing away a perfectly good one," she whispers back. Turning her head, she catches the corner of my mouth with a kiss and it feels like everything is going to be okay. It's all going to be alright.

Chapter 29

Maggie

"Guys, I'm still here," Sawyer says from behind us.

"We know," I say, smiling as I press my forehead against Maverick's jawline.

"Just making sure you didn't forget."

"We would never forget you," he says, lifting his chin and kissing the top of my head as he pulls away. "You look tired. About ready to call it a night?"

He's talking to Sawyer, but I know he means it for me, too, and yes. I am absolutely ready to go home, take a long shower and crawl into bed. I'm just not sure which home I'm going to.

Sawyer has worked here with us enough to know the routine for cleaning up and she starts without being told to or asking if she should. I hand her pans and bowls and utensils as she loads the dishwasher. Maverick treats the kitchen like he does the one at his house — scraping flour off the counters into the trash, wiping down all the surfaces, and then he reaches for the broom.

I'm really lucky. Some people aren't given the opportunity to be loved like this. It seems so simple, little tasks that I could manage like I do most other days when it's me and Lilah, but it's so huge because it's not my co-worker doing the job we've agreed to do. It's the guy I'm dating pitching in because I'm tired. It's his daughter stepping up because she knows the job goes faster if we work together.

I hide my smile as I take a tray of cookies out to place in the display for when we open in the morning. Delilah will be here in about four hours to get started on cupcakes, so I want this part done.

"Where are you sleeping tonight?" he asks, stepping through the café door from the kitchen, broom still in hand. As he begins sweeping up behind the counter, he asks, almost shyly, "I was wondering if you'd like to come home with us? You can drive your car, but, if I'm being honest, I haven't been sleeping great either and I think it's because your side of the bed is empty."

Is that a good idea? Probably not, but only for the fact I want to get up and get to the hospital first thing in the morning. Am I going to tell him yes? Absolutely. I need a good night of sleep and then I can adjust to my new normal of Gram not living at her house — my house — with me.

"I'd like that," I say, quietly, admitting out loud that I need him as much as he needs me. "Will Sawyer be okay with me staying over?"

He stops sweeping and leans his arm on the broom handle.

"I think we're going to have trouble keeping her from snuggling up between us," he says. I smile and laugh softly as I stand from the display case and close the door. Catching a glimpse of his face, though, the look he's giving me stops me in my tracks. "She might be sixteen, but don't put it past her. The first couple of nights without you, she cried herself to sleep. She's been as torn up as I have, but knowing she's the one who perpetuated the entire thing? She's been unbearable to live with at times this past week. She's been pretty miserable without you. We've been miserable with each other, too. Sawyer isn't the only one at fault. We should have done something about it before now, but I think deep down I thought you would just come home and I could apologize."

"You've already told me all of this. You both did. I don't want you to keep worrying about it," I say, shoving my hands in the front pocket of my apron. "Plus, this is your one and only lesson in me not apologizing if I know I am absolutely, without a doubt in my mind, not in the wrong. Only lesson. We're going to move forward from this. If I'm going to be part of your life and hers, I also need to be realistic of my expectations. Right? Isn't that what we said?"

"Yeah, but—"

"No buts. This is not going to be the thing that messes up our entire life. It's now in the past. We still have a lot of life to live, so ... conversation over," I say.

Stepping toward me, Maverick reaches for my face but bypasses my cheek and wraps his hand around the nape of my neck. His fingers curling into my hair, he pulls me toward him, slamming his mouth into mine in what can only be described as the best, most toe-curling kiss of my entire life.

"I love it when you're bossy," he says, breaking away from my lips and resting his forehead against mine. "Love it."

Chapter 30

Maverick

APRIL

Arriving at Maggie's house and not thinking about it as Gram's was awful and strange at first. It's taken me the last eight weeks to get used to it, but now that it's mid-April and I'm here everyday digging up the yard with my kid, it's not so bad.

We made the agreement once Gram moved into Becky's house that Maggie would split her time between my bed and her own. That lasted about a week before she realized she preferred good sleep over insomnia and started slowly taking over the half of my closet I had saved for her. I guess it was forward thinking when I built the house and made sure my bedroom had a closet twice as big as Sawyer's. The en suite bath is nice, too, but there are times I think she'd rather share a bathroom with the kid. She's never said anything about it, but when we spend Sunday mornings cleaning up around the house and I hear her and Sawyer talking about the messes I leave it makes me wonder.

For the record, the bathroom is probably the only place I don't immediately clean up when I'm done using it. There are beard trimmings in the sink that don't always make it down the drain when I shave and sometimes, I get toothpaste on the counter. I'd rather clean that up once a week than the dust from eye shadow and whatever else those two have going on when they get made up for the day or an evening out as a family.

And while I love seeing both my girls dressed up and feeling beautiful, I love them just as much as they are right now — dirt caked under their fingernails, messy hair, baseball caps, and filthy jeans. Maggie is absolutely in her element at the bakery and in the food truck, but she also fits perfectly here in the yard lugging wheelbarrows full of top soil and mulch. I've never known someone to be so comfortable in so many roles.

I catch myself staring as she bends over to pop another lily bulb in the ground.

"You're being creepy," Gram says beside me. She knocks her shoulder into the back of my arm and laughs as she walks past me to the camping chair we set up for her every day. "When are you going to ask her?"

"Ask her what?" I try to play it off like I don't know what she's talking about, but we both know. It's been on my mind more and more lately. Making Maggie a permanent fixture in our family is something we all want. I need her to be surprised when I ask, though.

"Don't be a smartass, Rick. If you're planning to ask her before I'm dead, you might want to get on that. I'm no spring chicken," she says, looking at me like I'm a foolish man.

Gram's had some rough days lately, but today she's here and that's important to all of us. It's more important than me asking for Maggie's hand in marriage on a whim without a plan.

"I haven't decided yet. I'd like to finish the gardens first," I say. "Problem is, by the time we're done here, I'm going to be swamped with the other jobs coming up and she's got a full schedule with the food truck and bakery expansion."

"I'm sure you'll come up with the perfect time," she says. Glancing in her direction, I see the mischievous side of Gram making an appearance. "You just let me know when you want to do it. I have something to give you."

I eye her suspiciously and nod, but before I can ask questions, Sawyer is walking over to get my opinion on the garden design now that it's coming to life.

"We need to make sure things are exactly how I want them. I only have a couple days of April break left and then I'll be at school all day and can't help," Sawyer says, dragging me away from Gram. "I don't want you messing up my hard work because you didn't give your input."

Laughing at her, I allow myself to be pulled around the yard as she points to what's being planted and where those things are going. Her enthusiasm for gardening is more than I could ask for. When she was born, I was just hoping I would have a little helper for a few years until she got bored with trees. What I got instead is a business partner and my kid as one of my best friends.

Lucky doesn't begin to describe the feelings I have today compared to where I was six months ago when she fell and sprained her ankle. The homecoming game is what kickstarted this entire phase of life and while we've endured literal pain and emotional suffering, I've had Maggie right by my side the entire time.

Everything changed that night.

All I had to do was taste the cupcake and talk to the girl, and my life was rewriting itself.

"Your brain is working overtime," Will says as he drops a wheelbarrow beside me. "What's got you all up in your head this time? Did we forget to put the weed barrier down?"

"What? No. Everything is fine," I say, turning toward Will and catching Gram's eye across the lawn. "I have a thing I need to take care of, though. Will you and the girls be okay handling this until I can get back?"

He huffs dramatically for effect, but laughs and tells me to get lost. They have everything under control and will probably work faster with me not hovering over them.

"I owe you one," I say, clapping him on the shoulder as I jog over to Gram. Once I'm in front of her, I reach my hand out and say, "Yeah. I'm ready. Whatchu got for me, Gram?"

Smiling like I've never seen before, she places her hand in my palm.

"Come. Let's go on an adventure, Maverick."

M.L. Pennock

Chapter 31

Maggie

He holds his hand out for Gram to take and gently lifts her to her feet. The smile on her face is all I need to see to know they're up to something, but I don't care. Just seeing her have a good day is worth all the shenanigans in the world.

"Where are they going?" Sawyer asks nobody in particular.

"Not sure, but wherever it is, they're gonna have fun, kiddo," Will says, shoveling a scoop of mulch from the wheelbarrow beside him. "Your dad has never been all work and no play."

"I know that. It's just …" she trails off.

Will and I look at one another, then at Sawyer.

"Nothing. It's nothing."

"If you say so," I respond, laughing.

I know I don't have to worry about Sawyer keeping secrets from me, but this is definitely toeing the line of secrecy. However, we're so close to finishing the flower bed and getting started on the vegetable patch I'm not going to let it get to me. Lifting my face to the sun and allowing it to warm my cheeks is as invigorating as doing the yardwork. I'm glad winter is (hopefully) over. In Western New York, it's not unheard of to have a snowstorm in May, so I'm just crossing my fingers we haven't jumped the gun on putting plants in the ground.

In the last several weeks things have gotten so much less complicated and I'm grateful. I've pretty much moved into Maverick and Sawyer's house and I sleep better, which was the deciding factor. We've taken time moving my things over, though if Sawyer had it her way, I would have been living there full-time the moment we moved Gram to my parents' house. I was the one holding out; I needed them to be sure they wanted me.

This week I've stayed at my house — which is still weird to say — one night and that was because I stopped to grab the extra coffee I've been hoarding in the kitchen. Maverick messaged me asking to stop and pick some up at the store on my way over, but why spend the money on new when I already had some? Exactly. But then I sat down on the couch to go through the mail and before I knew it, it was five in the morning, the alarm on my phone was going off, and I had sixteen missed calls and four text messages from Maverick. The last one read, "I assume you fell asleep at the house. See you in the morning. I love you."

Considering he's usually up by five, I called him immediately and told him I was on my way home.

Because that's what his house feels like. It's home.

Which brings me to this house. My house. Gram's home for more than fifty years. The home she and Grandpa built and brought babies home to.

"How would you feel about me renting this house out?" I ask Sawyer quietly. I haven't talked in depth about it with Maverick.

His sister also hasn't talked to him about her situation. And none of us has talked about the Alex situation yet, though we are all aware of it.

"Would that mean you'll be home every night instead of accidentally sleeping here?" she asks, laughter in her voice.

My body's need for sleep has become a running joke, so I shouldn't be surprised. The hours I work now that Gram is situated are back to their previous level of crazy, so I sleep when I can.

"That's exactly what it would mean."

"Then do it." Sawyer looks up at me from her kneeling position in the dirt with questions in her eyes.

I kneel down to get on her level and ask her what's on her mind.

"Who would rent it, though? This was Gram's house and I know it's important to you, so whoever rents from you is going to have to pass the vibe test," she says.

"Oh," I say, dragging the word out as I let her comment sink in. "I absolutely agree. I don't want you to worry too much about it. There are a couple people interested who I think pass the test, and would pass yours, too."

She cocks her head and scrunches up her face while thinking about anyone she might know who would be in need of housing. I want to tell her, but not without Maverick knowing first. It would really suck for him to find out from his daughter that his sister is moving to town and going to split my house with one of my friends — a man, no less — to make it more affordable for both of them. It's nice when things work out even when we didn't plan it that way.

"You aren't going to tell me who it is, are you?" she questions. Rolling her eyes at me, she adds, "Figures. Can you just please make sure they aren't going to have an issue with the garden? We're putting all this work into everything here. The last thing I want to have happen is tenants messing up what we've put in so much effort to create. Please?"

"Trust me. If we're not over here taking care of it, the people I have in mind will absolutely help out in the garden."

She smiles broadly and nods before getting back to work. That was almost too easy, but hopefully it's because she knows I'm not going to keep her hanging too long.

Harper has been subletting a one-bedroom apartment closer to her job, but she misses being "in the middle of nowhere," as she called it, so when the topic came up while we were having lunch with Gram and Mom one day she said she would take it if I was serious. The problem being, I had already discussed it with Alex as his lease is up at the end of this month. Trust me when I said I tried to talk her out of it because I don't want anything to turn messy. It could be like a freshman college roommate situation where they get stuck living together and then despise one another at the end of the first semester.

However, Harper was very convincing that it would be fine and insisted I ask Alex about the two of them sharing the house. Since Alex is trying to save a little extra for graduate school, the option to split the space here for less than they're both paying in rent elsewhere was too good to pass up for him.

Neither of them have a lot they're going to be moving in, so most of the furniture is staying. I need to pack up the kitchen and bathroom and the few things left in my bedroom, but other than that the house is pretty much move in ready when they are.

So, I guess my boyfriend's sister and my best guy friend are about to become roomies.

It's not weird. At all. Nope.

"Mags, can you help me stake out where we're putting the garden. Rick hasn't gotten to it yet," Will says, pulling me from my thoughts.

We measure and hammer markers in the ground, and I'm hoping deep down that when we till up the grass we're met with perfect soil. We've got tomatoes started in the greenhouse at the tree farm and I can practically taste them when I go out each day to check the seedlings. There are so many vegetables Sawyer and I have started, I was pretty sure Maverick would have a coronary when he saw them all. He surprised us both and instead pulled us close to him on either side, looked at our handiwork, and mumbled something about the business growing ... again.

I'm not entirely sure how I was so fortunate to meet a man who loves me and my crazy, but I'll keep him forever if I can.

My hands are deep in the dirt, covering more seeds and bulbs for the flowers that should start blooming in late spring or early summer, when I hear a throat clear behind me. Standing up and clapping my dirty palms together to knock the excess dirt from them, I turn around to find the throat clearing offender.

"Nothing is more irritating than someone doing —" and the rest of my complaint gets forgotten as I look up from my filthy fingers to find an equally filthy boy kneeling in the grass and holding a ring out in front of him.

"I know. I know you hate that sound and I knew it would get your attention faster than calling your name. Except if I had called you by your whole name," he says, a sly smirk on his face, "which I know you secretly like being called by me."

"Maybe I do," I say, placing my hands on my hips, my eyes never leaving his.

Gesturing to his position in front of me, his cheeks pink beneath the ball cap.

Sawyer stands with Gram near the edge of the flower bed and when I glance in their direction, Sawyer leans in and whispers something in her ear. They're tucked into one another, arm-in-arm, and I haven't seen Sawyer or my grandmother smile so big in a long time. I can feel their excitement from across the yard.

"Shhh. Just wait till she actually looks at the ring. That's going to be the real surprise," Gram says loud enough for me to hear as I turn my attention back to the man in front of me.

Maverick lifts his cap and turns it backward so he can get a really good look at me as he takes a deep breath and stakes his claim.

"Margaret Regina Florence Southard, will you do me the honor of being my wife?"

I want to make him wait, but I also can't wait to say yes and before the word finishes leaving my mouth he's up off the ground, pulling me into him and lifting me in the air. My hands find his face and his lips are crashing against mine as if we haven't held one another in years instead of just hours. Will whistles somewhere behind me and Gram and Sawyer are clasping each other's arms and, if it's possible, their smiles are even bigger.

Slowly he places me back on the ground and reaches for my left hand. Brushing the remaining dirt from my fingers, he holds it gingerly and carefully begins slipping the ring in place.

"You know, I don't need a ring to know I want you forever, but it does sweeten the deal a bit," I say before looking carefully at the band around my finger. My breath catches in my throat. And for the first time in a very long time, I'm actually speechless.

"Told you so!" I hear Gram yell out, followed by Sawyer's laughter.

Sitting perfectly on my hand is the same ring my grandfather used to propose to Gram. For years I asked her why she didn't wear it and what she was going to do with it. The arthritis in her hands and knuckles had gotten so bad and that was why she didn't wear it anymore. It was honest and believable, but she never told me what she was going to do with the ring Grandpa Jim gave her. I guess I now know.

While I've been carefully staring at my hand, memorizing every dip and curve of the band and the way the small diamond sits perfectly in the prongs, Sawyer has led Gram over to me.

"I kept my promise to your grandfather," she says, holding my hand in hers and fingering the setting. She looks at it lovingly and then, with a content smile, says, "He wanted to make sure that when the time was right, when I took it off for the last time, that I saved it for you. You were the last granddaughter, and you having this gift from us, from whoever knows exactly how to love you, was important to him."

Still at a loss for words, I wrap my arms around her once broad and strong shoulders and pull my grandmother into me. As I do so, I'm left facing the back of the house and catch my parents standing at the door, smiling like a couple of fools who knew this was coming. Mom wipes tears from her cheeks and my dad pulls her close to kiss the top of her head.

I wonder if they wish they were more involved in this moment across the lawn, but they're letting Gram and me have the moment we need. As I pull away from Gram, they make their way across the lawn to us. My father smiles and shakes Maverick's hand, then hugs Sawyer before hugging me.

"All I ask," Sawyer begins, garnering attention from all of us, "is that you don't make me wear a dress that's too floofy or pink. Deal?"

Putting on a shocked expression, I place my hand over my heart and say, "I would never!"

Sawyer looks skeptical as she takes in my face and body language.

"For real, kiddo, never. I can't imagine having to wear fluffy things. As much as I love weddings and everything that goes with them, the frilly dresses aren't my thing either, so it's a good thing you'll be there to help figure out all the details."

It's not that I've put a lot of thought into an actual wedding with Maverick, but of course I've thought about it a little. Sawyer is part of him and she's going to be part of me, which means she's going to get a say in some of the things we choose. I'm not particular about colors, but she is and that's something I've gotten to know about her. It's something I want her to help me with. Just like I want Delilah and Genevieve to help us figure out the cake situation. And I would like Alex to help with the music.

Sawyer reaches out to shake my hand and I know I look confused. When she huffs and doesn't move her hand, I place mine in it.

"Deal. I would love to help with the details. It's kind of my thing," she says, then gestures to the flowerbed. "I might be prone to considering the little things."

Pulling my soon-to-be daughter in for a hug, I whisper, "You certainly are. Speaking of little things, did you know about this?"

"Maaaaybe," she says, pulling me closer. "I didn't know he was going to do it today, though. Not until he and Gram wandered off. Then I put it all together."

"I heard my name," Gram says as she steps closer to us. "Two of my favorite girls. You probably didn't think I had it in me to pull something like this off, huh?"

Sawyer and I both go to argue with her, because we know she's capable of some wild things, but almost in silent agreement we stop. Gram gives us a look. The one that tells us we're foolish to have thought otherwise. It's the same look I would get from her when I was a kid thinking I was getting away with something ridiculous, like keeping toads as stowaways in a box in her garage.

"I am still a spry young lady, you know. Might have a bit of trouble with my mind sometimes, but I keep up," she claims, leaning on me for a small bit of support. "Don't test me, Margaret."

"I wouldn't dream of it, Gram."

Chapter 32

Maverick

Moving her in the rest of the way was worth the wait. I know, it was a short wait. Our relationship is still young, but the things we've been through together in the last eight-ish months have been enough to make us realize that if we talk to one another, everything is going to be alright. We are going to be just fine.

Plus, the sex has been phenomenal now that we don't have to schedule it. It would be nice if we weren't both exhausted all the time, though.

The ups and downs of figuring out new business adventures has been easier with her at home with us. We get family time with Sawyer every single day, and we go to bed together every single night. The wedding was planned in a weekend with minimal stress and now we just have to wait for the date to arrive. This is the least stressed either of us have been in months.

We relocated my sister to Maggie's house at the end of April and had a freak snowstorm in the midst of it all. Somehow all the flowers we planted earlier in the month were spared. Now that we're into the warmer days of May, we've seen that we didn't lose much, if anything at all. Harper has been working on the weekends to help Sawyer and Maggie plant the garden — some seeds are going straight in the ground and others we started weeks ago in the greenhouse. Watching all of them work together, watching Maggie and Sawyer at home, and seeing Sawyer and Gen together when I stop by the bakery or check on Mags while she's at a food truck event ... it all feels perfect. Even with Alex sharing the house with my sister, it still feels serendipitous.

Part of me can't help wondering if it's all going to fall apart as we begin the next chapter of our life.

"Mom texted me," Sawyer says.

We've all gathered at Harper and Alex's — Gram likes when we get together at her old house so we've made an effort to have a family dinner or game night there every now and again. It's cramped once all of us are there, but as the weather continues to get nicer and the chilly evenings dissipate, we can be outside more.

Sawyer's admission comes as she's shoving a toasted marshmallow into her mouth. All heads turn in her direction and Maggie's hand grips mine. Everyone here knows about Hannah and her antics.

Through the gooey fluff, she states, "She said she's moving."

The hold Maggie has on my fingers tightens as she asks, "Where is she moving?"

Our biggest concern has been that, now that we're getting married, Hannah is going to somehow magically be able to be a more present parent. That's the exact opposite of what Sawyer wants. She's given up trying to have a relationship with her mom and has made it clear she considers Hannah more of an acquaintance than a parent. I don't blame her. I'm sad it turned out this way, but I don't blame her.

"I didn't ask," Sawyer says, placing another marshmallow in the flame. Genevieve sits beside her, snuggled into a blanket and looking concerned for my daughter. Sawyer's been through a lot because of her mom, but Gen is no stranger to having an absentee parent and doesn't want Sawyer to experience that. It's been a conversation around the table at home when Gen is there for dinner with us, and I'm thankful everyday my daughter has a girlfriend who is supportive and mature enough to understand her situation.

Not in any way meaning to shock them, I say, "I did." Clearing my throat, I give Maggie's hand a little squeeze and lift it to my lips to kiss her knuckles before continuing. "I asked. Uh, she's moving to France. With the new guy."

"France!?" Sawyer and Maggie yell in unison, and all other conversations cease.

I take a long pull on my beer. Like I said, I can't help wondering when it's going to come apart at the seams ... but I do. I wonder regularly if it isn't going to turn into a huge mess. Maybe the distance will help clear my head since I still mourn the relationship I hoped Sawyer would have with her mom. Maybe it'll help Hannah realize she misses being near her daughter. Perhaps, and this is a big perhaps, everything will work out the way it's supposed to.

For now, though, I'm not going to worry about what or how Hannah feels. That's on her. Sawyer is content with the way things currently are, and for that, I'm happy. She's not pining for her mother's affection. Not when she's got an amazing stepmom who supports her in everything she does.

"None of us know how long it's going to last, but I bid her adieu and hope she has the life she deserves," I say.

"I'll toast to that," Sawyer says, raising her soda in the air. I watch her choosing her next words carefully, but it still floors me when she says, "I guess the only thing left to do is get you two married and start working on some baby sisters and brothers for me. I'm not getting any younger, you know."

Maggie gives my hand another little squeeze. We haven't been keeping secrets from anyone. Not really. We just haven't been asked the right questions.

"We'll get right on that, Pumpkin," I say, leaning into Maggie and kissing the top of her head.

Her smile is all I need right now. This is the blissful feeling that's been missing in my life, and I never would have found it if I hadn't said yes to selling trees at the homecoming football game or taken a chance on the little bakery on Main Street.

Chapter 33

Maggie

NOVEMBER

It's been six months since the garden bed proposal, four months since the wedding, and fifteen minutes since I told him my thoughts on the situation at the rental property.

"There's something going on with your sister and Alex," I said. "Something's changed between them."

"What? No. They're just roommates," he said, completely oblivious as he pulled the turkey from the oven.

But for the last fifteen minutes, he's been mumbling to himself while I mash the potatoes for Thanksgiving dinner. Our first year married and, of course, I offered to host. Because baking and cooking in this kitchen is my favorite thing to do when I'm home, especially since my wedding gift from Maverick was a state-of-the-art upgrade from the range he had. We installed a double wall oven, replaced the space from the oven with a wine fridge and chopping block, and built an island with an electric cooktop. We did all the work ourselves. It's been worth every penny, every moment of working side-by-side with my husband and daughter, and absolutely worth having it done on our terms in between busy days at the bakery, in the food truck, and designing or building new dream gardens.

"There's no way. They're just roommates," he says again, mostly to himself.

"They're not just roommates," Gen says as she enters the kitchen with empty cups from the other room.

"Who's not roommates?" Delilah asks when she comes in from the pantry carrying a stack of heavy-duty paper plates. "Are we doing this dinner on fine China or do you really want to do dishes later?"

"Fine China works for me," I respond.

"They're full of it," Maverick says to Lilah, but he looks a little ashen. "There is no way my sister and Alex are doing anything but sharing a house."

Lilah and I look at one another. She rolls her eyes and I laugh, because we both know Maverick is having trouble with Harper and Alex living together without having really known one another beforehand, say nothing about if they really are sharing a bed. It's not like it can't happen, he just doesn't want to think of the possibility that it is happening.

"Rick, you're delusional," Lilah says. "And I mean that with the utmost respect as my favorite brother-in-law type of person and my daughter's girlfriend's father."

He looks from Lilah to me to Genevieve to the door.

"Well, this is awkward."

We turn to find Harper and Alex standing in the archway between the kitchen and living room, far enough away they hopefully didn't hear the entire conversation. But looking at my husband's very red ears, I'm almost certain they heard most of it. He reads his sister's nonverbal cues better than anyone, with the exception of Bentley, so I know he's seeing something that I'm not.

"But, yeah, we're definitely sharing a house. Laundry soap, too. Pretty sure I caught him doing the dishes on my night, even. It's pretty domesticated," she says, pulling a bottle of wine toward her on the island and topping off her glass.

"Yup, just sharing a house. No worries, Rick," Alex says, walking over to help with the turkey. "Scout's honor."

As Maverick turns back to his task, Alex and Harper share a look that I don't miss and I wonder what this will mean for next Thanksgiving.

Because there is most definitely something going on.

I don't have time right now to consider all the possibilities. Our house is going to be full soon as Mom, Dad, and Gram walk through the front door. I see Maverick's parents pull into the driveway and Bentley is right behind them in his Chevy Silverado. They park beside the food truck where Maverick and I have stored a special dessert. We'll bring it in the house after dinner. We don't want anyone to see it until it's time.

Family meals are always lively, to the say the least, and it's never just eating. It's like a family reunion every time, and the gratitude of being able to do this big holiday meal together in our home is almost more than I can handle. By the time it's time to make coffee and set up dessert, I'm practically crawling out of my skin with excitement. Or nerves. It's probably a healthy dose of both.

The only ones who know there's more for dessert than the pies sitting on top of the washer and dryer are Delilah, Fisher, Genevieve, and Sawyer.

We couldn't keep it from them. They're a big part of how we've ended up where we are and what's happening behind the scenes. If it wasn't for their love and support, we wouldn't even be able to make the announcement.

Well, one of them.

As the evening begins winding down, everyone gathers in the kitchen — Mom and Sawyer are washing the glass dishes we dirtied, Maverick's mom and Harper are dividing up leftovers to send home with anyone not living at our house, and I've started pouring coffee.

"Are you ready for me and Maverick to carry in the desserts?" Fisher asks.

I nod and tell him I'll be out to help in a minute as Delilah, Genevieve, and Jax carry pies in from the laundry room.

"You good?" Lilah asks, bumping her hip into mine as she passes.

Again, I nod.

"Yeah, I think so."

"Think so?" she questions quietly in my ear so only I can hear her despite the room being crowded. She raises an eyebrow at me.

"Yes. I'm good. Just … getting my bearings. Fish already went out to start grabbing boxes, so I'm going to go help him," I say and as I step aside for Lilah to take my place at the counter where she can begin cutting pies, she wraps me up in a hug only a sister can offer … even if that sister is from a different family.

Having the friends I do, I've learned that family isn't always blood and found family is often the best kind to have. I'm glad I found mine.

Fisher and I pass one another as I walk out to the food truck. Maverick is waiting for me and as I step up inside, he places his hands on my face and leans into me for a kiss that I've been longing for all day. It's the kind that makes my knees weak and makes me wish we had more than a few minutes alone.

"We're ready for this?"

"We are. Sawyer is going to wet herself when she finds out we've been hiding this from her. Plus, our moms are both going to lose their minds."

"What about Gram?" he asks.

Biting my lip, I consider the fact my grandmother has had a rough few months, but know she's going to be head over heels in love with all of it.

"She's going to be happy and I hope she's still in good health when it all comes to fruition," I say.

"Me too, sweetheart, me too."

"Come on. Let's get the rest of these in the house," I say, picking up three bakery boxes. "I just hope I planned for the right amount of goodies."

Maverick snorts out a laugh behind me as if the four boxes he's carrying, plus the however many Fisher already took in the house, are going to be more than enough. Maybe they will. I mean, I labeled all of them, but I might have put Alex and Harper together, and I definitely have one for just Gen and Jax so they don't have to share with their mom and dad. Bentley has his own even though he's living with Mom and Dad Rogers still, but that doesn't mean he won't eat everything in there before leaving our house and want more to take home.

It's really a crapshoot with this family of ours. So, I always try to bake extra. It's just, these boxes are special.

Walking through the back door and into the kitchen, I set my boxes down on the counter beside the ones Fisher brought in and Maverick follows suit putting his beside mine.

"Alright, everyone!" Maverick yells above the noise of the entire family talking. He goes so far as to clap his hands together and raise his arms above his head so all the attention is on him. "I know it's Thanksgiving, and we're all in a season of gratitude. With that in mind, Maggie and I are especially grateful for all of you and your unwavering support of us, our family, and our business adventures."

He doesn't even need to look at me for me to know it's my turn.

"So, we've got a lot going on here," I say, unable to wipe the smile off my face. "Tomorrow, Christmas tree shopping officially starts, and that is always an exciting time for Maverick and Sawyer. This year I get the full experience because I live here now and will probably have my butt dragged out of bed at five in the morning. But, I'm okay with that … because that means I get to work on the next phase of doing life with Maverick and Sawyer."

I let it sink in a little because they all think they know, but they don't. Pulling Delilah into my side, I take a deep breath.

"Delilah and I are happy to announce we are going to be breaking ground on a second bakery location," I say. "The Bakery on Main is coming to the farm. We'll have room for extra stock, there will be an on-site bakery for future Christmas tree shoppers, and we've been playing around with bread recipes to help supply local restaurants."

Delilah links her free arm with Fisher's and I grasp Maverick's hand with mine, because only he knows what's next. Fisher and Delilah think I made special treat boxes for everyone just because it's the holiday.

Slipping away between Maverick and Delilah, I begin passing out bakery boxes.

"This is a little gift from me and Maverick to each of you for all you've done for us. We hope you love it."

One by one boxes begin to open. A little gasp here, a "holy shit" there, and, finally the best sound ever.

"Oh my god, are you serious right now!?" from a very excited Sawyer.

Playing with the tie on my apron and biting my lip, I do a non-verbal check-in with Maverick and elbow him in the side.

"The bakery isn't the only thing expanding," I say.

Epilogue

Maggie

SEVEN MONTHS LATER

"Hi there, sweet baby," she says, gently caressing his downy cheek. "It's so nice to meet you. Oh, Margaret, he is just the best little thing ever."

Gram is the first to come to the house to see us since we were discharged yesterday. Of course, Mom is in tow because Gram doesn't drive anymore, but she's giving my grandmother time to snuggle her newest great-grandchild. Mom, on the other hand, is taking a much-deserved break quietly drinking coffee in the kitchen.

"You are the best little gift I've ever received," she says to him.

Ashton's the only great-grand who lives close by, and I feel a little protective of the fact I grew up getting Gram all to myself and now he will, too. Sawyer is almost a senior in high school now, but she gets as much time with Gram as she wants as well. It's a different dynamic, though, because Sawyer is older and came into the family as a fully grown human.

Ashton Maverick — named as such because his daddy wanted to keep with the tree and wood theme he started with Sawyer — came out screaming after a short labor a week past his due date and in the midst of wedding season. Lilah and I are feeling fortunate my water didn't break while I was trying to finish up the last order I was working on. Was it the smartest move to keep working right up until he arrived? Maybe not, but I'll never regret it.

Everything got done around the house to prepare for him and, just like when we updated the kitchen and built the bakery extension at the farm, Maverick and I tag-teamed every step of the way. When I was working and she wasn't at school or on a job with her dad, Sawyer was at the bakery helping me, Lilah, and Genevieve. When I was working late into the night at home as my due date approached and then passed, Maverick was keeping a watchful eye. There were days Gram and Mom were with me the entire workday, too.

I know some people would feel overwhelmed or suffocated by all of that. I don't. I can't. A lot of days, Gram didn't know me but she knew I was a young mom who needed help folding baby clothes as we got ready for Ashton. If she didn't realize right away who I was, but was at the bakery with us, she at least knew she was in a kitchen and if nothing else, that's where she shines. I wish I had paid more attention to all the things she tried to teach me when I was younger. I'm grateful I have her for a little longer and can try to absorb as much as possible now. Sawyer, too. I've watched her flourish as she's steadily grown Sugar Shack Landscaping alongside her father, but like the rest of us she's kept a close watch on Gram. I catch her sometimes writing things down after being with Gram and when she shows me her notebooks, I'm rarely surprised that she's taking notes about plants and food they've talked about.

My grandmother has been invaluable to all of us. She has taught us more than we realize — about family, love, and even forgiveness.

"You remind me of my Jim," she says, still caught up in the moment with our newest addition. She sighs, contentedly, but I feel like there's something else there. "He was intense and stubborn, but, boy, did he love just as hard. I miss him every day."

My breath catches. I'm overcome with emotion. It's probably just a side effect of having just had a baby. Hormones and all that. Certainly, her mentioning my grandpa isn't going to be the thing that makes me cry today. I watch as Ashton scrunches his legs and stretches his arms as he yawns, and she touches his tiny toes.

"When I see him, I'll tell him all about you."

*****

Gram passed peacefully in her sleep when Ashton was a week old.
She knew.
She was spry and mobile and as authentic as ever up until her last night with us.
But she was tired. And she knew.
The funeral home is standing room only. All of us who own businesses on Main Street either closed for the afternoon or left the shops in the hands of people who never really knew Gram. Not the way we did, anyway.
Murph offers words of love and affirmation, even though Gram wasn't Catholic. He was a friend, and he talks about his time knowing Gram as if she was his favorite person. Will talks until his emotions take over and he

simply can't because he's laughing while telling a story. He laughs until he cries and ends with, "I'm going to miss you, Gram. You were one of the best friends I ever could have had."

Mom and the uncles sit together with Dad and the aunts behind them; they hold onto on another, because now it's just them.

But what surprises me is when Sawyer steps up to the front of the room and clears her throat.

"Hi. For those of you who don't know me, I'm Sawyer. Not to steal a line from Will, but Gram was one of my best friends, too. Sorry, Will," she says, smiling in his direction. "Um, I didn't get to know her nearly as long as most of you, but in the short amount of time I did get with her she taught me more about life than I could have hoped. She supported me in everything I did, even if she didn't understand it right away. Gram knew how to love and she was blessed with the ability to think forward, ahead of her time even, because she always made me feel accepted. In fact, if I were to take a wild guess, she made each and every one of you feel loved and accepted, too. Why? Well, because that's just who Gram was. No rhyme or reason to it as far as I can see.

"It's not just those things that make her special, though. This woman had knowledge and spunk and, God forbid you did something to irritate her, because she had attitude, too," Sawyer says, talking with her hands to articulate her emotions. "I hope we all leave here today with a little bit of Gram in our hearts that we can pull out when we need to. I hope my baby brother is fortunate to have inherited those traits from our mom, Grandma, and Gram. She was famous for everything she did … even if she was only famous to the people in this small town."

Acknowledgments

Where do I start? I love writing, but sometimes my writing time is scarce ... and sometimes, I'm just scared and don't push myself to work through it faster to get the book done. I aim for quality in my writing, not quantity, which is why I try to publish once a year and don't expect more from myself.

Consequently, this book has been in the works for almost three years, which is insane. I didn't realize it had been that long but, according to my notes, I started writing The Bakery on Main as my NaNoWriMo 2021 project. By November 2022, I had less than 25,000 words and the plot wasn't plotting. Plus, I was trying to get my act together to finish Foster to Family because that needed to come out first. I stopped writing this one altogether until I picked it up again in October 2023.

Even then it was touch and go. Sammy started preschool and my big kids went back to school, and it gave me time each day to work, but I didn't get started again on Maggie and Maverick's story until school had been in session for about a month. Figuring out my routine was not easy.

But then? Then NaNoWriMo came around again as it does each year and I found out my local group actually had virtual events and in-person events close to me that didn't require I drive into the City of Syracuse. I made it my goal to write every day in November, and I did. I had a few days that were only a few words (literally), but it counted. Every single word counted. The ones that popped into my head when I really didn't have time to write were important enough to the story that I made sure I put in the effort to add them to my document and then add them to my project page. I had already started doing that when I did my first write-in with the Syracuse NaNo group, but they made it easier to figure out how to find my flow.

Timers have become my best source of motivation along with the support I've had from family and friends ...

Marissa Frosch and Taylor Delong: The two of you were the big ones to help me get this book started with NaNo2021. I can't thank you enough for the sprints early on while I sat freezing my butt off waiting for my kids to finish team runs. Your friendship has been invaluable and I cannot wait to spend time with you again soon.

Syracuse Region NaNoWriMo: I might still be struggling after taking almost a year off from The Bakery on Main if I hadn't shown up for those write-ins. I look forward to meeting up again in a few months when I'm working on the next project.

My mobile hot spot: You make it feasible for me to work while I'm at the dojo or the ball field. Thanks for being an invention I didn't know I absolutely needed and was unable to figure out without the help of my middle schoolers.

My beta readers — Ron, Sean, Carrie, Vicci, Laura, Barb, and Bridgett: Thank you for taking time out of your busy schedules to read Maggie and Maverick's story. If there's one thing you know I'm good at, it's writing about family dynamic and not keeping everything romance-centric, so I hope this book lived up to your expectations.

Josie, Charlie, Ellie, and Sammy: Thank you for understanding when I need to work and only interrupting me for important things, like opening snacks and breaking up fights. I know this isn't a normal job, and you've never known me as the normal job parent, but this gives me opportunities I might not have otherwise. I get to be at all school functions. I'm able to take you to all your doctor's appointments. I'm home or just a call away when you need me to pick you up from the nurse's office or take you to a friend's house. And if I have to take a day off to go blueberry picking, usually my boss is pretty understanding. I love you.

Boy Wonder: I hope you know everyday how much I appreciate the life we're building together. It's not always easy, and it shouldn't be. Growth happens outside our comfort zones and in the 21 years we've known one another and been a couple, we have stepped outside repeatedly and grown exponentially. I write good men because I was raised by one and then was fortunate enough to find and marry one. Thank you for letting me ramble while working through plot issues and panic about my characters. Thank you for standing beside me while I chase my dreams. I love you.

For current me from past me: *high five* for thinking ahead and putting The Dude in 5-day preschool. Without your forward thinking, I wouldn't have had two hours a day, five days a week, to finally get this book done. Go us!

And finally, Mom: Thank you for not hiding the hardships and the wins from your years in geriatric nursing on both A Wing and the dementia unit. You devoted more than three decades of your life to helping your residents who found themselves slowly losing a fight many are unable to comprehend. I'm grateful everyday you allowed us to visit you at work and Dad let me go with him on Sundays when he cut the men's hair. It was an education in being human most kids don't get until they are much older; many don't get it at all.

Gram wasn't even supposed to have memory issues, or what is considered mild cognitive impairment, but when I started writing, her story shifted from a sassy grandmother to sassy with a side of her own struggle. While this book doesn't center around dementia, I hope I displayed well enough that dementia related illnesses affect everyone within orbit of the person battling these diseases. I deliberately chose to have Gram leave the story on her own terms and with her cognitive health decline slowly progressing. I wanted her entire community to remember her as she was — a little bit famous, even if it's just in a little town in Western New York.

For more information on Alzheimer's and dementia, please visit https://www.alz.org/

About the Author

M.L. Pennock is a former journalist turned author. She attended Alfred University, earning a Bachelor of Arts in English and communication studies, before going on to earn a Master of Arts in communications from SUNY College at Brockport. She lives in Central New York with her husband, four children, and Siberian Husky, Tikaani.

M.L. Pennock is the author of the To Have series and a spinoff series, Famous in a Small Town.

Visit facebook.com/mlpennock or mlpennock.com for more information about what she's working on next.

Made in the USA
Middletown, DE
22 June 2024

55940919R00167